CYLA PANIN

STALKING SHADOWS

AMULET BOOKS • NEW YORK

Cataloging-in-Publication Data has been applied for and may be obtained
from the Library of Congress.

ISBN 978-1-4197-5265-0

Text copyright © 2021 Cyla Panin
Illustrations copyright © 2021 Juliana Kolesova
Book design by Hana Anouk Nakamura

Published in 2021 by Amulet Books, an imprint of ABRAMS.

Printed and bound in U.S.A.
10 9 8 7 6 5 4 3 2 1

Amulet Books are available at special discounts when purchased in quantity
for premiums and promotions as well as fundraising or educational use.
Special editions can also be created to specification. For details, contact
specialsales@abramsbooks.com or the address below.

ABRAMS The Art of Books
195 Broadway, New York, NY 10007
abramsbooks.com

To my mom, who always believed this was possible

CHAPTER ONE

Sometimes she smelled like blood. It stained her, worming into her pores and spreading out under her skin. I pretended not to notice, but each time someone came close, I flinched. Worried that they'd discover her. That they'd take her away from me.

A sharp sting bit my hand and cleared the fog from my thoughts. A prickle from a cleaver leaf had nipped into the skin of my thumb. I flicked it out and took up my mortar, crushing and rolling the leaves and the honeysuckle buds in it under the pestle. A heady scent, green and sticky-sweet, curled up from my bowl.

"Don't waste it, Marie," Ama said. "I only found a couple bunches this morning."

"I'm not," I told my sister. But I ran the mortar around the bowl again and let the juices dribble down into the bottom. Then I dipped a pale, white finger in and lifted it to my nose.

"Like nectar," I said. "I wish I could taste it."

"Well, you can't." Ama bent over the scrubbed wood table and pushed my hand away from my face. "Or it might be you I come after tonight. Make sure you wash your fingers with the soap."

Ama's pointed nose and prominent cheekbones gave her a sharp quality I knew only ran skin deep. Her hair, dark and threaded with early gray, fell from its braid against her white skin. I wiped my hands on my apron and reached out to push a strand behind my sister's ear. Her face grew harder, the lines deeper when she was close to turning. The change curdled my stomach, but I'd never tell her that.

"You'd know me, even then. I'm not scared of you, Ama."

"You should be," she said, slamming down a tray of little glass bottles so they clinked against each other. The frayed ends of her voice trailed over my skin and left prickles in their wake. I fumbled as I took one of the bottles. They were cheap things, edges and planes cut into them by the maker so they'd sparkle in the sunlight. The ladies clamored for them and the men knew it, so they gave up their deniers too. That was what mattered to me.

I selected a glass dropper from a little tray at my elbow and used it to suck up a few drops of the honeysuckle juice mixture. Then I let them fall, one at a time, into a small glass bottle with a rounded belly.

"Here," Ama said, passing me the lavender water. "This one's popular lately. Even the farmer's wives have been wearing it."

"I'm not after a farmer's wife today," I said, but I took the flask anyway and poured a little in. The scents danced at the bottom when I swirled it, claiming each other.

When I was done, the lingering notes of flora clung to the neck of the bottle.

"Who did you choose?"

"Don't worry," I said. "There's enough meat on him."

I never told Ama beforehand. If she knew who the victim would be, she'd go all jittery when we saw them in town. Better for her to be in the dark. I could carry the burden of selection myself.

My sister dipped around the room—pinching a kerchief from the folded stack I'd placed near the washbasin, checking her reflection in the small, round mirror hanging from a nail by the door, prodding the firewood with an iron poker. Her fluttering movements were carefully practiced to seem easy and frivolous, like those of a rich merchant's daughter. She was so good at it now, at just fifteen, she forgot to stop doing it at home.

We'd watched the ladies in the shops together, how they lightly touched the baker's hand when he passed them their bread or gently murmured over a new fan in the atelier. We'd studied them over the shoulders of the men and through clouded panes of glass until we could mimic them with precision.

With no dowries, we had to rely on charms. Money was hard to earn. Charm could be more easily acquired, for Ama at least. I was never very good at any of it, but that wouldn't matter if she married properly to a good man who could give us a steady life.

The problem was, there was no one to teach her how to be the right kind of woman. Maman had died ten years ago trying to bring a dead baby into the world. I wanted Ama to be able to turn her head with an elegant extension of the neck and sweep her eyelashes onto her cheeks in just the right way to attract a good man. Papa couldn't help us. He didn't know anything about being accepted in this little town because he never had been—a cobbler's son with no talent of his own to sell, he'd relied on the strength of his arms and his love for the bite of fresh morning air and become a farmer. He hadn't been very good at that either.

Our tired cottage was testament to that. Maman had liked the brightness of the little house made of yellow plaster with windows set into it like two startled eyes. She'd told me that more than once when we'd been outside pulling away at the dirt and dropping seeds in the holes, but I imagined she was making the best of it for me.

The kitchen, the table, and the two padded chairs we kept before the fire were all in one room. Papa slept in the bedroom with a real bed, while Ama and I had a mattress filled with straw in the loft. We didn't always like sharing, but at least we stayed fairly warm in the winter from the heat of both of us in the bed.

And we'd done what we could to make it comfortable. With a little of the money we made selling perfumes, we bought a bit of cotton and sewed up pillowcases. I bargained for the ends of a roll of muslin from the seamstress and sewed them into soft curtains and an impractical tablecloth. I tried to add touches of home here and there, but no one had ever showed me how and I was afraid I was getting it all wrong.

Dirt stuck to the floorboards and the flagstone at the entry. Dust settled over our two earthenware candlesticks no matter how often I buffed them with a scrap of cloth. And I never could scrub away the black stains clawing their way up the fireplace.

I scraped at one now with the tip of my fingernail. The fire popped in the hearth, and I jumped out of the way of the sparks just in time. Smoke stung my nose—the chimney needed cleaning. Another task to add to my list after I sorted Ama out for this month.

I walked to the door and it whined over the stone floor as I pulled it open to let in some of the crisp late autumn air. I let it fill me, wash over me, numb me for a moment to what I had to do today: Mark another victim. Take another life. The top of the church spire rose over the peaked roofs of the village street. I hoped the warmth of the sun would be strong enough to last until we were ready to walk down the path to the market.

"Close the door now, Marie," Ama said. "It's cold."

It wasn't, not really, but her perception was growing more and more skewed each time she came back into her skin. It was more delicate and grew cold more easily than the fur.

"Papa needs to clean the chimney. It'll be a long time before the curtains air out," Ama said, fluffing the thin fabric hanging at one of the two windows in our cottage. "And what about us?" She lifted her arm and sniffed her wool sleeve.

I shook my head at her and gripped the iron door handle to pull it closed, then stopped. A little doll sat on the doorstep. Big eyes, clumsily stitched, it stared up at me over spikey, black-threaded teeth. A shiver started in my toes and rippled through my veins.

"Is that a . . . monster?" Ama said, pressing her chin on my shoulder. I hardened then, snuffing out my unease and letting the hot flame of anger lick my stomach. The little beast, a crude linen doll, was the second I'd seen in as many months. Someone had come from the village and dropped it in front of our door on purpose. There were no other cottages close enough beside us for it to have been meant for anyone else. Someone was trying to scare us.

"Market will be starting soon," I said, but Ama didn't look at me—her eyes were trained on the doll on the doorstep. "We should go."

I pinched the doll between my fingers and carried it over to the hearth, feeding it into the flames. The edges caught and the orange flames ate up the linen, leaving brittle black ash in their wake.

"Do think it's from a children's game? They must have been playing in the field."

Sometimes the village children did run through our empty patch of land, gone to grass. They'd dare each other to run into the trees bordering the field, counting how long each of them could stay in the shadows of the woods without fleeing. People died in there, even before Ama started to turn. Animals killed them or they simply never made it out. The mothers in our village had done a good job warning their children of the dangers—the wolves and the stags and the whispers of the forest witch's magic.

"You're probably right, Ama. It's just a game."

I took up a padded basket from the table, nestled the bottle of honeysuckle essence into the bottom, and added an assortment of rose and lavender water.

Ama tied her fichu around her neck and handed me mine, which I knotted with surprisingly steady hands.

"Let's go find your victim."

CHAPTER TWO

The square stank on market day. The yellow stones of the street took on the darker hues of spilled beer and watered blood. Unidentifiable guck stuck to my leather shoes, which I discreetly scraped off against the side of the well.

A whiff of fresh bread curled into my nostrils and I stood, one hand steadying myself against the well, to find a tray of rolls shoved right into my face.

"Two for you and your sister, Mademoiselle?" the baker asked.

"We're selling today, not buying." I held up my basket of tinkling glass bottles.

"Ah, les perfumeuse. My wife quite liked your lavender. I'll trade you three loaves for a bottle?"

"Desolée, it would need to be five," I said. Ama pinched my arm, and I closed my hand around her wrist and squeezed, hoping for silence.

"What?" she asked, swinging around and prying my fingers from her wrist as soon as the baker padded away with his tray. "Is it him?"

"And who would feed the village if the beast ate poor Henri?"

Ama pushed out her bottom lip, but her eyes twinkled. "Really, Marie . . . I'm ready to choose one."

I stopped short, foot hovering over another pile of unappetizing brown muck. People flowed around us all the same, like river water around a stone. There were routines to be kept to. Cheese to be weighed and bought, ribs cut from the pigs hanging in the butcher's shop. The children needed to wail and pull on their mother's hands until they received a conciliatory honey drop. Each market day was the same. The only thing that changed from time to time was if Ama would kill later that night.

She'd been on about this for months now—choosing her own victim. It was impossible, of course. The burden would be too heavy. She didn't understand that, because none of this was more than a game to her. I'd asked her what she remembered and her answer was this: the power, the taste of blood, the satiation.

That was it. She didn't recall the screams of agony or the glistening, glassy eyes. Remorse is ethereal for her. It comes and goes in light, wispy waves. It doesn't settle over her like the shroud I've come to wear.

"You don't want to choose," I said. "It wouldn't be any fun that way."

Ama's dark hair danced on her shoulders as she tossed her

head like a mad foal. "It would be! You just don't want to let me choose because you like being in control. You're only seventeen, not so much older than me."

The midday sun's weak rays barely warmed my wool sleeves, and I tucked the basket closer to my body. Mothers with babes tied to their backs crowded around the well and pulled water with chapped hands. The babies lay quiet, rocked by the rhythm of their mothers' work. I tried to imagine what it would feel like to have the warmth of a babe pressed tight against my back. Not mine, necessarily, but Ama's. I'd never know—never have that life—unless I kept my sister's secret contained.

Sudsy water drained down the cobblestones, shimmering with lye. Laundry maids rubbed and pulled linen against rock until the dirt fell away. Their chatter was as monotonous as their work. When we were just girls, there was a rash of killings of girls like that. Wolves, everyone thought. Even Papa took his pitchfork and joined the others as they searched for the culprit.

They were unsuccessful, but the killings had slowed so much that they were almost becoming shocking again. Then Ama turned and now the deaths were steady, one roughly every month. I didn't know what was responsible for the killings when we were children, but I certainly knew who was to blame now. Us. It was why the choice of victim was so important. I couldn't let Ama do it because she wasn't discreet enough. She'd go for someone exciting, but that kind of victim—like the starchy village priest or the weaver—would be very, very noticed.

A few fruit sellers rolled soft, brown apples around the bottoms of their barrels and called out promises of spiced apple wine. Vegetable peddlers lined up their carrots and cabbages beside one another in hopes they had the biggest, most robust stock. Ice already laced the leaves in the mornings, and soon we'd have only what we could pickle or keep in the cold cellar. A sharply green cabbage with frothy leaves almost claimed my attention, but Ama steered me away by the elbow.

"We're not here to shop, remember?"

"Soon it will be all beets and turnips, you know. You'll miss cabbage in a few months."

Ama's mouth turned down. "Will not."

I couldn't help a laugh. "Okay, well, maybe you won't . . ."

The threat of winter hung in the air like a silent omen. It was in the knitted scarves the wealthier families wore and the bright pink feet of the poorest village children. There were many things to fear, but winter was the worst in its surety. The ice and snow would come every year, without fail, and every year they'd take a few lives.

"Can you at least think about it?" Ama said.

"About the cabbage?"

"No! About tonight . . . the *you know*."

She couldn't even say *victim* out loud and yet she wanted to pick one?

"Do you want me to start listing all the reasons that's a bad idea?"

She rolled her eyes. "Please don't do that thing where you tick them off on your fingers."

"You're not taking this seriously, Ama!" I hissed at her.

Luckily there were lots of people out today, soaking up the last gifts of a golden autumn sun before it turned too bright and unforgiving and cold. No one was paying attention to us as we strolled arm in arm down the cobbled street. A row of farmers' stands started just beyond the steps of the church. Hastily built tables holding up jars of honey and baskets full of the last of this year's harvest. I steered Ama away from the honey stand with a bit of pressure on her arm. If I didn't, she'd go and take the lid off one of the jars and smell the stuff inside and beg me to use one of our few coins on something sweet that wouldn't even last us through the winter.

"Don't push, Marie," she said.

"I wasn't. I'm cold; I'm just trying to lean into you for warmth."

"You were not. You're trying to make sure I don't go after one of Madame Lorraine's honey pots. You know I wouldn't, not when Papa spent all that coin the other night. I'm more responsible than you think . . . that's why I should be allowed to choose who we give the honeysuckle oil to."

My teeth clenched together at the thought of Papa taking all my earnings from selling perfumes down to the ale house and staying there till every coin was gone. He'd known I'd been trying to save it and he'd not cared at all.

"Stop it, Ama. People will hear you."

I glanced around at the faces under white caps and brown hats. Did one of them put the doll on our doorstep?

"No one's listening, Marie. They care more about themselves than trying to eavesdrop on the likes of us."

A bare elbow, scaly and red, jutted into my side as we rounded the corner. The man lurched from the impact and roiled on unsteady feet. His unfamiliar face opened in surprise, and the sharp scent of ale hovered in the air around him.

"'Scuse," he slurred.

"Bit early for the tavern, isn't it?" Ama asked, steadying me with a firm grip.

The man pushed away her words with a meaty hand. He'd be perfect—alone, a drunkard, a vagrant probably, missed by no one. I slipped my hand into my basket and felt for the glass bottle etched with two horizontal lines. The cork held fast, so I jiggled it, unseen. Ama must have felt my movements, realized what I was doing, because she pulled away from me.

"No," she shot out of the corner of her mouth.

The man tried to grab at her elbow, but she yanked it away and shook out her black hair. The gray strands glinted in the sun like stray cobwebs.

"You think I'd let you touch me?"

The man's eyes widened at the bite in Ama's voice. "You couldn't stop me."

I dug my nails into the little cork and wriggled it free, palming the open bottle.

"Oh, she could," I said.

The man stared at us, rheumy eyes swiveling from Ama to me. Shock hardened his features, but there was excitement there too. In the space of his silence, the dry crack of wagon wheels on gravel crackled through the air. We all turned to see the blacksmith pulling a handcart heaped with rags toward the village green.

The air settled around us, thick and still. Something was wrong with the rags in the cart. They were piled too precisely and there was a patch of red on the brown homespun.

A body. A small one.

CHAPTER THREE

My fingertips tingled as I gripped Ama's shoulder and pulled her back to me. Something terrible had happened to a child—an accident with a scythe perhaps, or an axe swung too hard by unpracticed hands. Whatever had caused it, we were about to see the awful consequence.

Ama settled against my chest and looped my arm around her own. Her heart beat hard and hot against my wrist. Even if we couldn't escape it, neither of us relished suffering. Soon the silence would be replaced by screaming, and the sound would grate at my skin.

Others gathered, pulled in by some dark curiosity. The bottom of a white foot fell free from the mud-colored wool, and one of the older women gasped and clutched her shawl tightly under her chin.

Low heels clattered over the cobblestones, frenzied clips echoing against the honey-stoned walls of the crowded shops and townhouses. It was much too bright a morning for blood and screaming.

The sound, when it came, ripped free from the baker's wife in one keeling arc. Piercing. Painful. Her wail reverberated through my body. People around me shuddered and brought hands to their mouths as if they could keep their own horror in.

How did the woman know it was her child under the heap of rags? Did she sense a severed connection, cut like the umbilical cord that once tied them together? My hand twitched over Ama's and she moved her thumb against my palm in calming circles.

The baker's wife pulled at her white cap, at her cheeks, her hair. She stumbled toward the cart in jolting steps, both eager and hesitant. It was as if she needed to see but didn't want to know. Once she pulled the rags from her child's face, there would be no going back. It would be done. Her child, lost.

She inched back the rough wool over soft brown curls and half-moon lids. Though his eyelashes brushed the rounded tops of his cheeks, he didn't look asleep. Something imperceptible was missing. The absence of it—the flicker, the breath, the rose tones of blood and life—made my stomach twist and turn like river eels in a basket.

Fabric fell away from the boy's neck. I squeezed my eyes shut, but it was too late. I'd seen the ragged edges of the child's skin and the deep red hues of what lay beneath.

"Did you do it?" I whispered to Ama even though I wasn't sure I wanted to know the answer.

"No," she breathed, but the warmth of relief never spread through my chest. We'd agreed—no children. Not ever. And Ama hadn't even turned yet this month. But here was a dead child.

The question lingered in the back of my mind—if not Ama, who? My sister was the greatest threat in these mountains.

"Maurice," the baker's wife whimpered her son's name into his feathery hair. She hadn't even shorn it yet. He couldn't have been more than four years old.

The crowd stilled. The brisk morning wind whipped around us, loosening caps and scarves and carrying the tangy scent of blood. Ama sniffed and her pink tongue ran along her bottom lip. In a swell of panic, I gripped her closer. She shouldn't be so enthralled by the scent of blood in her human form. She strained against my arms, her body leaning toward the wound glistening where the boy's throat should have been.

"Ama, stop."

Faces turned toward us now, brows creased and eyes narrowed. One of these people put the monster doll at our doorstep. We were two women alone with only a drunkard father for protection. Suspicion fell to us like the yellowing leaves falling from the trees. Predictable.

I had to do something. I couldn't let these people's eyes rove over Ama, over me, until they saw through the façade I'd created for us. I'd been too careful to let it all fall apart. Ama was going to ruin everything if she couldn't keep herself under control.

Her heart beat urgently against my arm and I squeezed her closer to me, until my lips hovered just behind the delicate skin of her ear.

"Hold it in."

Ama breathed hard, letting out a noisy breath through her nose. Why was she reacting like this? This boy, this child, couldn't be one of her kills. My stomach clenched. Could it?

She turned only once every moon cycle, and tonight was the night. She couldn't have turned last night too. I would have known, would have heard . . . unless she'd snuck out while I was sleeping. But she wouldn't, she *wouldn't* hurt a child.

My sister trembled in my arms like the cold had gotten to her.

"Please tell me you didn't do this," I whispered.

Ama's elbow jabbed into my stomach. "I told you I felt the buzz this morning, that I'd turn tonight. When would I have done this? Do you really think I would have?"

I wanted to say no, tell her I didn't think she'd hurt a child because we'd agreed, but I couldn't. Every time Ama changed, she brought a little piece of the beast back with her. A heightened sense of smell, the desire to be under the canopy of the trees rather than in front of the hearth. How could I know who exactly she was now, what she would do?

The baker tumbled toward his wife, dropping his tray so the bread rolled onto the hard dirt. He gripped his son's still hands.

"How many more?" he shouted over the top of the cart. A few people stomped their boots against the growing cold.

"How many more victims before we take action? A beast stalks our village. Will we let our women and children die?"

"This is the first child," the cobbler said. Others nodded and mumbled, but still more stayed silent with their eyes on their feet. I could almost smell their fear.

"Maurice was playing yesterday and now he's dead. He won't be the last." The truth of the baker's words settled in my bones. Maurice's killer, whoever it was, had a taste for blood now—young blood—and blood was addictive. Ama's body twitched in its desire to be closer to the drying stains on the boy's clothes, but I held her still and stepped on the heel of her boot to remind her where we were. *Keep it together. Everyone's watching.*

The clop of hooves on cobblestone drew my eyes away from Maurice and his sobbing mother. A black horse dipped its head and reared as it approached the cart, but its rider urged the animal forward.

Atop the horse, Sebastian LaClaire held tightly to the reins with hands gloved in black leather. Brown eyes swept over the scene, set in a tawny face—almost the color of the patches on a new fawn's back. He wore no hat and his black hair curled loosely over his shoulders. His deep blue jacket frayed at the edges. Even lords were left wanting when harvests were bad year after year. He'd inherited his estate from his father a year ago when he'd been the same age I was now, and he looked too young to help a mother crying for her child.

The woman spared only a glance for Sebastian before

pulling her dirty apron up and scrunching it to her eyes to catch her tears. I hoped Ama felt at least a quarter of the sour guilt rippling through my belly. I'd tried so hard to make sure no one anybody cared about would be hurt. I'd done the best I could with a sister-turned-monster. Still, maybe it wasn't enough.

CHAPTER FOUR

ebastian swung down from his horse and held his reins in one hand. With the other, he reached out for the baker's wife's shaking shoulder.

"Madame. What happened?"

The woman flinched away from Sebastian's hand. He didn't react to her refusal of his touch, only bent down further so he could look her in the eyes. His own softened, almost pleading.

"Tell me, please."

"Can't you see?" shrieked the woman. "The beast has killed my son... my only son. He was just doing what I told him to do and he died. And you've done nothing to stop it. You don't protect us."

Sebastian's face darkened as he gazed into the cart. He clenched his hands into fists at his side. It did not look as if for show. He seemed truly angry. He could have punished the baker's wife for her insolence for the way she talked to him, but I suspected his rage was more internal. He hadn't saved his villagers or his own parents when they'd died. He'd failed to be the hero. And worse, everyone thought he was a killer, that he'd murdered his own parents to take his father's title.

But I knew that wasn't true.

His parents' killer stood shivering not three paces from him now, and I would never let him catch her.

"What will we do?" the butcher said, his eyes lingering on the little boy's empty face. Maurice's eyes should have been lit up with the pleasure of running through the marketplace with his friends. His lips should have been curled up in a smile, but instead they pulled back from his teeth in a grimace. Did my sister do that to him? Terrify him as he died?

The townspeople's voices came together in a low din. Everyone seemed to have a solution—send a letter to the king for help, dispatch a messenger to the next village, collect anything that could be used as a weapon, hunt the beast.

Sebastian seized on that and threw his own voice out over the crows.

"Emméline Poitres is our greatest hunter; she carries on her father's legacy now that he's gone." Sebastian pointed to the young woman and she stepped forward. Her hair had been braided back from her face, and she wore a slim-cut dress with trousers showing under the shortened hem. I envied her that, the confidence to wear something that went against all the rules, a dress that allowed her to be herself. I envied her many things, actually—a father who'd loved her before he died, a revered position in town, a thriving business breeding the best hunting dogs in the valley, even her impressive height.

Usually, I was below her attention. If she did notice me, it was only to sneer about my cheap dresses and strange sister. In an odd way, though, I wished she knew what I'd come up with, how I'd kept the beast under my control this last year. If Emméline knew the truth of it, I think she would have respected me.

Sebastian gave her a tight smile that didn't reach his eyes. I liked him a little more for that.

"Our best hunter will kill the beast and make our valley safe again," he said.

A few villagers shouted their approval, but others nodded less enthusiastically. There'd been killings in this valley for as long as anyone could remember. Emméline and her father before her hadn't succeeded in eradicating all the dangerous things in these woods, and she and her hunting hounds would never even come close to catching Ama. My sister was too fast for her, too smart. She was different from the wolves Emméline was used to killing.

"It's too late!" wailed Maurice's mother. "My baby is gone! She won't save us from this monster . . . this beast!"

"Don't doubt that I *will* kill that beast," Emméline said.

Sebastian nodded at her and raised his voice out over the

crowd. "Trust in Emméline and trust in *me*. We won't let the animal live."

"But you have! It lives and we die."

"And no surprise either. No girl is going to be the one who kills the beast," Maurice's father said.

"You'd be surprised what this girl can do." Emméline stepped toward him, spittle flying from her lips.

Maurice's mother ignored them all and collapsed into sobs again. Her eyes squeezed shut and snot trailed between her nose and mouth. Sebastian bowed his head. He'd failed these people. *His* people. He shifted from well-made boot to well-made boot on the slick cobblestones and refused to look at us.

"Who will clean the body?" he asked finally, and looked to the woman next to him. "Clarice?"

The midwife shook her head. "Those wounds are cursed."

"Nonsense. Two sols to the person who will prepare the body. We must bury him before the ground freezes."

The priest swept through the crowd, his great black sleeves flapping like a crow's wings as he made the sign of the cross.

"Forgive me, my lord, but I should like to examine the body first," Père Danil said. "For marks of evil."

At the mention of evil, Maurice's mother keened again and gripped her son's sleeves. I let go of my sister and stepped forward. I couldn't have the priest examining the boy's body. If Ama had done it, the teeth marks would show. But it was more than that. If my sister had really killed this little boy, I'd failed—failed at protecting her and Maurice both. The only thing I could do for the boy now was to clean the blood from his skin, and I wanted to do him this last kindness.

"I'll do it. I'll clean the body," I said, pushing through the crowd toward the cart.

Sebastian's eyes landed on me with a blow. I didn't think he'd ever looked straight at me before, and a frisson of energy passed over my skin as he nodded his head at me.

"Your name?" he asked.

"Marie Michaud."

"Sinner," someone whispered, and the word hung in the air. I dared another look into Sebastian's clear eyes. There was no reprimand there, no threat—just curiosity. Fine. He could look and wonder. I'd been called worse before. If I sold enough perfumes and kept Ama's secret, I'd be considered respectable by the time Ama was ready to marry. They'd have to accept us with coin in our pocket and the right fashions on our backs.

"Michèle," Sebastian called to the blacksmith, "take the boy to Marie's house."

"I want to help," Maurice's mother said, grabbing onto her child's arm. "Please."

"It'll be hard, Claudette," the midwife said. "Better to let Marie do it."

Claudette nodded but held fast to Maurice's arm as the blacksmith pulled the handcart down the lane. My heart beat faster and the slow heat of grief climbed through me. This was horrible to watch.

Eventually, the woman lost pace with her son and fell to her knees in the muck of the street. Ama tripped forward and pulled Claudette up by the elbows. The woman fell into Ama's arms and sobbed onto her wool-clad shoulder, staining the green fabric with the salt of her tears. She sniffed in and pulled back suddenly, eyes wide.

"You don't smell right . . . like raw meat," she said, and let go of Ama as if my sister burned to the touch. Fear licked my belly. Suspicion stalked us from the shadows.

For a year, I'd focused on protecting Ama's secret and minimizing her destruction, but that wasn't enough anymore. If she'd done this terrible thing, I was losing the battle with the beast, and that couldn't happen yet. I wasn't ready.

Ama looped her arm through the handle of our basket and hurried back to me. The little glass bottles tinkled again, but the sound enticed no one. It rang too cold.

Much of the crowd dispersed, but Sebastian lingered, stroking the thick neck of his horse. He watched as a few townspeople approached Maurice's mother and ushered her toward the church. Père Danil welcomed them with a grim twist of his lips as he stood on the stone steps. After the priest followed them inside, Sebastian finally pulled himself onto his horse. A gray cloud ate up what had been left of the afternoon sun and the stained glass window above the wide church doors stared down at us like a dull eye.

"We never marked a victim," Ama said as she watched Sebastian ride away.

"I know, I'm sorry. You'll have to make do with rabbits tonight."

Ama pulled a face. "I always wake up hungry when it's rabbits. There's no animal in the valley big enough for me. And the manacles? You know how they burn my wrists. No one ever sticks *you* in the cellar."

The casual tone in her voice irked me—no, not irked; it *scared* me.

"I don't need to be locked in the cellar because I don't eat people." I pushed a few strands of hair out of my eyes. "Anyway, the village has had enough excitement today. We don't need another killing tonight. Come on, let's clean up this mess."

I almost said *your mess*. But Ama merely shrugged and skipped away down the cobbled lane with the basket swinging haphazardly from her arm.

CHAPTER FIVE

I was not prepared to see the body up close. It was inescapable from here—I couldn't squint my eyes and blur the edges of the gore. The boy lay on our scrubbed wood table, the smell of death leaking from him, oozing into the cracks in our plastered walls. There wasn't enough lavender in the world to rid us of the tang of blood and urine.

"Here," Ama said as she pushed a bowl of water into my hands. "You do it."

Of course, the dirty work was mine to do. Ama was good at leaving everything for me take care of, and as I grabbed a cloth from the sideboard, a little sting of resentment zipped through me.

But just as my irritation settled into my muscles, Ama came to stand behind me and rubbed the tightness from my shoulders. Even when I was angry, I still needed her. When she'd been gone working at the big house last year, I'd felt the shape of her missing from my life.

I'd known, even then, Papa had debts. He racked them up at the tavern, the bakery, even the cobbler's shop when Ama's feet outgrew her boots. What I hadn't realized was the debt holders could petition Monseigneur LaClaire and *he* could pay them back and have Papa's debts pass into his hands. So Papa owed Monseigneur but had no way to pay.

I didn't know who suggested it. Perhaps Monseigneur LaClaire demanded immediate payment in kind or perhaps Papa offered, knowing it would be one less mouth to feed for a while. He told me later Monseigneur had asked specifically for Ama, but I still didn't know if I believed him. I'd never thought Papa really loved me, but he had even less time for Ama. She looked too much like Maman, I thought.

He took Ama to the manor in the night. I didn't even wake up when he pulled her from our bed, when her spot beside me grew cold.

Morning light inched over my face until I was forced to open my eyelids. It was then I realized. Ama never woke before me.

"Where is she?" I asked.

Papa slumped against the wall and pulled his scarf from his throat. He let it fall to the floor in a lumpy red puddle. He pushed his great, meaty thumbs into his eyes and rubbed, as if trying to clear his vision. As if he couldn't stand what he saw.

"Papa, please…"

"I had no choice, Marie."

A feeling like ice cut through me. Ama was beautiful, and

being beautiful was a dangerous thing for a girl. I was less so. My pale brown hair like a faded imprint of her raven strands. My white face less likely to blush a nice, healthy pink. My light brown eyes not nearly as striking as her dark ones.

"You sold her, didn't you?"

Papa ran a hand over his face. The deep lines in his forehead caught beads of sweat. "It's not what you think. She'll be a servant, nothing more. And she'll come home when the debt is paid."

A small shudder of relief ran through my belly, but it wasn't enough. Ama was still gone. And without her, I was utterly alone. I didn't have any friends in the village. The good ones wouldn't talk to me, and I wouldn't talk to the vagrants. I was stuck in this in-between I would never have been in if Maman had lived longer and Papa hadn't turned to drink. But things were as they were. And now my sister, my only friend, had been stolen from me.

"They'll work her hard up there in the big house," I said.

Papa scratched a freckle beside his left eye, and the familiar gesture tugged at my heart in a way I hated. I should have been all stone toward him after what he'd done, but it wasn't that easy.

He leaned against the wall, palms turned out. "It's done."

"Marie." Ama slammed the bowl of water onto the table, and the soft sunlight of that morning dissolved to the orange glow of a late afternoon fire crackling in the hearth.

She grabbed the rag from my hand and pushed it deep into the bowl. The clear liquid sloshed over the side and pooled in the grains of the table.

"I said I'd do it." I snatched the rag back and squeezed out the excess water. Ama's hands were dirty enough without touching the boy she might have killed.

Maurice stared up accusingly from the table. His round eyes glimmered dully in the firelight. I'd have to sew them shut, and threading the lids together without hitting the eyeball would not be easy—or enjoyable—work.

Suspicion crept like heat up the back of my neck. I took a breath in through my nose and let it leak slowly from my lips. I steadied myself enough to say, "Look at the shredding of the skin. Only an animal could have done that."

"What other beast stalks these mountains and kills like this? I thought I was the only one," Ama said from where she leaned against the stones of the hearth. It still smelled like smoke in there. My sister traced little circles into her right palm, something she did to comfort herself. I wanted to comfort her too, but I couldn't. Not while I cleaned the body of a child she might have killed.

In truth, this didn't look quite like one of Ama's kills. Her long front teeth usually punctured large holes in her victim's skin, and her claws left jagged cuts behind. This boy's wounds were a bit too shallow—and Ama didn't usually leave this much meat on the bone.

"You're the only one who trades feet for paws, but there are other animals hiding in the trees. Wolves, lynxes . . ."

"When has anyone ever brought a lynx out of the woods?" she said.

"You're saying it *was* you?"

"No! I wouldn't do this to a child, Marie. You know that."

Ama stood up straight now and wrapped her arms around herself. "I'll go chop a few logs for you before you lock me up in the cellar. I think it will be cold tonight."

Do I know she wouldn't do this? I thought about it as I worked. Before she turned for the first time, I wouldn't have thought Ama capable of killing anyone at all. Now the monster inside her seemed to be eating away more and more of her gentleness with every kill.

I glanced out the window as Ama's shape blurred past. She pushed the door with one hand and used her hip to edge it wider open, her arms full of logs topped with a rabbit that still had most of its brown fur.

"Here," she said, dropping the stack into the wood basket, rabbit and all.

I snatched up the dead animal.

"Lots of wood and one rabbit from the trap," she said.

It was a peace offering, no—more than that. It was a bribe. I knew from the way she leaned over Maurice's body and found my gaze with hers. Her eyes burned into me, little yellow flecks glinted in the low light from the candle beside my elbow.

"I don't want to be in the cellar."

"Well, we didn't get to mark a victim, so we've no choice."

"Yes, we have. You're choosing to chain me up."

"So you don't kill anyone again!"

Ama scoffed. "You mean so I don't kill anyone important that the villagers would go asking about."

Annoyance turned my belly. It was a delicate balance,

what we did. Feeding the beast and keeping the villagers at bay was no small task, and in truth, it was left to me. Ama never worried about who died. She just followed my lead and tore out the throats I prepared for her. The least she could do was be grateful.

"They're already suspicious, Ama," I said. "That monster doll on the step was no coincidence. And with Papa gone right now, we can't take any chances."

"The doll was prank, that's it. Someone's trying to taunt us for fun."

"Yes, and what happens when those taunts turn into accusations and they come with their pitchforks? What then?"

"Then I eat them." Ama's eyes flashed gold again.

"This isn't a joke."

"Who said I'm joking?"

CHAPTER SIX

The knotted wood of the cellar door had swelled in the misty rain. It stuck and I had to pull hard, both hands gripping the cold metal handles, until there was a squeak of hinges and one of the doors finally came free.

The scent of damp earth unfurled around us with heady notes of clay and a hint of sulfer.

"You first," Ama said.

I pointed the toe of my boot and touched it to the first sagging step. I scooped up the lantern and swung it forward, casting long shadows against the mud-packed walls. The low light caught the chains fastened to the floor and the iron glinted blue-black.

"I'll stay until it starts and then I'll come back the moment you're yourself again. You'll barely remember being down here," I said to fight back the sour guilt in my stomach. Ama hated this place and I couldn't blame her.

"I'll know I'm stuck here in this hole."

"Once the beast comes, you, *Ama*, won't be bothered."

"We aren't separate you know, the beast and me. We're entwined. I remember more each time."

Her words turned my blood to ice. I stopped short and swung around to face her in the dim light of my oil lantern.

"Why didn't you tell me before?"

"Because when I talk about what happens to me, fear shadows your eyes."

I hadn't thought she'd noticed—she rarely seemed to truly look at me these days. It wasn't the same as it had been between us before she went away. We were older now, and though the tie between our hearts was still there, we seemed to need each other a little less.

I pulled a twist of paper from my pocket and unwrapped a dab of lard, and it gave under my finger like slippery dough. I bent down and rubbed the glistening fat around the inside of all four manacles—two for her wrists and two for her ankles. At least the iron wouldn't chafe her skin.

"I need to know these things, Ama. I need to know *every-thing.*"

"What difference does it make?"

"Because I'm going to find a way to stop it ... but first I need to figure out what *it* is. I need to figure out what happened to you at the big house."

Ama pushed her hair away from her face, running her hands along the top of her head. There were small changes since this started, but I noticed them—sharper edges to her face, a manic light in her eyes. And always, the whiff of blood.

The first time I saw her transform, I thought she'd kill me, but she only sniffed me, ran a claw along my cheek, and bounded into the dark after better prey. I'd thought the perfumes ingenious. I taught Ama the scents and she recognized them even when the beast took her. We marked vagrants and thieves—she satisfied her taste for blood and warm meat and no one complained about those who went missing. I had it under control. Until now.

Maurice shouldn't have died like this, scraped away from life by sharp points of an animal's claw. His wounds were cleaner and more precise than Ama's usual victims, but perhaps she was getting better at killing? She'd had enough practice by now. And if I suspected my own sister to be a child killer and did nothing about it—what did that make me?

I wouldn't be that person. Already I did things I never thought I'd do. I lifted my finger and dabbed a man's neck with scented oil knowing full well that same throat would be torn later that night. I chose who lived and who died like some kind of vengeful Roman goddess. But I did it for her—for Ama—and it always seemed a fair exchange.

The child was different. Nothing about his death felt fair, and Ama's calm unsettled me. It was as if she wasn't touched with remorse, as if the sight of his blood had done nothing to chasten her. She pouted a little when I moved to fasten the shackles around her thin wrists.

"You might as well be naked. You're going to ruin that chemise, and we don't have many more to replace it," I said.

"It's pouring rain! I don't want to freeze while I wait."

"Fine, but we're going to have to sell twice as many bottles of scent to afford new linen."

"I'll be a good little saleswoman next week. I promise."

Ama looked up at me with the big round eyes of a child, and my own rolled into the back of my head. I couldn't help the smile tugging at my lips. My sister made everything sound so easy, and I wanted it to be true, so sometimes I believed her. We needed to sell scent, so she'd sell scent. We needed more firewood, so she'd go into the forest and collect sticks from the ground. Ama always saw the easiest solution. It was me who got stuck in the muddy details, and I often needed my sister to pull me out.

But as I smiled at her now, my heart skipped a beat. A band of amber rimmed the familiar dark brown of her irises. It began.

I ignored the distant growls as I sponged blood off Maurice's throat. It plumed in the bowl of water, making it unclean.

His mother would always remember him like this. His torn body would haunt her nightmares and daydreams both. That's the cruelest thing the mind does, isn't it? Fraying the edges of all the good and leaving us with perfectly clear memories of the worst days of our lives. I'd tried to hold on to everything that made my sister *her*—but in the end, I'd only see the glowing gold of her animal eyes and remember the smell of blood on her skin.

I scrubbed faster, washing away the dirt behind Maurice's knees and using a knife to pry the grime from under his fingernails. He'd probably never been this clean before. I needed to deliver him to his mother so I could go to the big house and collect my sols—enough for bread and meat and to put one aside. Though, of course, it wasn't only coin I was after.

Somewhere in the shadowy corridors, among the forgotten furniture draped with white cloths, there was a library—the only one in the village. Sebastian's mother had always kept a little blue book with her on a chain hanging from her belt. Ama told me she'd seen Madame LaClaire writing in it, singing the little songs contained in its pages. It *had* to be Sebastian's mother who turned my sister into a monster. It wasn't songs my sister had heard but spells. Ama had gone into her house a normal girl and come out part monster. Madame's book was my only chance to break the curse she created.

If Ama had been cursed in that house, she could be cured there too. And even though it hardly mattered since the deed had been done, I wanted to know *why* Ama had been cursed. Why my sister? Why had Sebastian's mother done this?

I'd felt bad for the great lady when I was little. She'd been shunned by the same people I had. We were poor and she was rich, yes, but we both hurt.

It was easy to see in her face whenever she *did* end up

coming to church. She'd step out of the heavy wooden doors and the villagers would back away from her as if even the hem of her dress might have been poison. Sometimes they'd whispered behind their hands as she walked away. And yet, she had always held her head high—even if her eyes and cheeks had been wan and pinched.

When Papa sold Ama to that house, I'd dared to hope Sebastian's mother might be kind to another of the village's castaways. I hadn't believed her to be a witch. Everyone here was too superstitious. Eager, even, to believe there was more than what they saw in front of them.

It was because she was an outsider, of course, born on an island called Martinique. It was easy for Père Danil to turn the villagers against her without any extended family to shield her. He'd say how she must be such a great mother to spend all her time caring for her invalid youngest son instead of coming to church every Sunday. So caring, so maternal.

So dangerous.

The whispers of *witch* had started before I can even remember. Always behind her back—she *was* married to the lord of the big house. I was never sure if I believed the rumors. They seemed like the same kind of insubstantial threat that the other kids made, taunting me about the woods witch coming out of trees to claim me in the night. Something to make you shiver when you lay in bed but nothing more.

Then Ama came home a fourteen-year-old monster, and who else could have made her that way? My sister had tumbled through the door of our cottage—naked and pink from cold—with blood crusted around her mouth and under her fingernails. When news of the lord's and lady's deaths cascaded through the village the next morning, I thought there was a connection to the state Ama was in. When I saw her turn for the first time, I realized what must have happened. Someone in that house had made Ama a monster and she'd made that someone pay.

From the time Ama came home, I'd taken care of her. I drove chains into the floor of the cold cellar and taught her the scent we'd use to mark her victims. I'd watched the clouds drift over the moon through one of the small windows of our cottage while I knew my sister was out there, tasting blood. I spent that time planning how to keep her safe.

But now, I wouldn't let Ama kill any more children and threaten everything. This had gone on for too long.

I would finish cleaning Maurice and go to Sebastian for my payment. He had a young brother who never came to the village. Consumption, some said. I could offer my help, my services in making him better. I could get Sebastian to let me stay in the house just long enough to uncover its secrets. It had all started there, and it was where I needed to go to find out how to undo the curse.

Sebastian would probably be hesitant to let me in, but I knew what it was to watch a sibling suffer. I didn't think it would take much convincing at all if I made the right promises.

CHAPTER SEVEN

My skin rose in gooseflesh, painfully squeezing each hair on my arms and legs, and I shivered. My legs ached as if I'd been squatting down planting carrot seeds all day. I unfolded them from underneath me and pushed myself up to a sitting position with the palms of my hands against the cold, rough floor.

"What are you doing, Marie?"

Ama sat, legs pulled up to her, wrists and ankles trapped by iron manacles. The cellar was revealed haphazardly as the candle in the holder near Ama's foot guttered.

Had I decided to come and check on her in the middle of the night? Even so, that doesn't explain why I'm naked.

"How long have you been yourself?" I asked while pulling my hair forward so it fell over my breasts. It didn't usually bother me to be naked around my sister, but a strange sense of vulnerability made me want to cover up.

"Not long. I woke to find you sleeping here." Ama combed through her tangled hair with her fingers. "Were you sleep-walking again last night? Are you that worried about me, Marie? You don't need to be."

That was probably it. I'd been worried about Ama, about what she was becoming, and I must have started walking in my sleep again. Did I wear a nightgown to bed? I thought I'd just stripped my dress off and fallen onto my mattress, too exhausted to stay awake even long enough to change. At least I could have grabbed a cloak before coming out here though. I certainly didn't thank my nighttime self now as I shivered on the cold earthen floor of the cellar.

"Is this in solidarity?" Ama gestured, the chains clanging as she moved. "I wake up cold and naked, so you do too?"

I adjusted my hair again and shrugged. "I was so tired last night, I barely remember taking my chemise off."

"Well, since you're here, can you unlock me?"

"Oh, sorry."

I put a finger through the ring of keys hanging by the door and freed my sister from her irons. She rubbed at her wrists, even though they weren't red and raw. The fat had worked.

"Come on," I said. "Let's have something warm to drink. I need to talk to you about something."

Ama bounded ahead of me and ran up the steps out of the cellar. I didn't worry about anyone seeing us naked—no one really came out this far without good reason.

As I passed through the doors, I noticed claw marks, long

scratches deep in the wood. I hadn't thought the chains could reach that far. I'd have to check them again.

The house welcomed us with the glowing embers of last night's fire. We pulled on new chemises before Ama poured a little ale from the barrel into a pot, tipping the barrel onto its side to coax the liquid out, and warmed it over the fire. I sliced thick oat bread, and we both ignored Maurice's body taking up most of the kitchen table.

"So, what do you want to talk about?" Ama asked as she passed me a cup of warm ale.

I took a sip and instantly regretted it. The tip of my tongue went numb from the heat.

"I need to leave for a little while. A few weeks at most. We need coin for the winter, to make it through."

The lie fell steadily from my tongue and Ama stared at me.

"That's what Papa's gone to do . . . work in the next village and bring back coin. Why would you need to do that as well? We'll sell the perfumes."

"It won't be enough for food to last us through. And do you really think Papa will bring the money back? No, he'll drink it away first."

Ama put her cup down near Maurice's foot and stuck out a finger to touch his toe. I wanted to slap her hand away.

"Well, where are you going to go? Who would hire you? And what about the next time I change?"

"I should be back before it happens again, but if I'm not, lock yourself in the cellar and keep the keys nearby so when you're human again you can use them. I'm going to the big house, to beg work as a kitchen maid."

Ama's eyes widened. "You can't, Marie."

"As you said, nowhere else here would hire me."

"Marie, you must be joking. You know what happened to me when I worked there. I came back like this! What if something bad happens to you too?"

"Nothing will happen to me. It's just the young lords there now and a few servants, right? Nothing to be scared of."

"Well, I *am* scared. For you and for me. I didn't like being apart from you when I went to work there before and I don't want to be apart from you now." Ama reached across the table and hooked my smallest finger with hers. "Don't leave me here on my own. It's going to start getting dark so early."

For someone who roamed the woods at night at least once a month in the body of a beast, Ama as a girl was quite terrified of the dark. She got stuck in the images she thought she saw in shadowy corners. Monsters coming to get her.

"You can light the candles as soon as the sun starts to go down."

"Really?" Ama said.

Usually I forbade it. We only lit the candles when we could barely see enough to move around the cottage anymore. Light was a luxury and we had to be sparing.

"That doesn't make it all right, you know," Ama said.

"It will be fine and it won't be for long, I promise, and I'll write to you when I can."

"I don't like it at all. And I'll be bored here without you."

It was her way of saying she'd miss me but she accepted that I was set on going. I reached out and wrapped my fingers around hers.

"I'm sure you'll find something to keep you busy."

Ama smiled. "Always."

I packed while she puttered around the cottage—polishing our three china teacups, counting out spools of thread, crushing lavender in our mortar. I gathered what little I'd need.

"Help me load Maurice into the cart."

Ama set down the pestle and it rolled along the table. *Thunk. Thunk. Thunk.*

"He's heavy."

"That's why I need your help."

Is she hesitating because she does *feel bad about what she's done? Is it hard for her to have to be here for the after?*

We loaded the boy in like a sack of meal. He actually wasn't very heavy, but he was stiff and hard to maneuver. I tried not to think of him as a child. It was easier to pretend he was nothing special at all.

I lifted the handles of the cart and looked back toward Ama. She stood in the doorway to the cottage, a cloth stained red slung over her shoulder.

"I love you," I said.

"I need you," she replied, and turned back into the house.

Iridescent bubbles of blue and pink skimmed the top of the puddle outside the baker's door. Cheap soap and a bit of oil from cleaning the pans. The weathered wood door, always open to release the heady scent of baking bread, stood firmly closed against the steel-gray sky and the prying eyes of villagers.

I'd slung a cloth over Maurice and tied it down to the slats of the cart, but the boy's toes still peeked through. His clothes were in a bag next to his body—I could have kept them and sold the boots at least, but it felt cruel to do so. What if Maurice's mother had nothing else to remember her son by?

I knocked twice with light raps and the door swung open a little.

"Do you have him?" Maurice's mother whispered through the gap.

"He's in the cart."

"He'll be buried tomorrow."

The thought of Maurice at the bottom of a hole made my stomach squirm. "I can take him to the churchyard now if you like."

"No." The woman reached out and grabbed my sleeve so hard her nails bit into my arm. "He's mine for tonight and then never mine again. I want him to sleep in his bed."

Sleep. It would be easy to pretend, with Maurice lying there with his eyes closed under the covers, that he was all right. It would be easy to fool yourself into believing, even for one night, that he wasn't gone. I couldn't deny this poor woman her indulgence.

"I'll help you carry him in."

I wasn't sure she'd be able to do it—I thought maybe once she grabbed his cold wrists, she'd lose her nerve. But she gripped each arm steadily and I lifted his ankles and together we got him to his bed. His mother covered his nakedness and the jagged tear at his throat with a thin red blanket.

"There," she said, tucking the fabric close to his body. "Now he won't be cold."

I swallowed to ease the burning ache in my throat and touched Maurice's stiff, frozen fingers one last time. He was too young to be gone.

"Emméline's making a plan, you know," Maurice's mother said. "The young lord said she's training. It's about time he gets someone to help us, but I wasn't really expecting it from him after what he did to his parents."

"We don't know he did anything to his parents. And what do you mean Emméline's making a plan?"

"The young lord told her he'll give her a great reward if she kills the beast that's been hunting us. Maurice is the fifteenth to die since last year."

The number was too high. Ama surely couldn't have killed that many since she came back. But then, exaggerations always made a better story.

"Vagrants and thieves for the most part. Few locals die," I said.

"Enough do."

Her words struck me like the frozen rain threatening in the dark clouds above. There was only *one* local who mattered to her and he was dead. Nothing I said would change that.

"We don't know what's doing the killing. It might be a pack of wolves. It might be we've just had bad luck."

"Bad luck," Maurice's mother murmured, trying and failing to lift her son's stiffened arm to her breast. She relented and let it go before dragging her own sleeve against her eyes. Two wets drops fell onto Maurice's gray skin.

"We'll find the beast that killed our baby and hang it in the square," she said. "We'll slice it down the middle until the innards fall out. It will be nothing but a shell, a coat destined for the back of the king. We'll do that to the animal because we can. That's the natural order. We kill them. They don't kill us."

My skin prickled and fear brewed in my gut. They'd be after her now—after Ama. And Emméline was planning and training and trying to figure out how to kill my sister and earn her prize.

CHAPTER EIGHT

ime is a weapon turned against us, I realized as Maurice's mother led me from the house. I had to figure out how my sister had been cursed before Emméline began her hunt.

Sebastian's mother was dead, but the book must still be somewhere in the house. Père Danil had preached about the evils of spell books given to witches by the devil and wouldn't have allowed her to be buried with such an item.

But . . . what if something evil still lingered there too? If it got to me somehow, if it made me a monster too, who would fix things?

Papa mostly ignored what happened to Ama. When he saw her the first time, the beast fading into a girl outside our cottage, he fell to his knees in front of the little wooden cross that hung from a nail beside the hearth. He muttered incoherent prayers while tears slid down his cheeks. Then he made a point to leave us as often as he could. Carting late vegetables into another town, going north to look for work. Any reason, any excuse to be away from his tainted daughter. If he couldn't be away from us, he'd drink himself into a state where we didn't matter, where we barely existed to him at all.

I was the only one who tried to make sure we'd have a future. If I were to be cursed too, that would be the end of it.

If they discovered Ama's secret and killed her, that would be the end of me.

"Does Master Sebastian have my coins?" I asked Maurice's mother.

She pursed her lips at my question and shut the door in my face. I couldn't fault her that. Her only son was dead and I'd just asked about money.

The wind whipped fallen leaves against my shins as I hurried away from the baker's house. A thin layer of ice frosted the cobblestones. Townhouses crowded together like they could lean on each other for warmth. A wooden sign for the atelier swung on rusted hinges with a grating squeak.

The streets were empty.

It wasn't just the promise of bad weather keeping everyone tucked up into their houses. Something else lingered in the air—a whiff of fear. I, however, had nothing to be afraid of. I knew the monster intimately.

Unless, of course, I didn't.

Maybe I just didn't want to believe my sister could do such a thing, but I couldn't help wondering if something else had killed Maurice. The kill didn't look right, and there were other animals in the forest with long claws. I sighed and pushed my hair back into my hood. It was easy to talk yourself into something when you wanted it so badly.

The trees thickened as I left the village street and crunched over the dying grass. There was a large drive up to the big house, but it was rutted with half-frozen mud, so I walked alongside it on the green. The sky above was a steady gray, but the wind had drifted away. The animals in the forest had gone silent. Everything was utterly still. I had the impression of being contained, like standing inside the glass globe Père Danil had shown the children at Christmas, before turning it over and releasing the little flecks of fake snow over the minuscule town.

I pushed out a loud breath just to hear it and see the little cloud of white appear in front of my mouth. The world was still real. I was still alive.

The house sat on a hill overlooking the town, and its blank windows stared down at me like Maurice's expressionless eyes had as I cleaned him. It wasn't in disrepair, but a whiff of neglect came off the chipped paint and brown ivy clinging to the walls. Sebastian must have dismissed the gardener. Perhaps he needed to make economies like so many others in town. Except, for him, it was not having his rosebushes trimmed; for others, it was choosing which meal to skip that day.

I continued toward the house. Something had happened to my sister here. Dark magic must collect in the corners of rooms like dust. My feet slowed. I knew I needed to go in there, that the house was the only place I'd find answers and a cure for Ama, but my skin prickled with fear. The place stood solitary on its hill, the woods leaning away, as if the very trees had tried to run from it. I wanted to run too.

My stiff fingers fumbled on the slick metal pull chain beside the wooden door. I tugged it and a bell trilled inside. The door swung open immediately.

"Oui?"

The voice reached me before its owner peered around the door. An older woman with fleecy white hair hid half her pale face in the shadows.

"I'm here to see Master Sebastian."

"Non, he's not here. You are Marie, yes?"

My name slipped from her lips and fell like a stone. A shiver tingled down my spine, but I shook it off. This was silly. It was only the rain and the squeak of the door and the strange white film clinging to one of the woman's eyes playing tricks on me—frightening me without cause. I'd seen worse than this.

"I'm Marie, yes. I was told to come here to collect my sols after I delivered Maurice to his mother."

The woman gave no indication she knew who Maurice or his mother were, but she extended a shaking hand with two coins tucked in her palm.

"He thanks you for your service."

Damn. The old woman kept the door opened only wide enough for half her body to be visible. I couldn't even see inside the house.

"I have some herbs," I said as I pulled the little bag from the pocket of my dress and tucked away the coins. "I think they'd be helpful to the young master. The lord's brother?"

The woman narrowed her eyes and showed me her graying teeth. "No peddlers!" she said, and slammed the door.

I waited until I heard the bolt slide into place before skirting the face of the house. I wasn't going to leave just because that old woman had slammed a door in my face. There would be another way in, another route to Sebastian.

The house seemed untouchable in its grandeur, but if you looked closely, you could see the cracks in the façade. Thin lines like spiderwebs ran the length of the plaster—where it wasn't peeling. The faded dark blue shutters clacked in the wind. It was the biggest house I'd ever seen, but even it wasn't impervious to the sun beating into the valley in summertime or the wind and snow of winter. It broke down against the elements, just like my little cottage did.

A curling iron gate leaned against the side of the wall with its latch hanging open. I pushed on the intricately wrought black vines and it scraped against cobblestones. A shadow shot up from behind the gate and my heart thudded in my ears. A bird, probably, disturbed by the noise. I pressed on.

Overgrown grass clumped under the iron and the gate stuck. There was only enough room to squeeze through sideways. The sharp fingers of wayward branches grabbed at my dress.

I turned, stuck in between the gate and the wall of the

house. A scream rose through my throat but I gritted my teeth against it. There were no fingers, no hand. Just thorns sticking in my dress, pulling me back.

Drops from last night's rain clung to the rose petals. The gray-black morning drained the color from their petals, but their smell couldn't be shaded. This was the house's private garden, so there had to be a way in from outside.

Gravel crunched under my boots with every step on the well-laid paths. Water pooled along the ridges from last night, threatening to drown the roses. Someone should have planned these gardens better and devised a drainage system. Nothing could be left to its own devices and survive.

An owl called from a tree with hoots like soft burs. I wrapped the trailing ends of my scarf around my numbed fingers. Ama was probably warm right now, resting in bed after a night chained in the cellar. Resentment nipped at me but I couldn't let it take hold. Not when I was trying to find the courage to get inside the house and tell my lie.

The hanging branches of a willow sheltered a stone bench a few feet down the path. The seat dipped in the middle—proof it was well-used. Did Sebastian's mother sit here, flipping through her spell book, scribbling down the words that would turn my sister into a monster? It was easy to imagine her here, in a dress saturated with color, her hair loose over her shoulders, letting the breeze comb through it. I could almost see her, the shift of her smile as she penned the word that, once uttered, would turn my sister into a monster. The satisfaction in her eyes.

A shiver crept over the back of my neck like a long-legged spider. I had to get out of there. My boots slipped on the loose gravel of the ordered pathways as I turned at the end of the path, sinking deeper into the garden with each step. The rosebushes struck me with unkempt branches, and the sweet smell of the petals choked me.

Then, out of nowhere, a little boy stood in the middle of the path. I skidded right into him.

CHAPTER NINE

ur bodies collided with a soft thump and he fell to his knees. His face twisted in what looked like annoyance rather than pain. I reached out a hand and pulled him up anyway. He seemed a few years older than the boy whose body I'd just cleaned. In stark contrast to Maurice's cold, gray skin, life flushed this child's brown cheeks with a hint of red. His dark, solemn eyes avoided mine.

I wasn't good with children. The way some women in our village knelt down to talk to them in smooth voices didn't come naturally to me, but here was the boy I'd been hoping to use as a way into this house. I could at least bend my knees and crouch to his level.

"What's your name?" I asked when I realized I didn't know. This boy hadn't been paraded through the village by his parents like Sebastian had been.

The child shrank from my voice, and I backed away from

him on my heels. Scaring him already wouldn't win me any favors with his brother.

"It's all right. You don't have to answer."

He contemplated my boots for a moment before reaching out a small hand and slowly, gently, pushing it into mine. I squeezed his cold fingers and my heart warmed. His touch was a comfort among the shadows blanketing the garden. The little boy coughed and red spittle flew out onto his dark blue sleeve.

"Come here." I stood and pulled him to me without thinking. An impulse born of secondhand guilt. Whoever had the care of him shouldn't have left him out here among the thorns.

I retraced my steps along the gravel path with light footsteps trailing behind me. He followed without question, with a trust I hadn't earned. Part of me yearned to tell him to be more careful—but of course, his faith in me could be used to my advantage.

My chest tightened with each corner we turned, but I didn't picture Madame LaClaire there again. Her bench sat empty with raindrops pooling in the middle of the seat. The boy never flinched or slowed. He wasn't scared here.

A sigh of relief escaped me when I found the garden gate. My steps quickened and the child's did too. I grabbed his hand again when we skirted the corner of the house and dragged him toward the great front door. Thankfully, he didn't resist.

A thin layer of ice slicked the chain of the bell and my

fingers slipped as I pulled. Chimes sounded deep in the belly of the house and I prayed it would be Sebastian who answered this time, but the door swung open to reveal the same woman who'd turned me away earlier.

Her deep-set eyes widened, even the milky one, as she took in the boy beside me. "Master Lucien. Whatever are you doing out here?"

"He was on the drive," I lied. "Thought I'd bring him back to you."

The woman reached out for Lucien and pulled him gently to her side. Then the wrinkles around her mouth deepened.

"What are you still doing here?"

I went on as though she hadn't spoken. "Lucien has consumption, doesn't he?"

A veil dropped over the woman's eyes. "I already told you, we don't want peddlers here."

"I'm not selling anything, but I could help him," I said.

The woman almost rolled her eyes but then narrowed them instead. Tears glimmered at the corners. "How?"

I had her. She was interested in me now—interested in what I could do for Lucien. They'd probably seen as many doctors as could be persuaded down into our valley. Obviously, none of them had been able to help the boy.

I brought her a whiff of hope. Something they hadn't tried before. I'd prayed Sebastian would fall into the trap just as easily.

"I'll only speak with the lord." I said. "Now, are you going to let me inside?"

The hall swallowed me up. A wide staircase framed with dark mahogany wood stretched up toward the second-level gallery. Faded images of angels with dusty blue robes and feathery wings stared down at me from the ceiling with huge, bulging eyes. The artist hadn't been very good. The angels didn't make me feel welcome or safe—instead my skin tingled with the urge to turn around. I wouldn't though. Not when I was this close to a cure for Ama.

A large clock stood sentry by the door, its great brass ticker swinging back and forth with a heavy sound. Weak light trailed in from the two windows and illuminated specks of dust drifting up from the carpet with each step the servant woman took. She wrapped her hand around a small candelabra and pulled it from an alcove.

"Come with me."

Lucien had grabbed back onto my hand. How strange that he should cling to a stranger in his own home. Pity welled in my chest, but I took a breath and forced it down. There was no room for weakness here.

"Are you taking me to Master Sebastian?"

The woman gave me a sad smile, exposing a gap where one of her front teeth should have been. The rest of her teeth were graying in bright red gums.

"Don't play games with him, Miss. He's known enough heartache already."

I swallowed on a dry throat. That was exactly what I

planned to do with him—play a game. And I was making up the rules as I went, which didn't sit well with me. I preferred well-laid plans and hedging my bets. But I didn't have time for any of that now. I had to figure out what happened to Ama in this house before the hunters came for her. Before she killed another child.

Something deep and dark had happened within these walls, some kind of magic I barely wanted to imagine. What had Ama seen, what had she felt on that night? Had she trusted her mistress and been betrayed? Had she seen it coming? Anger and fear warred in my heart. My sister had been hurt here. Would I be hurt in this house too?

"I only want to help," I said, to hear the sound of my voice in the too-quiet hall.

"That's true of very few people in this world," the old woman said, leading me on anyway.

Floorboards creaked beneath thick carpets as the servant woman led me into a dark, wood-paneled room. A great dining table crowded the space with its legion of spindly wood chairs upholstered with faded brocade. Black scorch marks marred the carved stones of a hearth big enough to walk into. Embers glowed orange and red among the ashes littering the iron grate. A kettle hung from a hook over the fire.

"More water, Master?" The old woman said as way of greeting.

Sebastian, head bent over papers, hair trailing over his shoulders and into the ink pot beside him, didn't look up. He dipped the nib of his pen into the black liquid and scratched something out on one of the papers in front of him.

"Bastian." Lucien's small voice startled me and I let go of his hand. The older brother raised black eyebrows and tore his gaze away from his work. His eyes widened a little as they swept over me. I lifted the side of my skirt and bent my knees in the barest shadow of a curtsy.

"Didn't Madame Écrue give you your coins?" Sebastian asked.

My voice caught in my dry throat. "That's not why I'm here."

He set down his pen and rubbed a hand over his lightly freckled cheeks. "What do you want?"

"I found him outside on the drive. He was coughing."

Sebastian gave me a tight smile but held himself in an elegant pose like some kind of untouchable statue.

"It's the rain. He's always worse after it rains," he said, and looked back down at his papers. "Go with Madame Écrue for a posset, Lucien."

The old woman and the young boy turned from the room without even a moment's hesitation. They obeyed Sebastian without question. I wondered if that was out of fear or respect, or maybe out of love.

"I can help him," I said.

Sebastian blinked and then looked up at me again. "No, you can't."

The light in the room flickered with the dancing flames in the hearth. I looked around to see Madame Écrue gazing at her feet, face tight. Lucien stuck his fingers in his mouth like a much younger child, and sadness crept through me as the housekeeper led him away. I probably couldn't help him, not enough. I might be able to lessen his symptoms for a while, but children who coughed blood rarely lasted long.

"I *can* help," I said. "There are plants...herbs that can make a difference."

"Doctors have tried. Nothing works."

"I'm not a doctor, but I know things they don't."

"A bold claim." Sebastian pushed his chair away from the table with a screech of wood against wood. "What do you want, girl? Patronage for your shop?"

I want to know if someone in this house cursed my sister and turned her into a beast. I want your mother's book of spells. The words sat gingerly, foolishly, on the tip of my tongue, but I bit them back.

"My sister can run our perfume business. This will be a challenge for me...and I like a challenge. I'll stay here with Lucien and make him better."

A grim smile tightened Sebastian's face. "If you know what he has, you know he can't get better. No one survives consumption. He'll die...it's just a matter of how long he has left."

He was right, of course, though I'd hoped there'd be more reckless optimism in him. But I could change tack.

"And how do you want those months, or even years, to be? Painful? Do you want Lucien to be too weak to enjoy the last of his life?"

Sebastian gripped the back of his chair and his face strained against the tears wetting his eyes. The firelight threw him into stark relief and sharpened his grief. His sadness, his hopelessness . . . it was the same thing I'd felt so many times while watching the beast take over my sister. We were both losing our siblings to something attacking their bodies and minds. I couldn't beat back the consumption from Lucien's body, but I could give him some kind of comfort. I could ease his pain. More than that, I wanted to. I could help the little boy while looking for the book of spells.

Sebastian glanced up at me from under his dark brows and then he was on me, pulling at my arms, gripping my hands. His desperation rolled off of him like a pungent scent. "Please promise, please. Take his pain away at least."

I extricated myself and stumbled back into the darker corner of the dining room, where Sebastian couldn't reach me. My stomach clenched at his sudden intensity and I had to swallow down the lump in my throat. He scared me, but I knew I looked the same on the inside—wild and determined and dangerous. We shared that, at least.

"Yes, I can take the pain away. I can make him comfortable—give him energy even—if you let me stay here. Not as a servant either."

He stared at me. "Why?"

Lies slipped to the end of my tongue, but none of them would be as convincing as a piece of the truth.

"I want to live in a big house and have a full belly." I

shrugged. "Plus, I know what it's like to watch someone you love suffer."

A wave of some emotion—pity?—ghosted over Sebastian's face and he gave a tight nod.

"You'll stay until he's gone, then, to lessen his pain."

I started to shake my head. Consumption was unpredictable. It could be months or even years. I only had a month before Ama turned again. I had to agree knowing it was a lie.

"All right," I said.

The fire was snuffed out suddenly by a gust of wind from the open window, and the paneled walls of the room swallowed what was left of the light. My heart beat faster, but I held my face still. I wouldn't show Sebastian even a hint of fear.

"It's a promise."

"Good."

He took his seat again, sweeping his coattails out of the way. Madame Écrue came back in with Lucien trailing at her heels. She made a noise in her throat and held a hand out toward the door. Sebastian took up his pen, even with no light to see his scribbling. Lucien took easy steps toward the head of the looming table, and I was surprised when he slipped under Sebastian's welcoming arm. They looked so alike. Twins separated by time. Until a racking cough crumpled Lucien's body. Sebastian rubbed his back and pushed a handkerchief into his hand.

I followed Madame out of the room and left them to their shadows.

CHAPTER TEN

The house groaned in the wind as Madame Écrue led me through a gallery with slow, deliberate steps. The soft carpet cushioned my boots but the dust tainted its elegance. A large stained glass window loomed at the end of the hall. In the absence of the sun, the colors faded to duller tones.

The scene was a hunt—a boar streaming away from a pack of riders. The beast's glass eyes betrayed nothing, and I prayed it would be so resolute with hunters on my tail. The fear lurked in the back of my mind as it always did—that they'd come for us, for Ama. That I'd let my terror freeze my limbs, make me useless.

I walked on, still gazing up at the window, and treaded sharply on the back of Madame Écrue's heel.

"Sorry," I said, and stepped back.

The old woman stood quite still and I braced myself for

a scolding, but none came. She made no reaction at all to the toe of my boot scraping against the delicate skin of the back of her foot, left exposed by her slippers.

"Don't stop here, your room is this way." Madame Écrue's voice was as papery as her skin. She turned away from me, down the hall. "It was Mademoiselle's before what happened."

Mademoiselle. Not Madame.

It seemed Madame Écrue had been here longer than I'd thought—perhaps she'd been Sebastian's mother's maid. She could have sailed from the islands with her. She might prove to be an invaluable resource. Who else would know where to find Sebastian's mother's book of spells if not her childhood maid?

Staying in the bedroom of a dead woman wasn't very appealing, but it seemed a likely place to find some of the house's secrets. That was something. I hurried in front of Madame Écrue in the direction she pointed. At the end of the corridor, a set of double doors stood open. Cold, fresh air swept over me as I crossed the threshold. Someone had opened a window. They couldn't have known I was coming and yet it looked as though they'd prepared.

On a small mahogany table near the door, a white porcelain water pitcher sat beside a bowl painted with blooming roses. Dust coated the carpets in here same as the entry hall and dining room, but the colors and patterns underneath the thin layer of gray were more vibrant.

I soaked up the room, taking in the velvet curtains, silk bed hangings, and hand-painted wallpaper. I'd never in my life been so close to wealth. I almost didn't want to touch any-thing. Almost.

The green pattern of birds on the wallpaper begged to be examined. The wings seemed to rise and fall with my every breath, and the brushstrokes tickled my fingertips when I ran them across one bird in flight.

A creak in the floorboards told me Madame Écrue was growing impatient, shifting her weight from foot to foot. I left the wallpaper and turned to run my hand along the slip-pery stretch of pink silk on the bed. Then I stopped and the cold rushed over me like freezing rain. Pressed down into the silk on the left side of the bed was the distinct imprint of a woman's body. Even the shape of her hair left curves on the embroidered pillowcase.

But I blinked and it was gone. The coverlet was perfectly smooth and the pillow plumped and waiting.

I whirled around. "Why this room?"

"Master Sebastian said he wanted you in here."

"In his dead mother's room?"

Emotion caught in Madame Écrue's face, tightening the deep groove between her brows. "It's one of the nicer rooms in the house. He's always been a kind boy."

The old woman stalked over to the heavy velvet curtains and pulled them open fast, so the tassels bobbed and swayed. Thick tree branches stood in silhouette against the fading light. The rain had stopped.

"You know the family well?" I asked.

"What does it matter to you? You're here to make Lucien

feel better. Occupy yourself with that and not with impertinent questions," she said, and backed out of the room, pulling the doors shut behind her.

The cure, the book of spells, was here somewhere, perhaps in this very room. Anything else I offered Ama would only be a temporary solution—potions and tricks and chains. Nothing would hold her forever.

With every morning came an opportunity, and I would find mine.

✻

Dawn broke cold. The sheets tangled around me, and sweat pooled in the hollow of my neck. Sometime in the night, I'd stripped off my dress and even my chemise. Gooseflesh marred my bare skin.

I pushed the bedclothes off in one big, damp heap. I'd slept restlessly, dreaming of faceless women and the yellow eyes of wolves. I'd never stayed the night anywhere but my own cottage and it seemed both my mind and my body had rebelled against the idea. I'd even scratched my own arms and legs in my fitful sleep, leaving little trails of broken skin.

The window stood open to the deep blue dawn, and cold air poured in. I swung my feet over the side of the bed and tripped toward it on tired legs. My body ached for more sleep. I wanted nothing more than to crawl back into bed and pull the covers over my head and ignore everything I knew needed to be done.

I pushed the panes closed and dropped the latch so it wouldn't blow open again. This room wasn't as high up as I'd thought. I could have easily jumped from the window and landed in the soft grass on the side of the house. It made me worried that someone—anyone—could have hoisted themselves up through the window with relative ease. I'd be sure to secure the latch before I went to sleep.

The scent of dying leaves and the frost-tipped morning lingered. I shook the sleep from my body like a dog and pulled on my chemise. I didn't know how early Sebastian typically rose from bed, but I wanted time to explore without his eyes on me.

The quiet of early morning draped the hall. I'd expected servants, or Madame Écrue at least, to be scurrying around the house at this hour. Maybe she was and the place was so big I simply couldn't hear her.

How did Sebastian and Lucien live in this dark, expansive house? There was no warmth, only the cold glitter of fine things. Already I missed the closeness of home. With two rooms and a loft, there wasn't anywhere for anyone to go, so Ama and I would sit close together by the fire and read aloud from one of our two books while we waited for Papa to come home from the tavern. Once he stumbled in and drew the bolt over the door, Ama and I would slip under the thin blankets on our bed in the loft and I'd listen to the pattern of her breathing until I fell asleep.

It had been hard to sleep without her beside me. The only times I ever did were when she was out hunting. I always slept fitfully then too, tossing and turning all night. I often woke sweaty and more tired than when I fell asleep.

But I had to get my wits about me this morning—I had to earn my place here, and Sebastian's goodwill, so he'd be more likely to share his secrets. He must have known about his mother's power if the townspeople did. He could help me find the book of spells to break the curse, and then I wouldn't have to lie sleepless in my bed while Ama killed people anymore. He wanted to protect his town, and I could help him do it. That might be enough to convince him.

The first rays of morning light filtered in soft blues and greens through the stained glass window at the end of the gallery. I stretched my hand out and the faint colors washed over my skin. It was as beautiful as something in the church, and I wondered who had made it for the family. Where does one buy such a thing? Many of the cottages dotting the edge of town didn't even have glass windows, let alone works of art, to keep the cold wind at bay.

Almost everything in our cottage served a function. There was very little there for beauty's sake. But here, that seemed the point. The carpets, which I hadn't fully taken in before, were woven with intricate, spreading patterns of vines and flowers. Expensive colors, ones whose dyes were not easily found, shone up at me from underneath my boots. These people walked on their wealth. It was outrageous, but I couldn't stop myself from luxuriating in the loveliness all around me. The paneled walls, the sweeping stairs, the smooth lines of the carved banisters—I admired it all, despite dust that had settled over the dark wood. Everything was made with purpose, to draw the eye.

I trailed along the hall at the bottom of the stairs, in search of the kitchens. I wanted to make Lucien a tonic for his cough to at least show Sebastian I was good for some of my word. I'd do my best to help Lucien while I was here. I may not be able to offer a lasting cure, but I could ease his pain a bit.

My fingers fell into a small gap in the paneling when I ran my hand along the wall. The servants' door. It gave under a gentle push and revealed a white plastered stairwell leading down into the bowels of the house. The kitchens would be in the basement—Ama had told me about them—and led directly to the kitchen garden in the yard. I wasn't sure what herbs would still be clinging to life in this particularly cold autumn, but I'd check for some chamomile. That, mixed with a dollop of honey, would make a soothing tea.

A big wooden table stood proud on a floor of flagstones swept clean. The great hearth yawned cold and empty but for a hook for the pot and an iron oven for the bread. I'd have thought a kitchen maid would have already been stoking a fire high to boil cups of chocolate for her master's breakfast. Something about this house gave me a strange feeling at the bottom of my belly. There wasn't as much life here as there should be.

"What are you doing down here?"

I gasped and shot out a hand to grip the edge of the table,

but it was just Madame Écrue coming through the garden door with a little basket of firewood.

"I'm looking for some honey to make Master Lucien tea."

Madame Écrue dropped her load of wood into the larger basket by the hearth. The logs thudded into each other as they fell and one rolled off onto the stone floor. She bent with a hand to the small of her back to pick it up. It was cruel that she should do all this work. She'd been employed in a big house a long time—there should be much younger servants to do the hard work for her now.

"Check the larder," Madame Écrue said. "There's a pot in there."

I stepped around the table and ducked into an opening in the wall. The air cooled as I pulled open a door and went into the pantry. Rough wooden shelves lined the walls with nothing more on them than a couple earthen jars, a cheese, and a joint of ham. Not at all what I thought a lord's larder would look like. I'd expected it to be stuffed with food I'd never even seen before. I went a little deeper in and peered all the way to the back of the empty shelves. A crack ran along the plaster wall that made me think of another hidden door. I reached out a hand to push it experimentally when Madame Écrue's white cap and pale face suddenly peered into the pantry.

"Find it? It's the brown pot with the white lid."

I grabbed for the jar she described and hastily joined her back in the kitchen with the feeling of being caught by a grown-up—even though I hadn't been doing anything wrong.

"What herbs do you keep in the garden?" I asked when I set the honey on the table.

"Not much now. The mistress was the one who tended to them. I've not had the time."

"Chamomile?"

Madame Écrue spared me a tight smile as she pulled out a bowl and poured in a measure of flour. "None of that, I'm afraid. I've some dried tea in that tin over there. Boil some up and mix in the honey for Master Lucien, if you wish."

It didn't surprise me Sebastian's mother kept the herb garden—witches needed their stores, and any story I'd ever heard said they used them to make potions and elixirs. Learning plant lore was a risk. Women who have a way with plants were often the first to bear whispers against them. Especially if they were alone. Lucky for me, I had my father—a man, even if the townspeople held him in no great esteem. He offered Ama and me a little protection we wouldn't have had on our own. I had to—grudgingly—acknowledge that.

I made the tea with no more words for Madame Écrue. If I started asking her about her mistress now, or the secrets of this house, she'd make sure I was tossed out before I could learn anything. When I was done with the tea, I held the steaming cup in my hands and turned to the old woman.

"Will Master Lucien be in bed?"

Madame Écrue didn't stop in her work. She kneaded the dough with easy, practiced movements and shrugged. "I never know where he'll be."

Oh good. I might be carrying this cup of tea around the house till suppertime trying to find him.

"And Master Sebastian?"

"In the garden."

Well, at least he's a little more predictable than his brother.

CHAPTER ELEVEN

I went out through the front door and found the gate into the rose garden. My unease with the place melted away in the bright light of morning. Little birds flew in bursts of fluttering wings from bush to bush, and some came to their companions from the trees overhead. Sebastian sat on the stone bench under the willow, reading a letter. The long, thin branches of the tree swayed in the breeze and dappled the weak sunlight.

The heat from the mug in my left hand started to seep into my skin and I transferred it to my right. Sebastian looked up at the movement.

"You're up."

I nodded a bit foolishly. "I've made a tea for Lucien, to help with his cough. Where is he?"

Sebastian's lips turned up in a smile as the rosebushes rustled behind him. Lucien burst from between them and jumped at me with a playful growl. I couldn't help but give a little yelp. He laughed.

"It's a good morning," Sebastian said, looking at his little brother. The sunlight illuminated the warmth in his brown eyes.

"I see that. Perhaps he doesn't need the tea."

Lucien took a small step toward me and made a face. "What's in it?"

I crouched down to his level, careful not to spill any of the hot liquid. "Honey."

An easy smile bloomed on the little boy's face, which he quickly hid with a forced cough. "I think I still need it."

Sebastian laughed and dropped his letter on the bench beside him. "All right, Lucien. Come sit here and drink it."

Lucien climbed up beside his brother using both hands to hoist himself onto the bench. I carefully handed him the tea.

"Blow on it."

He blew too hard and a spray of tea flew from the cup. Lucien chanced a look at his brother but Sebastian only laughed. It was a peek behind the veil, something I'd never seen from the stoic young lord before. Easy smiles and bright eyes.

Maybe this was the true Sebastian, at home in his garden. The morning was indeed lovely. The strength of the sun chased away the bite from the breeze and warmed my skin through my dress. At this time of year, any warm day could be the last before a long winter. Water pooled in the gravel path from yesterday's rain, but my boots were thick enough to keep my toes dry.

"What are you reading?" I asked Sebastian, to buy myself a little time.

He glanced up at me in surprise and I realized it was quite bad manners to ask someone about their private correspondence. I stewed in the silence of my misstep for a moment, but Sebastian smiled mildly and picked up the letter beside him.

"Nothing important."

The paper was thick, stiff in his hand. A deep red wax seal had been split down the middle. I remembered Maurice's mother's claim that Sebastian had sent to the king for help. Could this be the reply?

"Have you offered Emméline a reward for killing the beast?"

Lucien took a big slurp of tea and Sebastian shoved the letter into his pocket.

"I think it was the beast who killed my parents," Sebastian said. "And now a child in the village . . . I *need* Emméline to get rid of it for us."

"Why don't you hunt it yourself? You *are* the lord here. It's your job to protect us."

I was taunting him and that was stupid, because I didn't actually want him to go out into the woods with his musket. That would be no better for Ama.

Lucien looked up at both of us and giggled. "Bastian can't hunt! He's no good."

Sebastian grinned and shook his head. He didn't seem to be angry at his little brother for revealing this information; instead, he tucked a piece of Lucien's hair behind his ear. The gesture reminded me of when Ama would lace up my dress and tap a little pattern down my back with her finger. Just a touch, a reminder of love.

"He's right. I was never good at it. Papa used to get so frustrated with me when he'd take me out."

"So, what's the prize you're offering Emméline? She hasn't killed it yet; why do you think money will change that?"

He sat up a little straighter on the bench. "I don't think that."

"So, it's not money?"

"No, it's not. Emméline's father left her a good business. Money's not what she's after."

"Then what?" *What would incite her? What does she want that she doesn't already have?*

Sebastian glanced around the garden, his eyes flitting from wilting rose to wilting rose like butterflies. "I can't say. It wouldn't be fair to her. In any case, it's in the whole town's best interest that she have a very good reason to want to kill the beast."

It certainly isn't *in my or Ama's best interest.* I tried to imagine what might make Emméline more determined than she already was. If not money, prestige? She was known as the best hunter in the village and had been since her father died. But in the end, it didn't matter *what* she wanted—just that she was planning to kill my sister to get it.

The shadow cast by the bench onto the gravel had shifted slightly to the left—the morning slipping away. Time was precious now, and I had to figure out what had happened to Ama here before she killed someone else or Emméline killed her.

Lucien sat quietly, his legs swinging as he alternately blew on and sipped his cup of tea. I wanted to find out exactly how sick he was and what would set him off. I didn't want to hurt him, but if he didn't have any episodes at all, I wouldn't be able to heal him and earn Sebastian's trust. Beyond the wall of the rose garden, the grounds stretched out to meet the woods. The tops of a few broad-leafed trees were visible from where we sat.

"Are those fruit trees?" I asked, even though I knew the answer. All the village children had made games of running into the orchard and picking up a fallen apple or two before the grand people in the house noticed. No one ever got caught—Sebastian's parents had probably known about our tricks and kindly let us have our castoff fruit.

Sebastian glanced over his shoulder, craned his neck. "Yes, apple trees. My mother loved apples."

"They're my sister's favorite too," I said, to make a link between us, a commonality. In any case, I wasn't lying this time. When we were younger, Ama had loved to climb to the highest limbs of apple trees and pluck the fruit there.

It's the sweetest, she'd said.

I wondered if Lucien liked climbing too.

"Almost done with that tea, Master Lucien? Why don't we take a walk through the orchard?"

He cradled the cup in his hands and looked up at me. "Sebastian said you're to make me feel better. No other doctor has taken me for a walk."

I bent down to his level, my boots crunching on the gravel. His eyes were perfect in the way that only children's can be. The whites almost too white, the brown around the iris as soft as goose down. No telltale red lines shooting through or bags gathered under his eyes.

"I'm not a doctor, but I will make you feel better. A brisk walk is the perfect way to start the morning."

I meant it, because how could I not? He was a child, innocent in all this. If he was in pain and I could help, I did want to. My using him didn't change that. It was contradictory, yes, but my manipulations wouldn't cause him any real harm. I'd make sure of that.

"Do you normally do that? Walk in the morning?" Lucien asked.

I supposed I did. Walk to the well for water, walk to the edge of the trees for kindling, walk to the cellar to find Ama cold and naked inside.

"I do sometimes."

Sebastian didn't look convinced about my plan, so I didn't give him any more time to object. I took the cup from Lucien and set it on the bench beside him before gently pulling him to his feet.

"Come now, little one. Let's go find ourselves an adventure."

He grinned and giggled as we followed the path to a

wrought iron gate. I glanced back at Sebastian, and he stared at me with an intensity that brought heat to my cheeks and made my stomach swoop in a not altogether unpleasant way.

That couldn't be—I had to stop that silly feeling right away. I had work to do here, and it would be unwise to grow soft toward the lord of the house. He was far out of my path, anyway. Save Ama from her curse and find her a husband and live in the freedom of being a spinster aunt. That was my road, and I couldn't let warm brown eyes throw me off.

I dropped my gaze toward the gravel path, but I couldn't help feeling Sebastian's gaze burning into my back as I led his brother away from him.

CHAPTER TWELVE

I loved the smell of apples in the autumn. They were at their most perfect, round and firm with juice. The orchard wasn't large, with just two rows of five trees each. Calling it an orchard was probably being generous—it was more like a copse or a smattering. When I'd come here as a child though, the rows of apple trees had seemed to go on forever. The trees themselves were giants holding on to their treasure.

Now Lucien looked up at them and a little spark jumped into his eyes.

"Do you ever climb them?" I asked.

He immediately dropped his head so I couldn't see, but I imagined the spark died out.

"I can't."

"You can't or you're not allowed?"

He shrugged. "Maman didn't like me to because it made me cough."

His mother. The woman who turned Ama into a beast. Hearing about how she cared for her son seemed strange to me. How could she love him and have so little care for others—for Ama?

"Well, you're not coughing now," I said. "How old are you?"

"Seven."

"Seven! You really should try if you haven't already climbed a tree at seven years old. My sister always said the best apples were at the top."

Lucien glanced around as if he was expecting Sebastian or Madame Écrue to pop around a trunk and scold him.

"I'll give you a boost," I said.

"Do you really think I can?" Lucien asked.

He looked up at the tree in front of us, with its thick branches perfect for climbing.

"Here." I bent at the knees and cupped my hands. "Catch that low branch and then climb."

Lucien slowly put one boot into my hands and gripped my shoulders.

"Up you go!" I said as I boosted him.

He clung to the rough bark of the branch and pulled himself up. He was stronger than I had expected.

"Just watch your feet and go a bit higher."

He did, eyes carefully planning his route before he made any movements.

"Are you watching, Marie?"

The pride in his voice made my breath catch. This was nothing, everyday play for all the other children. For Lucien, it was something special, because he was being robbed of his childhood, slowly, one bloodied handkerchief at a time.

I knew how it felt to have to stick to another set of rules, the shadow of all the things you needed to do following you through each game. Papa tried when we were little, after Maman died, but he didn't even know how to cook a simple supper or wash and darn our clothes. No one had ever thought to teach him, because he was a man. I learned quickly, experimenting until I got some things right. We didn't starve and I always made sure we had clean clothes to wear, washing our linens down in the stream.

Lucien's life wasn't quite like that, but he had to protect himself more than others did, shield himself from all the normal things that had become dangerous.

I was glad he climbed confidently. He turned around, arms outstretched and holding carefully to two branches.

"Look at me! I can see over the top of the garden wall from here."

"Was it your mother's garden?"

"Yes."

"What do you remember about her?"

I put up a hand to shield my eyes from the late morning sun so I could see Lucien's face better. He scrunched his features, perhaps trying to coax forward his memories.

"She always smelled like the roses and her curled hair always tickled my cheeks when she hugged me."

"Those are nice things to remember."

He nodded and shifted his weight, finding his balance again.

If he could remember those things, maybe he could remember something else too.

"I used to see her, all of you, at church sometimes. When she came, I liked to look at what dress she was wearing."

Lucien gazed off toward the garden. I was losing him.

"She often had a little book with her—blue, I think it was."

"Oh, yes. I remember that."

"Do you?"

He nodded again. "My arms are getting tired."

Lucien remembered the book itself, but did he have any idea what was inside? And he'd already been sick when his mother died. How much had he noticed going on in the house?

"All right. Look first and decide where you'll put your feet on the way back down. There's a good, strong knot to step on," I said, pointing out a thick swirl of wood at the base of the branch Lucien stood on. The crisp breeze had blown some color into his cheeks. He didn't look very ill at all.

Lucien carefully placed one boot on the knot in the bark I'd suggested. He glanced down, head turning this way and that as he searched for another foothold. A little trickle of sweat running from the edge of his hair down his neck told me he was scared. Any village boy would be an expert tree climber at this age, but I knew without having to ask no one had ever taught him. I could barely hear his breathing, so it wasn't labored. He didn't cough and spit blood onto the ground. His face, when he turned it to me, shone with fear. Not illness.

"Take a breath, Lucien. You're not even very high up and you're not going to fall."

He closed his eyes as if he could block out the space between him and the ground. "Come up here! Please!"

I pressed my hands against the trunk and the bark was familiar under my touch. I hadn't climbed a tree since I was much younger—it wouldn't be appropriate now—but I'd been quite good at it as a child. I looked back over my shoulder toward the garden wall. There was no one around to see me hitch up my skirts.

"Oh, all right. Just stay still. I'm coming."

It all came back to me easily. One hand here, one foot there. My dress was longer than those I'd worn as a child and I imagined doing this in breeches would be much easier, but it only took a minute before I settled myself onto a branch just below Lucien.

"Open your eyes, it's all right. I'm right here."

He shook his head, squeezing his eyelids tightly closed.

"Don't think about where you are, Lucien. Tell me about something nice instead . . . tell me about your maman."

It was a bit cruel to use this moment to get what I wanted out of him, but I didn't have time to let opportunities pass me by. In any case, the distraction would allow him to relax and then I'd coax him down the tree.

"Maman?"

"Yes, we were talking about her beautiful dresses at church and that little blue book she carried…"

He nodded and the movement made him hug the branch he clung to even tighter. My heart squeezed for him. It wasn't an easy thing to be so afraid in this world.

"Come on, Lucien. It's all right…just tell me about her. Forget where you are."

"She…she always hugged me extra tight in the morning so I'd be ready to face a new day."

Good, a memory. It's a start.

"And what about that little book? The one she sometimes wore hanging from her belt," I prompted.

"Can you help me down now, please?"

"You're almost ready. Tell me about the book and you'll be calm enough to climb down."

I was so close, and I wasn't going to lose this chance. He was perfectly safe holding on to the branch, and I was right here below him, ready to catch him if he fell.

"She just always had it with her. I couldn't read the words in it yet but I liked the pictures."

"Pictures?"

"Leaves and swirls, a lady sitting at the edge of a tree… pretty things."

It didn't sound like a prayer book. I'd never seen one illustrated like that. A spell book though…well, I didn't know what one was supposed to look like, but pictures of leaves and ladies sounded close to my expectations. And if Madame LaClaire always had it with her just like Ama said, it had to have been very important to her. Perhaps too dangerous even to let out of her sight.

"That sounds nice, Lucien. Did she ever read it to you?"

Did she share her magic with her son? Did she try to heal him with her spells?

He shook his head. "It was just for her and that lady. They always had it on the table between them when she came for a cup of chocolate. She showed things to Maman."

So, there is someone else involved too, someone who knows about the little blue book and what it contains.

"Who was the woman? Madame Écrue?"

Lucien tightened his grip on the branch. "No, Madame was always with me. Why are you asking? She was just Maman's tutor or something."

Tutor? So perhaps Madame LaClaire hadn't come here with her own knowledge of magic. Another woman might have taught her. The only other person around here with rumors attached to her like that was the Woods Witch, but no one was even sure she was real. It was a start though, a path I could go down. Sebastian would know who the woman was—he'd been old enough to know more. I just needed to figure out an innocent way to ask him.

"All right, let's get you down now, Lucien. Take a deep breath, nice and calm."

I reached out a hand for him, but his deep breath turned into a sharp inhale and sputtering cough. Wet droplets landed on my fingers. I pulled my hand back to look—spittle and blood.

"Lucien!"

He lost his hold on the branch above. I braced him, hands holding the small of his back. He was heavier than I'd expected. My left foot slipped.

"Grab on again," I said. "Then I'll ease you down."

"I can't!"

"Yes, you can! Summon up all your strength, Lucien!"

He gripped the branch again and his weight left my hands. I breathed out and repositioned myself so I could guide Lucien's way back to the ground. He was *not* going to fall out of this tree. Healing broken bones wasn't the way I wanted to prove myself. Not very subtle.

"Okay, bring your right foot down. I'll guide you with my hand, don't worry . . . just keep looking straight ahead."

"At the bark?"

"I don't care what you look at as long as it's not your feet!"

I took the heel of his boot in my palm and placed it in the crook of a branch. His fear made this so much harder for him. It tightened his muscles and made it almost impossible for me to pull his leg straight enough to reach the next foothold. If he could just let go of it, he'd be down on the ground already.

"There! Now the other."

He slipped and screamed, "Marie!"

"I'm right here, Lucien. You're still hanging on, aren't you?"

I guided his boot back to a safe spot. We were almost back to the ground. I could jump the rest of the way easily and would need to move to allow Lucien to finish his descent.

"I'm going to get my feet on the ground so I can hold you, all right?"

Lucien nodded, eyes squeezed shut now.

"You're going to have to look though. You can't do it with your eyes closed."

"I can't open them!"

"You can, Lucien, I promise. It's not as scary as you've made it out to be in your head."

He wasn't even that far from the ground. A fall now might mean a bruise and a sore back or knee at worst. I let go of Lucien's boot and turned carefully to face away from the tree before launching myself away from the trunk and back to the ground. The impact jolted through me.

"Look here, Lucien, I'm down! Now I'll hold you while you climb down the rest of the way."

I reached my arms up to try and grab on to his hips.

"Should I let go?"

His eyes were still scrunched up, tightly closed.

"No, open your eyes and look where you're going!"

"I can't! It's too scary!"

Then Lucien let go of the branch. I wasn't ready. His

weight knocked me to the ground and he fell on top of me, punching the air out of my lungs.

He rolled away, coughing. The guttural sound of it suggested fluid somewhere it shouldn't be. His sleeve, already marked with little brown stains, had brilliant new splotches the color of rubies I'd seen in paintings in the church. He was worse than I'd thought, but I *would* make him feel better. There was truth in what I'd told Sebastian—I knew my remedies.

Lucien tamed his cough and stretched out a little hand to help me up.

"You saved me, Marie."

Not yet, but I will.

"You did well for your first time climbing a tree," I said.

Lucien's cheeks were already pink from the coughing spell, but he dipped his head a little and wouldn't meet my eyes. "I didn't, I know it. I'm no good at that kind of stuff."

"Well, I think you did just fine. Now, should we go find something to soothe your throat?"

He looked up at me, eyes sparkling. "More honey tea?"

I laughed. "Maybe."

The skies above had turned gray while we were climbing. The air smelled fresh, a pre-cleanse meaning rain or snow had rinsed the world behind us and would soon be here.

"What's the quickest way back in?" I asked.

Lucien seemed to consider this. "The kitchen door."

"Good, let's go."

As we went through the grass fading from green to gold, I glanced back at the garden gate. There in the shadow formed by the space between the gate and the wall, Sebastian stood. Staring at us. Face blank. *How long has he been there?*

I shook off a prickle of unease and followed Lucien back into the house I'd tied myself to—the place that made my sister a monster.

CHAPTER THIRTEEN

adame Écrue took Lucien's cheeks in her hands when we finally came through the door to the kitchen.

"What were you doing? His color is high," she said, pinning me with a sharp stare.

"Just playing in the orchard," I said.

Lucien wriggled out of her grasp. "I climbed a tree! A real tall one too."

Madame Écrue went whiter than her cap. I was going to be on her bad side already and I'd only just arrived. That wasn't good. I wasn't sure if Sebastian's mother would have told her maid about her spell book, but the woman seemed like she didn't miss much.

"Are those new spots on your sleeve, Master Lucien? Did you have a coughing fit?" she asked.

"No," Lucien said, trying and failing to discreetly tuck his arm behind his back.

Madame Écrue took a wooden spoon from the table and dipped it in a big pot hanging over the fire. The whole room filled with the sweet smell of cooking carrots and onions. My stomach gave an audible rumble, but neither Lucien nor the older woman paid any attention to me.

Lucien stood in silence, his chin tipped down toward his toes. He looked more ashamed than if Madame Écrue had started yelling and taken the spoon to his bottom.

"Madame . . ." he said.

"Yes, Master Lucien?" she replied without turning around.

Her apron strings were tied in a tight knot behind her back. I suspected she was just as strict with Lucien as she was with her apron, but he closed the space between them and leaned his head against her.

I yearned for someone to take a little bit of my weight like that. Ama's curse added to my burdens, and she only sometimes offered to help hold me up. It wasn't that she didn't care—I knew if I asked her directly to look after me more, she would—it was more that I didn't want to have to ask. Ama didn't notice other people in that way though, not without being prodded. My moods didn't seep into her skin like hers did into mine.

Madame Écrue and Lucien obviously had a different relationship. I leaned against the great big table and tried to make myself small in their moment. The older woman broke eventually and turned around to offer Lucien a hug.

"You know I worry," she said. "Your maman charged me with taking care of you, and I want you to be safe."

"I know," Lucien said, his reply muffled by Madame Écrue's brown dress.

It was good that he'd had the fit and she'd seen the results, even if it put me firmly in the column of people she didn't like. She'd be happier when I made a poultice to clear his lungs, and that would likely earn me more trust than sweet manners.

"You go up to bed, now," Madame Écrue said to Lucien. "I'll bring you some tea."

"I'll make him a poultice," I said, and they both turned to me, startled, like they'd forgotten I was there.

"It's what I'm here for, to help Lucien," I went on.

Madame Écrue looked at me, one hand balled into a fist on her hip, the other holding the wooden spoon dripping broth onto the floor. "Yes, you *are* supposed to help him, but all you've done so far is make him worse!"

She was right, of course. I had taken Lucien out to the orchard to test what would happen if he worked his body, but I had every intention of making sure he wasn't really hurt in any way.

"It's my first day here; you can't expect things to happen that quickly. But if you let me make my poultice, I can almost guarantee Lucien will be able to sleep better tonight."

Lucien tugged on Madame Écrue's arm, the one holding the spoon, and got a few drops of broth on his head. "It was fun, Madame! Marie was just showing me how to climb trees and I never get to—"

"Enough," the older woman broke in.

Lucien fell silent and let go of her arm.

"You go to bed, Master Lucien. Rest and I'll be up soon."

She may have been a servant, but Madame Écrue obviously held sway in this house. Lucien retreated from the kitchen with his eyes on his boots and my heart pained for him. He just wanted to play.

"Happy now?" Madame Écrue asked.

"Not particularly, no. But I'm not the one who just sent Lucien out of here like a scolded puppy."

She returned to stirring the stew. "I know what's best for him."

Ah, I'm coming into her territory—caring for Lucien is her job. I understood the sharpness to her words better now because I knew what it was like to be protective of someone.

"Look, Madame. I'm just here to give Lucien my remedies. You clearly love the boy and I'm not here to intrude."

The woman stayed perfectly still for a breath, then shrugged.

"Yes, I do love him. Both of them."

Acknowledgment, that's what she wanted. She'd cared for these boys since their mother and father had died, and I thought she wanted me to know she was more than their housekeeper.

"I'll be able to do my best for Lucien with your help. I'll need to know where the ingredients are kept so I can make my poultice."

"Yes, all right, I'll help you. Check the store cupboard."
She pointed with her spoon.

I opened the cupboard she indicated and glanced over the
bundles of rose petals and the sacks of fine-milled flour.

"Any onions?" I asked. The midwife in the village taught
me that when I went to her once about a chest cold—onions
lift the cough out of lungs.

Madame Écrue turned and glanced toward a string of
onions hanging from the ceiling by the wash basin. I hadn't
missed them—I'd just hoped there were more in the pantry and that she'd direct me there instead. I wanted to see
it again and look for signs Madame LaClaire may have been
mixing things for spells.

"Sorry," I said. "They were hiding in the shadows."

The woman nodded and took an earthenware bowl from
the shelf near the window. She began to ladle in stew. "Here,
dinner. Supper's after dark."

I took the proffered bowl and pulled out one of the chairs
around the big table. The onions and poultice would have to
wait because my stomach was nearly caving in on itself at the
smell of the rich stew. Carrots and even potatoes peeked out
from the gravy.

Madame Écrue put a spoon down on the table, just a bit
out of my reach. I leaned over to grab it.

"Thank you," I said.

She turned to leave, not helping herself to a bowl of
stew. She probably didn't want to sit across the table and
eat with me and I couldn't blame her. I'd rather be alone

with my thoughts than sitting through dinner making awkward conversation with her. But there was something I
wanted first.

"Wait, actually I have something to ask," I said.

She paused. "What is it?"

"Paper and a pen? I want to write a letter to my sister."

It looked like Madame Écrue *just* stopped herself from
rolling her eyes at the last moment. "What would you need to
write about? You have news after a day?"

"I just want her to know where I am. It's mostly just the
two of us at home, me and Ama."

I watched, intently, for recognition in Madame Écrue's
eyes at the name of my sister. Something flashed across them
and she pulled in her cheeks, giving her the look of a starving
woman for just a moment.

"You're Ama's sister?"

So she wasn't going to try and pretend my sister had never
been here. I supposed that was smart, since I obviously knew
my little sister had been placed here as a servant. I wondered
if Sebastian remembered her too. He hadn't acknowledged
her in town, but there'd been much more important things
for him to tend to at the time.

"Yes, I am. She served here for a little while only a year
ago, but I wasn't sure if you'd remember her."

Madame Écrue placed a hand against the doorframe but
her posture remained steady.

"I remember."

"Did she work with you here, in the kitchens?"

I already knew she had, but it seemed like a good question to ask to keep the woman talking.

"In the kitchens and in the bedrooms lighting fires. She had more spirit than you seem to though. She caused me trouble."

What kind of trouble? I wanted to ask. *The kind where she suddenly turned into a monster and killed your employers?* There was more in Madame Écrue's face than the memory of a disobedient serving girl. She'd paled—her white skin was almost translucent now. That was enough for today.

"So, can I have some paper?"

Madame Écrue let go of her hold on the doorframe and wiped her hands on her apron. They left damp streaks.

"I'll leave some in your room."

"Thank you."

She left me to my stew and I picked out the pieces of venison first, chewing each slowly and savoring the juices. I rarely had meat. Ama did, but not in stews, of course.

"Marie?"

I dropped my spoon into my bowl with a small splash of gravy. Sebastian stood in the doorway behind me.

"Sorry, you startled me," I said.

"Thinking deeply?"

He pulled out the chair beside mine and sat down as if we'd been friends all our lives.

"I guess I was," I said.

A little drop of stew had splattered onto the table and Sebastian wiped it away with his thumb. What was he doing down here? I expected lords of big houses didn't spend too much time in the kitchen.

"Why are you eating down here, alone?" he said.

I pulled my bowl a little closer to me, which was silly because he obviously wasn't going to take it away. It was just a simple question.

"Madame Écrue gave me some stew, told me to sit."

A smile lit his face.

"She's traditional, Madame."

"What do you mean by that?" I asked.

"I've told her you're not a servant here. You should be eating in the dining room with me and Lucien—not here in the kitchens."

"Oh." I hadn't expected that. Actually, I hadn't thought twice about sitting down to eat my dinner here because this room and this table resembled my own cottage much more than the dining room filled with its delicate, fussy furniture.

"Don't worry, I'll let you finish your dinner in peace. But you'll join us from now on and come to breakfast in the morning?"

I nodded. "If you want me to."

"I do. I want to get to know the person who is taking care of my brother."

His words brought back the image of him standing near the garden wall, watching Lucien and me climb down the apple tree. Unease prickled over my skin, even though Sebastian smiled at me now.

"I'm glad you'll eat with us," he said.

"Sebastian?"

"Yes?"

"Lucien's fine, you know. He's in his room resting and I'm going to bring up an onion poultice after I eat. He wanted to climb and I think the fresh air is good for him. He's perfectly fine, perfectly safe with me."

Sebastian stood from his chair, a squeak of wood against the stone floor. He stood behind my chair and leaned over me, placing one hand on either side of my arms, boxing me in. He bent his head so his eyes looked directly into mine. A little spark of panic flared in my chest.

"He'd better be safe, Marie. He'd better be."

The scent of rose petals lingered in my nose. He must favor perfume like his mother did. Sebastian pushed himself back up and walked out of the kitchen without another word. His threat thickened the air around me.

CHAPTER FOURTEEN

The soft hooting of an owl reached me through my dreams.

I stretched, my legs aching from climbing the apple tree the day before. That's when I noticed I was outside.

I was also naked, because my chemise had been sweaty and I'd taken it off before climbing under the fine covers on Madame LaClaire's old bed. I wrapped my arms around my breasts and bent my knees to cover myself as best I could, shivering. The lawn stretched out in front of me, rimmed by wide-canopied ash trees. Behind me, the bedroom window had been unlatched. It was odd, having the lady of the house's bedroom down here instead of upstairs with the others. This great big window with diamond-shaped, leaded panes, opened out onto this quiet stretch of grass and trees.

She might have come out here for some time on her own,

slipping through the window from her bedroom without anyone else knowing.

Now I stepped over the small ledge of that same window and pulled it closed behind me. I must have been walking in my sleep again.

I dove under the blankets, chilled right through to the bone. Sleepwalking in a house I barely knew was a terrible idea, but I didn't have any control over it. I'd have to make sure to calm myself better before falling asleep—no more thinking about Ama or how she was faring while I was away from her.

My letter to my sister sat waiting on the little stationery desk in the corner of the room. Madame Écrue had left thin white paper there along with a nib pen and ink. My letters weren't fine, not like I'd seen in the church, but they were legible. Ama was used to my writing anyway, and hers was similar—we'd both learned what letters looked like in the village school and then Papa taught us to make the shapes ourselves. We never had enough practice to be really good at it though. We didn't have anyone to send letters to.

I stood and slipped my chemise over my head and sat down on the little chair to look back over the words. *I miss you, please keep the chimney clean, don't bring attention to yourself if you go into town.*

I wasn't good at putting my thoughts down on paper. This letter was really nothing more than a list of things to do and not do. There wasn't anything real I could put in here anyway—*make sure you don't kill anyone else while I'm gone.* There was time before she should turn again; I'd only been here in Sebastian's house for three days.

I folded the letter and held a stick of wax over the candle flame. It dripped onto the line where the two sides of the paper met. There was a plain little seal in one of the drawers of the desk that I pressed into the wax. I hoped Ama would hear my voice in the letter.

I went down to breakfast a bit late. Sebastian wasn't there, and I assumed he'd finished eating and went on with the business of his day, whatever that was. Yesterday, I'd walked by his study and he'd been sitting at a large desk looking through a stack of papers. There were books behind him, lined up in a built-in bookcase. I couldn't stop long enough to look for one with a blue spine without Sebastian looking up and seeing me, but I planned to sneak in there later to check.

Lucien was at the table, eating some sort of pastry and licking the powdered sugar from his fingers. He looked up at the sound of my shoes clicking on the floor.

"Good morning, Marie."

"How did you sleep?" I asked.

He shrugged. "Same as always."

I'd learned Lucien had a hard time breathing well during sleep. He often burst out into coughing fits I could hear through the ceiling. Even my best onion poultice wasn't enough to keep it from happening—no matter how hard I wished it.

"We'll try a new tea tonight, all right?" I said.

"As long as it tastes good."

"I can't promise that, but I can always sweeten it with honey."

"Maman never made bitter tea," he said.

He kept his eyes on the half-eaten puff pastry on his plate. His mother must have known her herbs.

I took my own pastry from the plate and tried not to gulp down the saliva filling my mouth. I hadn't tasted anything like this in a very long time. The first bite made my mouth hurt with the intense sweetness, but the second was a dream.

"I know what will perk you up this morning, Lucien," I said.

The little boy wiped the rest of the powdered sugar clinging to his fingers right across his knee-breeches, leaving behind a ghostly trail of white on the dark wool.

"What?"

"I think we should play a game."

His eyes lit up and he gave me a smile that showed the top of one front tooth just peeking out of his pink gums.

"A game! Do you know any good ones?"

I returned his smile because I couldn't help it—his was infectious. He made me feel a little lighter when his face was bright.

"My sister and I played all the best games when we were little."

"Sebastian always says he's too old to play with me. But Emméline does sometimes when she visits."

"Does she come often?"

He shrugged.

I wasn't shocked to know she was a friend of the family. It made sense, what with her papa being the richest man in town next to the lord of the big house. Sebastian *did* know her, which meant he probably knew exactly what to offer her to hunt the beast.

"Marie?"

I blinked hard to clear my head. "Sorry, Lucien. Yes, let's play a game."

"What's your favorite?"

Hide-and-seek was, in fact, a good game. A big house like this was the perfect place to play it too. Ama and I had always run out of good spots in the cottage. There were only so many times we could hide under the table or wrap up in blankets on our bed in the loft before it got boring.

"Have you ever heard of hide-and-seek?"

Lucien shook his head. *Why does Sebastian never play with his little brother? Perhaps his papers, running the estate, the village, takes up too much time.*

"Well, I count and you go hide. Then I look for you until I find your hiding place and we start again but with you as the counter and me as the hider."

"That does sound good!" Lucien smiled up at me, his tongue poking through where one of his front teeth was missing.

"It is, trust me. All right, I'll start with the counting and you run along and hide somewhere. Not too far away though; your house is big enough that I might never find you."

He nodded, his face hardened into a very serious expression, and ran out of the dining room.

I covered my eyes and counted loud enough so he'd be able to hear me even if he'd gone down the hall.

"One, two, three, four ..."

This time I'd find him quickly, pausing to look in a few places to make it convincing. Then it would be my turn to hide.

"Ready or not, here I come!" I called.

Lucien giggled from somewhere down the hall, leaving a trail with his voice for me to follow. The parlor looked empty—the spaces under the sofas would make good hiding spots though. I crept back into the hall on tiptoe, my body remembering how to play the game even if I wasn't consciously trying to be quiet.

"Where could Lucien be?"

No giggle this time. He was learning.

The music room curtains looked odd, too full on the left side. I pretended to look under the bench in front of the fortepiano.

"Lucien? Are you here?"

On tiptoe again, I padded over to the bulging curtain. Stopped. Then ripped it open.

"Arrghhh!" Lucien jumped out with a monster's scream, hands made into claws. My heart leapt into my throat.

"Lucien!"

"I scared you, didn't I?"

He did a little dance of victory. I pressed my hands into my hips and offered him a smile.

"You did, you got me. But now it's your turn to count and I'll be the one hiding."

His own smile slipped a little. "Are you going to scare me?"

So now he doesn't want to take what he gave, hm? Children seemed to be like that—wanting all the fun with none of the unpleasant stuff. *Did Maurice, the boy who'd been torn apart, play hide-and-seek? Did he ever jump out and scare someone? And how scared was he when the thing that killed him went from a noise in the shadows to a real-life monster?* I wanted so badly to know it hadn't been my sister who'd terrorized him like that.

I knelt down so my eyes were level with Lucien's. "I promise I won't jump out and scare you."

"Truly?"

"Truly. Let's just have fun, all right?"

He nodded and grinned. "I can count all the way to a hundred, you know."

"Good!"

That would give me more than enough time to sneak to another part of the house.

"Close your eyes," I said. "Start counting!"

I slipped through the open music room door and ran right into Sebastian. My nose crunched against his chest. He startled and grabbed my shoulders.

"What are you doing?" he asked.

"Me? What are *you* doing?"

Sebastian smirked. "Well, I do live here."

He released my shoulders and I stumbled back. He'd given me a sarcastic answer, not the real one. This was the second time I'd seen him stalking around while I was with Lucien. He didn't trust me yet.

"Pause the counting, Lucien," I shouted back through the door.

"Counting?" Sebastian said.

"We're playing hide-and-seek."

Lucien came to the door then, slinking out to stand at Sebastian's feet.

"It's fun, and I don't have to run or anything," he said.

Sebastian's eyes softened and he put a hand on Lucien's shoulder.

"I'm glad you're playing."

"Good, because it's my turn to count!"

Lucien dove back into the music room and started counting loudly again. I rocked on my heels, not sure what to say next. I wanted to tell him he could trust me, that I wouldn't hurt Lucien, but voicing it would probably make him think I was lying.

"You'd better hide before he's done counting," he said.

"Yes."

He was in my way. I wanted to get to his study, but he'd wonder why I was going in that direction instead of hiding in the dining room. At least I knew he wasn't in his study at the moment; that was something. I had to make him think I was going to hide in the dining room and then sneak back out after he left—all before Lucien came looking for me.

"Don't tell Lucien where I've gone. Steer him away from the dining room," I said.

"I won't spoil the fun, promise."

"Then you better get on," I said.

Sebastian's smile vanished. Maybe that was too far.

"Be careful with him, Marie."

"I am being careful."

His lips turned up but it wasn't really a smile. His eyes stayed serious. Sebastian looked like a person who'd had too much placed on shoulders not yet broad enough to hold the weight. He almost stooped under it all, and that was something that drew me to him. My shoulders hurt sometimes too. If things were different, I could tell him the truth and he might understand—but they weren't.

I turned from him and went toward the dining room, listening for the sound of his footsteps as he walked away. When they grew fainter, I swung back around to see which way he went as he left the hall. Lucien was up to sixty now. My heart pounded too loudly in my chest. I had forty seconds to sneak away.

CHAPTER FIFTEEN

The room was draped in darker hues than the rest of the house, but I suspected that wasn't Sebastian's doing. This space would have belonged to his father before him, and he'd have been responsible for the shiny, deep-red wood desk and the wall of books bound in soft brown leather behind it.

A ledger was flipped open on the desk. Neat columns of script lined up like soldiers on the page. Reading script like this was harder than reading the evenly set letters made by a printing press, but I saw quickly it was an account book. Numbers indicating the expenses of the estate, many of them with a little tick in front of them I was pretty sure meant *minus* or *negative*.

Sebastian's clothes had been a clue. So were the lack of servants. There was Madame Écrue, a couple male servants who seemed to work in the yard, and a young scrap of a girl who made up the fires in the mornings and helped Madame Écrue cook. There must have been someone to take care of Sebastian's horse in the stables too. But I'd always thought there would be more people, more life, in a great big house like this. The LaClaires hadn't left much for their sons.

Sebastian just had to live with it, like everything else in his life, it seemed—a crumbling estate, bad harvests, a sick brother. All left to him by parents everyone else thought he'd killed. If I hadn't known about Ama, would I have thought so too? Not if I'd ever been here, in this house. No one would kill their parents to inherit these burdens.

I strained my ears to listen for Lucien but I couldn't hear counting anymore. It would be best if he didn't discover me here and I didn't have to answer questions about why I'd come this far to hide. The books visible in the built-in bookshelf had all been bound in the same brown leather. I stood up on the small stool behind the desk and slipped my hand along each row, in between the books, looking for a skinny blue spine. Nothing, but that wasn't surprising. Why would Sebastian leave his mother's personal book among his father's trade books?

It was more likely hidden away in the desk somewhere. I opened the thin drawer at the top, but there was nothing except writing instruments—sand and blotting paper, wax and another plain seal. The next drawer down was completely empty except for a little sack doll with lopsided stitched eyes. Lucien's? Or maybe it had belonged to Sebastian when he was a child. I gave it a squeeze because it reminded me of one I'd once made for Ama and dropped it back in the drawer.

The third drawer was empty save for a locket, a big one like something a lady might wear around her neck. I pressed a little silver clasp and it popped open. Two miniatures were nestled within. One was Madame LaClaire and the other was my mother.

No, that couldn't be right. It was a small painting, and lots of women had brown hair and brown eyes. Not many had that particular shape of the nose though, or the pointy chin. Was it really her? But how? Why? My mother hadn't known Madame LaClaire.

Sweat prickled under my arms and at the back of my knees. My stomach tightened. This couldn't be happening. There simply couldn't be a portrait of my mother in Sebastian's house. We were no one.

I brought the locket closer to my face, looking so hard my eyes hurt. It wasn't her; it couldn't be. I didn't remember well enough what she looked like, and the only picture we had of her was painted before she was married. She looked more like Ama in the painting at home, and this person in the locket didn't look like my sister. I was mistaken; I had to be. Madame LaClaire might have had someone in her life she cared for enough to commission a miniature and a locket, but that person wasn't my mother.

The necklace thunked at the bottom of the drawer when I returned it. I held myself against the desk and willed my muscles to unclench, the sweating to stop. There was nothing to be upset about here, nothing to be nervous about—except Sebastian finding me looking through his things. The book wasn't here, and the locket had nothing to do with me or my family. Just a trinket Sebastian kept.

"Marie!"

Lucien's shriek, ripped from the silence, made all the blood in my veins run cold. I ran out of the study and back down the hall toward the music room.

"Lucien!"

"Marie!" he answered from somewhere farther, fear curdling his voice.

"I'm coming, just stay there!"

Where is he? Not in the dining room or the music room.

"Where are you? Keep talking to me!"

"I'm with the boots!"

With the boots? I didn't know what that meant, but I followed the sound of his voice to the sitting room. A door set into that wall, even covered with the same pale green wallpaper, had been opened. I stepped through and discovered another hall, one plastered in plain white. The servants would come through here. It was a good thing Lucien had left the door open or I wouldn't have been able to hear him at all.

Off the hall, before the stairs down to the kitchen, there was a little room full of leather boots. Lucien huddled under a small table outfitted with rags and a few jars of polish. A whole room to polish boots. If I weren't looking at it, I wouldn't believe it.

"Lucien, come here," I said, crouching down. "What's wrong? You were supposed to be finding me."

"I tried! I thought you must be very good at hiding and I went through the secret door in the sitting room to find you."

My stomach churned uncomfortably. I was the reason he gripped his knees with white-knuckled hands. I'd made him scared.

"I'm so sorry, Lucien."

I dropped down beside him and extended a couple fingers to touch the back of his hand. He let me, so I took his whole hand in mine.

"I didn't mean to go so far. But there's nothing to be scared of. This is your house, your . . . boot room, isn't it? You know everything here."

He leaned against me, his head pressing into my shoulder. I was glad to be able to comfort him now, to make up for what I'd done.

"It's not what's in here. It's what's out there," he said, pointing to the closed window. The sun had traveled across the sky since morning, throwing off a pale afternoon light. Beyond the window, the woods shadowed the edge of the lawn.

"What's out there? There's nothing, Lucien. It's still daylight. The animals don't even come out during the day."

"I heard something, scratching on the window. Just like I used to."

Is he scared of Ama? Did he hear her the night she killed his parents? I pulled him in closer. He would never be at risk from her, I could promise him that.

"There's nothing out there, nothing like you heard before."

He shifted away from me a bit and looked up into my eyes. "You don't know that. It went on and on. Maman said she'd make me a protector, but she died."

Make him a protector? That was an odd phrase, but Lucien was only a child. He probably didn't remember right. It was the other thing he'd said, how it happened over and over again, that worried me. I was fairly certain Ama had only spent one night here as a beast.

"When did this used to happen, Lucien?"

He shrugged. "I was little. I didn't even eat in the dining room yet, just in the nursery with Madame. I heard things outside the windows. Howls and scratching."

The timing wasn't right for it to be Ama. He would have been older than that when my sister killed his parents and might have been prowling the estate. But howls were easily explained.

"It sounds like it was wolves," I said.

"It wasn't wolves." Lucien pushed me away then and stood. He wiped his nose across his sleeve, leaving a shiny trail of snot behind. "You don't believe me."

"I do! I'm sorry. I swear I believe you, Lucien."

This little boy had only a brother and a housekeeper for company. I didn't want to be a person he couldn't trust.

"I want to go to bed now," he said.

"But you're not coughing. You're fine."

"Madame would want me to."

He wanted to hide, from me and from whatever had scared him. I let him because it was the least I could do. It had been my game that caused this mess after all.

"All right, go on then," I said.

Lucien led me out of the boot room and back through the servant's hallway to the sitting room. I closed the secret door behind us. It really did look like part of the wall.

"Marie?"

I turned to see Lucien staring at me like he had something very important to say.

"Yes, Lucien?"

"Please don't tell Sebastian I was scared."

My heart hurt for him. Lucien was told he was sick, that he needed to rest all the time and couldn't climb apple trees, but he still wanted to be brave for Sebastian. I knelt down and took Lucien by the shoulders so I could look square into his eyes.

"I won't tell, I promise. But there's nothing wrong with being scared. I'm scared all the time." Of Ama being taken away from me, of her being found out, of her being the one who killed the little boy in the village, of the freedom I wanted slipping away.

"You are?" Lucien's eyes grew round.

I nodded. "Everyone gets scared, Lucien."

"*They* don't."

"Who?"

Lucien looked back out the window, mouth open, and poked his tongue through the gap where his missing tooth was again. This time I could tell it wasn't excitement that made him do it. It was fear.

"The monsters."

CHAPTER SIXTEEN

There'd always been deaths in the woods. We shared the valley with wolves and we all learned not to go into the trees alone, especially not at night. It wasn't usual for wolves to get as close to a house as Lucien described, but that was probably his young mind creating stories from a seed of truth. The wolves howled in the woods and he heard them from the house, and branches hit the window in his room when it was windy, creating scratching noises. He hadn't needed a protector. His maman had probably just been talking about herself, telling her child she'd protect him from the scary sounds of the night.

The picture in the locket wasn't so easy to explain away though. The image of the woman who looked so similar to my mother haunted me while I made tea and poultices, while I sat with Lucien in his room on his harder days, while I ate in the silent dining room with him and Sebastian. I didn't think the woman in the picture was my mother, but I wanted to know who she was and why she'd been so important to Madame LaClaire. If she was still living, she might know something about my sister's curse.

I couldn't ask Sebastian straight out, because then he'd know I'd been snooping in his study. I tried a few leading conversations with Lucien, but he didn't seem to remember his mother having a close friend with white skin and brown hair.

Three weeks had slipped away, and I wasn't any closer to finding the little blue spell book. My letter to Ama had gone unanswered and fear brewed in my gut. She might have just been angry at me for leaving and that was why she was ignoring me, but my sister wasn't usually that petty. I'd write her another letter today pleading with her to answer. I needed to know she was safe.

After a breakfast of porridge and cream, Lucien led me into the library. It was in the west wing of the house, a big room lined with shelves of books—bound with deep red leather tooled with gold—and a plush chair under a window that looked out over the lawn. I breathed in the smell of paper and leather. We owned two books. Occasionally I'd buy a chapbook from the pedlary if I had an extra coin and thought Ama might enjoy it.

Papa kept our books leaning against each other on the shelf above the hearth. They had been my mother's—two novels her parents had given her to bring to her new house when she wed my father. Papa had refused to read them to us as children because he'd said they'd give us foolish ideas, but when we were older, Ama and I both read *La Vie de Marianne* and *Roxana*, which my grandparents must not have actually read before giving to my mother. We were both quite shocked by the content. When Papa was out, we read passages out loud by the fire and giggled until our sides hurt.

I'd never seen so many books in one place before, and I'd never seen them arranged like this.

Lucien gave no sign of delight at this vast collection of thoughts and stories—he was accustomed to it. He went straight for the second book on the third shelf and pried it free.

"I want to read this one." He stroked the red leather cover with his little hand.

"All right. Come near the window."

A stream of light illuminated the stuffed chair. Lucien bolted for it but waited for me to sit down before he pulled himself into my lap. He was small for a child of seven years. He settled in and leaned against my shoulder while I flipped the book open.

Histoires ou Contes du Temps Passé
Les Contes de ma Mère l'Oye
Charles Perrault

I'd never heard the name before, but the frontispiece was the lively illustration of a cluster of children huddled around an old woman.

"Here," Lucien said, and deftly riffled through the pages until he found the one he wanted.

"Le Petit Chaperon Rouge," I read.

"It's my favorite."

"Why's that?"

"Because it's scary."

I'd never heard this story before, so I didn't know what the scary bits were, but Lucien's face lit up with excitement.

"Are you sure you want to read it?" I asked. I didn't want a repeat of the boot room incident.

He nodded. "Please?"

We'd fallen into a routine, and I suspected the shape of Lucien's days had been well worn before I came. Breakfast, tea to help his cough, letter practice with Madame Écrue before dinner, rest before supper. Sometimes we went out onto the lawn with two wooden chairs if the wind didn't bite too much.

We talked a lot, but he never asked to climb apple trees again. Instead, he told me of all the things crossing his young mind. What wolves eat, how he'd watched a white grub caught on his windowsill turn into a fly, how he planned to illustrate a book with ink pens for Sebastian for New Year's. I listened with attention. He made up for not being able to explore the world by questioning everything in his little corner of it, and I found that fascinating.

Even though I didn't want him to be scared, I wasn't going to stop him traveling the world the only way he could—through stories.

"All right, then," I said, and settled Lucien back against my shoulder. "Let's read it."

Il était une fois une petite fille de village, la plus éveillée qu'on eût su voir: sa mère en était folle, et sa mère-grand plus folle encore. Cette bonne femme lui fit faire un petit chaperon rouge qui lui seyait si bien, que partout on l'appelait le petit Chaperon rouge.

It wasn't a long story, but the words still chilled me to the bone. A little girl in a red cape, off in the woods alone, and a monster posing as a human.

"Do the voices!" Lucien demanded when I reached the part where the wolf speaks.

I stared down at him, and he must have seen the horror on my face, because his smile melted away.

"What is it?"

"Why did you pick this story?"

He frowned. "I told you, it's my favorite. I'll do the voices if you don't want to."

I nodded wordlessly and Lucien began to recite from memory, the lines of the wolf in a deep growling voice I'd have thought completely beyond him. Despite myself, laughter bubbled through my lips at his little face screwed up into such a scowl.

A noise at the door made me glance up to see Sebastian watching us. My chest tightened as I wondered how long he'd been standing there.

"I see you've met Le Petit Chaperon Rouge," he said.

"Oh yes, what a tale."

Sebastian nodded. "Quite dark."

"It's scary!" Lucien cried in his wolf voice as he slid from my legs and dove at his brother. They tumbled together on the soft carpet in front of the cold fireplace, Lucien crawling on top of Sebastian and pinning him down with a great howl.

My heart warmed at the sight. It was easy to imagine, for a moment, this was my family. I still barely knew Sebastian, but Lucien had carved out a place in my heart. Sebastian clearly loved Lucien and that opened a door to him that would have otherwise stayed closed. I saw him as more than the lord of this estate and our village. He was a young man who loved his brother, who was soft when Lucien needed to lean against him. A simple daydream took hold—a husband and son playing together on my hearthrug while I watched on with quiet contentment. It would be so natural, so simple, to have a family like that.

But the spell broke abruptly when a great cough racked Lucien's small body. He rolled off Sebastian and clutched his stomach as he coughed and coughed and red spittle flew from his mouth onto the carpet. This wasn't my family. It was a sick child and a rich nobleman, and I had no real place among them. I didn't *want* a place among them. I wanted to cure Ama and get on with our lives.

I was on my knees now, the book forgotten. Lucien's face paled and splotches of red stood out against the whites of his eyes.

"I'll take him to his room," Sebastian said. "Brew something to help him! You're here to make him better."

The accusation in his voice stung, but he was right to be suspicious.

Sebastian scooped his brother into his arms and struggled

with him out of the library. I sat still a while, not sure what to do next. I could make up another tea with honey to temporarily soothe Lucien's throat, but the effects wouldn't last. Instead, I took the opportunity to pull every book from the library shelves and look inside.

I knew, before I even reached the last shelf, that I wouldn't find the book of spells here. How silly of me to think the witch might have just hidden it among the family's books. Nothing was that simple.

In the end, I brought Lucien a cup of rose-hip tea with honey and Sebastian and I watched him drink it without much hope of its success.

CHAPTER SEVENTEEN

I tried to imagined what Ama must have been doing while I wrote her the letter. Mixing perfumes, cooking little stews of vegetables over the fire. I wondered if she missed me as I missed her.

Please answer this letter, Ama. I need to know you're all right. It's been good here, and I've almost earned enough money to keep us through the rest of the winter. My teas and poultices are helping young Master Lucien, and I'll be coming home soon . . . before the monthlies take you.

If Madame Écrue tried to read it before she sent it with the courier, she'd just think I was talking about Ama's period, not her transformation.

Have you chopped enough wood for the week? Don't put it off, Ama, or you'll wind up cold.

A wave of sadness washed over me and I had to put the pen down. I missed her. Lucien had tucked himself in my heart, yes, but Ama was my sister. She'd been my constant for as long as I could remember, and the last time we'd been apart for this long, I'd felt my soul splinter. I'd have to go home in the next week, breaking my promise to Sebastian. Ama would turn, so I needed to either mark her prey or lock her in the cellar and feed her a rabbit if I could catch one, knowing it wouldn't be enough. She weakened when we did that too many times in a row, which was why I let her kill at all. To keep her healthy, to keep her safe.

If I left here for good without the book of spells, we'd be no better off than when I came here. This was my only chance to figure out what had happened to her. Secrets whispered behind the walls of this house like scurrying mice. I just had to catch the right one. There had to be a way to go back just for a few nights without breaking the promise I'd made to Sebastian. I needed him to welcome me back if I couldn't find the book before next week.

Ama had always said I was the best hunter out of the two of us. I couldn't help but remember the first time we'd killed an animal. *One warm spring, Papa had found the right kind of wood and fashioned us a slingshot. Only one, of course, because he'd never think to try and avoid squabbles between us. We fought over it, but I insisted it should be mine since I was the eldest. Ama didn't swallow that, but I was still bigger than her then and easily pinned her down and wrestled the slingshot from her hands. After sulking for a few minutes, she slipped down beside me in the long grass and we waited, holding our breath, for a rabbit to come.*

Ama saw it first. She tapped my shoulder and stuck out her stubby fingers. I pulled the ball back, straining against the tension. Ama grabbed my wrist, helping me drag the line back even farther. I counted under my breath . . . one, two, three. Then we both let go.

The rabbit fell, and my heart swelled with excitement. Meat for the pot. Ama shook my shoulders, grinning so wide I could see her missing milk tooth.

"You're a huntress," she said.

We scurried out from our hiding spot and picked up the rabbit together—me holding its ears and Ama grasping its hind legs.

I might have been the huntress that day, but we were a team. I couldn't be me without her, and I had to figure out a way to bring her back to me for good.

Answer me, Ama. Please.

I let the ink dry and sealed the letter, ready for the courier to take into town, and then collapsed on my bed. I would have fallen asleep if not for the knock at my door.

Sebastian stood behind it.

"Lucien?" I asked, heart beating too quickly.

I should have stayed with him in his room, sat on the edge of his bed, held the teacup to his lips.

"No, he's fine. Sleeping."

My shoulders relaxed and a warm rush of relief spread through me. Lucien was all right. Everything was fine.

"You scared me," I said.

Color rose in Sebastian's cheeks. He had high, fine cheekbones and expressive eyes. I'd noticed how easy it was to get lost in them. More than once I'd had to remind myself to look away, much to my embarrassment.

"I'm sorry, I didn't mean to scare you," he said. "Actually, I came here to ask you a favor."

"Oh? Another poultice?"

"Not that. I, uh, well it's Madame Écrue's birthday tomorrow and I wondered if you might help me with her present."

Help him with her present? What help could I be? Even though his estate seemed to be in trouble, money-wise, he still had much more of it than anyone in the village. He could buy whatever he wanted for his housekeeper's birthday.

"What can I help with?"

He leaned against the doorframe, eyes on his feet.

"I want to make her a perfume, and I've heard you're very good at that."

A scent. I wrapped my arms around myself, holding in the colony of butterflies suddenly fluttering in my stomach. He'd heard I was good at making perfumes and he wanted me to help him make one instead of using his coin to buy something for Madame Écrue. It was sweet.

"Of course I'll help."

"Now?"

I glanced back at the bed and said goodbye to the nap I'd been planning. This would be better. Even though I'd tried speaking with Sebastian at the dining table or when we'd been together in Lucien's room, he hadn't been very open to conversation. While Lucien had been young and sick when his parents were alive, Sebastian had been old enough to know what was going on. He might know a lot more about his mother's magic and Ama's transformation than he realized. Making a perfume with him would be a great time to finally get him to talk.

"I hope it's not too much trouble, Marie," he said.

"No trouble at all." I stood and brushed off my dress. "I'd love to help."

CHAPTER EIGHTEEN

I brought Sebastian out to the garden, but it was slowly being strangled by the late autumn frosts. Where lavender once grew, there were now just stalks, yellowing and bent, flowers gone. It was likely Madame Écrue had some dried buds put away though.

"There's not much left right now, it's not an ideal time for picking ingredients," I said.

Sebastian surveyed the small kitchen garden with a grimace. "Well, we can't use the roses in the walled garden. Madame won't want perfume that smelled like my mother's . . . it would make her sad."

"All right, no roses then. Do you know where else we could find something?"

Sebastian shook his head. "We don't have another garden."

"What about a storeroom? Perhaps where herbs or dried flowers are kept to make scented pouches and the like."

I hoped he'd reveal something I could use. Madame LaClaire must have had a place where she brought her spells to life and I still hadn't found it. Any story I'd ever heard about the Woods Witch mentioned her brewing potions over her fire. It seemed like a requisite to magic making. If there *was* a room with potion ingredients in this house, the blue spell book might be there.

"Madame keeps things in the pantry."

I nodded but my stomach sank. I already knew about the pantry and it wasn't what I was looking for.

"Well, let's go have a look."

Madame Écrue *did* keep a couple small sacks of dried lavender, just as I thought she would. Dried wasn't as good as fresh for making scents, but I'd be able to squeeze some of the oil out. It would make a calming, comforting perfume if we used just enough of the flower. I turned to back out of the small room, almost bumping into Sebastian. He swerved to his right and I moved to my left and we ended up almost chest to chest again.

"Sorry," he said, rubbing his hand on the back of his neck. "You first."

I dropped my eyes to stop my cheeks from burning and the sweat from gathering under my arms. The floorboards in the pantry were uneven, and as I stepped around Sebastian, my foot hit a loose one right along the wall. Then another. This part of the room didn't have any shelves, which was odd considering nothing was hung here either—no meat or strings of onions. Maybe there had been once.

"Can you pass me that mortar and pestle?" I said when we

were both safely out of the pantry and once again standing a few feet apart.

Sebastian looked around and I thought he might not know what a mortar and pestle was, but his eyes landed on it eventually.

"Are your parents perfume makers too?" he said.

"No. Well, my mother passed a long time ago. My father's a farmer when the weather's right."

Sebastian hoisted himself up onto the table to watch me work. Not very refined for a lord, but I liked how casual the gesture was. As if we'd been sitting together in the kitchen, working and talking all our lives.

"How'd you learn to do it then?" he said.

"I'll tell you a secret—it's really not that hard." I dropped the dried lavender in the mortar and ground it up, sniffing to see if the scent of it would be potent enough. "I like combining scents when I have the right flowers and oils, but a simple perfume is easy to make. It's putting them in pretty bottles with ribbons tied round that make the women in town want them."

He smiled. "You know how to sell then. That's impressive."

"For a woman?"

"For anyone. I wish I could say I had a skill all my own, but there's nothing special I can do."

It didn't seem like he was hoping I'd object; he wasn't reaching for anything. His smile settled but his features were still soft. It was because he wasn't trying to force me into a compliment that I decided to give one.

"You care for Lucien with a lot of purpose. I've not seen many people do something like that before."

Sebastian dug one fingernail under his thumbnail, fidgeting with his hands. "Wouldn't anyone do that for their family? Wouldn't you take care of your sister if she needed it?"

He didn't know how far I'd gone to take care of Ama, how many things I'd done I thought would be impossible.

"I would. But that doesn't take away from the tenderness you show Lucien."

He shrugged. "So, what's next after you crush the lavender?"

"We let it soak in some water for a few hours before putting the whole lot through some muslin cloth."

"Oh."

"What?"

Sebastian smiled again. "It does sound pretty easy."

"Told you."

Talking with him came easily, easier even than with Lucien. The silences between our words weren't as comfortable as those with Ama, but they were close. I liked being with him. It was that simple. It would have been even better if I didn't need something from him.

"Did your mother teach you anything about remedies or cooking?" I asked.

"No, not really. We had a cook back then, and Maman spent time here with her, but I never really did. Why do you ask?"

I picked up the pestle from the mortar, lavender oil slick on the bottom of it. "You knew what this was."

"Oh," Sebastian laughed. "That's all Madame Écrue. After Maman died, she'd let me be down here when I was sad. We didn't have a cook anymore either, so she taught me a few things."

Madame Écrue seemed all tangled up in this somehow. Either she knew something or she'd been part of what happened to Ama. Unless Madame LaClaire had been a really good liar, which *was* possible, she would have had a hard time keeping something like being a witch from her maid.

"What did you learn from her?"

His eyes rose to the right as he seemed to comb through his memories. "How to knead bread and take the small bones out of fish so Lucien doesn't choke on them."

Fish was a treat at home, reserved for days of celebration, and I never knew how to cook them properly. I always just fried the fish in its skin in the iron pan with a bit of salt and a scoop of lard. It was tasty enough, even if we had to pick the brittle bones from our teeth.

"That would be tedious," I said. "I never bothered."

"No? Do you know how to cook, then?"

"Not well. My mother died before she could teach me, but I've kept my sister and myself from starving."

"Do you take care of everything in your house?" Sebastian asked. "What about your father?"

I ground the last of the lavender buds, squeezing the oil out under my pestle. The thought of Papa brought extra strength into my arms. Anger did that to me, fused me, made me stronger.

"He's not around much," I said. "He's not a very good farmer, so he goes to other towns and villages for day laboring."

Sebastian nodded but kept his eyes on my face, studying my features as if trying to find some clue in the way my eyebrows came together.

"What are you wondering?" I asked.

Pink tinged his cheeks, but he didn't shy away from me.

"I wanted to know if you felt it too, this . . . I don't know . . . this sense of responsibility. Before my parents died, I didn't know much about it. Now it's all I can feel. Lucien, the village, the estate. I have to take care of it all."

I'd imagined Sebastian's shoulders carrying a heavy burden, and now I knew they did. He'd shared that with me, and I wanted him in a sharing mood.

"It's the same with me. Papa gave up after Maman died, and then even more when Ama came here as a servant. It all rests with me now."

"Your sister was a servant here?" He slipped down from the table and leaned closer to me. "When?"

Madame Écrue knew, but I suppose there was no reason for Sebastian to take notice of the servants working in the kitchens—especially not then when they had more people serving them.

"She just came here to work a year ago," I said with a shrug. "A kitchen maid."

"Madame must know her then."

"She does."

Sebastian clapped his hands together, a little smile on his face. "How strange you have a connection to this house already. Your sister worked in this very kitchen and now you're here helping Lucien. I like little coincidences like that."

It wasn't a coincidence at all, but better to let him think there was some divine innocence to the situation. I just happened to come to him for work and to get out of my small cottage. To prove myself and my remedies. No reason other than those.

"Can you fill a bowl with water?" I asked.

"Yes, of course."

More serious now, he spooned out water from the bucket near the door into an earthenware bowl. I took it from him and dumped in everything from the mortar, crushed buds and oil, scraping down the inside with my finger.

"Now what?" Sebastian said.

"We let it sit like this, overnight is best, and then we strain it tomorrow."

"Right, okay. So, we're done for now?"

Something in the lilt of his voice hinted at disappointment. I didn't want this to end yet either. For one, I hadn't found out anything about his mother or her spell book. But there was something else too. I'd enjoyed it, the talking and the easy way Sebastian sat on the table while I ground the lavender.

"Well actually, I was wondering if you could help *me* with something now?"

Sebastian's brown eyes warmed. "Of course. What is it?"

"I want to try something new for Lucien, something I think might really work to help him get better, but I don't have the recipe. Madame Écrue mentioned your mother had a book for things like that. She said it was small with a blue binding."

This was risky. If Sebastian knew anything at all about what the book really was, he'd grow suspicious of me. He could also simply ask Madame Écrue and find out I'd lied to him.

But the potential reward outweighed the risk. We'd just talked more with each other than at any other time during the weeks I'd been here. If he was ever going to be open with me, it was now.

His eyes flicked upward to the right again while he thought. "I know what you're talking about, but I don't think Maman had recipes in there. She didn't cook, as I said."

"But you know the book?"

I'd seen it with my own eyes, hanging from Madame LaClaire's belt after church on Sundays, but to hear Sebastian confirm it gave me a little thrill. The book was significant and it was here, somewhere.

"I know it, but I don't know what happened to it after Maman died. Perhaps it's with some of her other things in her room."

My shoulders fell as I pushed all the air out of my lungs.

The disappointment was heavy. It wasn't in her room. I'd searched when I was supposed to be asleep, and I hadn't found anything.

"It's not." I let the words slip out before I realized it and cursed myself. Sebastian didn't need to know I was looking for the book or doing anything other than taking care of Lucien.

"Don't worry, Marie, you can stop looking for it. I'm certain Maman didn't know anything about which herbs to put in a tea. That wasn't what the book was for."

"What was it for, then?"

Sebastian gave me a long look. *Have I gone too far? Asked too much?* He could simply expel me from the house and I'd have no other chance to find the spell book without breaking back in.

"It was just her . . . journal is the right word, perhaps. She wrote little stories in it, poems, songs."

Spells. Lucien had seen them too—songs and little drawings. It had existed. Unless someone had stolen or burned it—and it wasn't likely Sebastian would have done that if he thought the book was his mother's journal—it would still be here.

"Shall we meet back here tomorrow morning to finish our perfume?" he asked.

I nodded as I wiped my oil-stained hands on my skirt, not even caring about how impossible it would be to remove the stain. Now I knew from both brothers that their mother wrote in the blue book. I should have felt relief, but I didn't—only hot swirls of panic in my chest.

As we left the kitchen, the loose floorboard in the pantry kept nagging at my mind, snagging my other thoughts. It could be nothing, but the bare wall in the same place was also strange. I'd get up early in the morning, earlier than Madame Ècrue, and have a look. There was nothing else to do. I had to get that book in my hands, and I was running out of time.

CHAPTER NINETEEN

Cold, gray ash was heaped high in the grate at the bottom of the kitchen's smoke-stained hearth. Little puffs of white outlined each breath I took. Bowls and cups and spoons crusted with yellow littered the big wooden table, the scent of last night's dinner clinging to them.

I stepped into the pantry off the kitchen. The temperature dropped and gooseflesh beaded over my skin. The joint of ham still hung from a peg in the wall and a barrel of apples took up much of the floor space, their scent sweetening the air. Madame Écrue must have hired a village man to pick them from the withering orchard. I bent down to breathe in the sweet smell oozing from the overripe fruit.

The empty wall was only an arm's length to the other side. The floorboard creaked when I took a step away from the barrel of fruit, and I shot a look toward the light of the kitchen, but I was still alone.

I put my foot down carefully and edged it along where the floor met the wall. Solid, solid, solid . . . not solid. There was a space between the floorboards and the back wall of the pantry. I knew there was something weird about this shelf-less wall and the loose board. I ran my fingers along the back of the plaster and felt a smooth break. With the full weight of my body, I pushed against the wall until it gave with a great moan and swung back like a door.

It was the workroom I'd been looking for. Excitement shot through me. Madame Écrue had been lying when she'd said there was no such place, and Sebastian likely just didn't know about it. Glass bottles and clay jars crowded a long, rough table. Flat knives and empty mortars and broken pestles stared up at me with a sense of betrayal. *Let us be useful,* they seemed to say.

I put my hand on the table and the buzz of energy hummed up my arm, rippling my skin into gooseflesh. She must have been happy here, Sebastian's mother.

Bundles of dried flowers hung from the ceiling and I trailed my fingers through them, rustling the stiff leaves. A thick stem with shriveled blooms caught my eye—foxglove. A few drops of foxglove nectar would render the drinker sick and slow the beats of their heart.

Some women learned a little plant lore at their mothers' knees, but I barely remembered my mother.

I did remember the void, though, the chasm left behind when Papa sent my sister away. I'd wandered the hours without her, lost in the relentlessness of the sunrise. Always another day, another endless stretch of light. My body needed to be fed, but I had no taste for food. The sweet spring air would whisper against my skin, but I didn't tilt my face to the warming rays of the sun. I would turn from them and dig into the mud with my fingernails, ripping and tearing until my blood mingled with the dirt and I felt something.

Roots burrowed deep into the soil and I was envious of their cold isolation. I had yanked them from the ground and gathered up the green stalks and white tips still humming with life. I slit my knife into their cores and squeezed until their lifeblood dripped white and sticky from my fingers.

I'd collect the sap in little bottles. When the sun finally retreated beyond the mountains and the stars fell across the sky like broken glass, I would lie back in the grass outside our cabin and tip the neck of the bottles to my lips. I tasted each drop of nectar with numb curiosity. What would this one do to me?

One morning, I woke and wanted more than that. I had collected my plants with purpose and arranged them on our table and hid them when my father came home and leaned his scythe near the door. Day after day, I catalogued the plants, wrote their names, and tested the combinations.

The work consumed me. It was what I thought of when the cold sting of each morning made me open my eyes. It helped me find the strength to swing my legs over the side of the bed and stand on the cool floorboards.

By the time Ama had come back, I'd known more about herbs than about her.

Back in the pantry, the wall clicked into place behind me as I brought the dried stalk of foxglove out into the kitchen. It was a good idea to have something like this on hand.

The house woke with creaks and shivers. The whispers of feet over plush carpets, the scrape of boots against flagstone. The master and his servants meeting the day.

I slipped into the melody, padding out of the kitchen with the foxglove tucked in my pocket. A candelabra guttered as I hurried past on the servants' stairs. I didn't want to be discovered here, so I took the first door out into the foyer and tiptoed toward the dining room.

Fresh snow leaned up against the large picture window, crowding the view, and white-blue veins of frost crackled over the glass. It was the kind of cold you could see, touch. Sebastian leaned with one hand against the stone facing of the hearth, his trousers glowing orange with the light from the low fire.

"Good morning," I said. "I checked the lavender water. It's ready now. You just need to squeeze it through the muslin into a bottle."

He turned quickly and the naked expression of surprise on his face told me he hadn't heard me come in.

"Oh, I thought you were going to do it with me?"

I splayed my hands. "You don't need me; you're a master perfumer now."

Sebastian chuckled and an awkward little silence settled around us.

"It snowed, finally," he said unnecessarily, gesturing toward the window.

"Yes."

"I thought we'd have a little celebration tonight. A party, of sorts, for Madame Écrue's birthday. I'll give her the perfume we made."

"That would be lovely, I'm sure." I sounded like Ama when she tried on her best manners and tight, expensive accent. Even Sebastian didn't sound like her approximation of an aristocrat. I had to stop doing that immediately. "What can I do for the party?"

"You've already helped me make Madame's present, that's enough."

I shrugged. "It was easy."

He raised an eyebrow. "For you. Not everyone can make perfumes that smell so lovely. It's a skill, a talent."

There was no honey in his voice—no added sweetness. It didn't seem like he was saying it just to be nice. His words landed with the warmth of truth and fueled the heat that rose in my cheeks.

"Thank you," I said, trying to surreptitiously grip the tall back of the chair in front of me. My legs weren't quite up to the challenge of holding my weight.

Sebastian put his hand over mine for only a moment. The warmth of his skin there and then gone.

"You're welcome."

We stared at each other, tangled in a moment I didn't quite understand but didn't want to end.

"Marie!"

Lucien burst into the dining room with all the energy of a healthy young child. Sebastian and I broke off and both welcomed Lucien with a smile.

These kinds of mornings were my favorite—where Lucien was happy and well. It didn't always last, from what I'd seen anyway, but I liked to indulge those good moods.

"Good morning, Master Lucien. And what are we going to do today?"

He rolled his brown eyes. "Don't call me 'Master.'"

"Would you prefer 'My Small Lord'?"

Lucien giggled, the sparkling laugh starting in his belly and flowing free. Sebastian rubbed Lucien's curls, tighter than his own.

"You two stay out of the kitchen today, all right?" Sebastian said.

"Who's cooking the supper for the party if not Madame Écrue?" I asked. It didn't seem very fair that she would have to cook for us as part of her birthday celebration.

"I've hired a couple women in from the village to cook," Sebastian said. "So, steer clear and let them get to it, all right, Lucien?"

He wasn't stern, but Sebastian was firm with his brother. As if he took his role of head of the family almost a little too seriously to convince himself it was indeed true. I knew being the responsible one wasn't easy. Ama only listened to me half the time, but she paid attention when it was important, like when we'd decided on how to select her victims and keep her secret.

"Come on then, Lucien," I said. "Show me something new in this house, somewhere I haven't been yet."

He grinned, his cheeks plumping up like apples. "Like a secret?"

Sebastian put his hands on his brother's shoulders and pulled him in to rest against the front of his legs. Lucien pushed his head back into Sebastian's stomach—a backward hug.

"Don't make Marie a promise you can't keep, Lucien. We don't have any secrets here."

Everyone had secrets, every family, every house. This one was no exception, and people who claimed there was nothing to find were often hiding the most. I already knew there was something here, but did Sebastian know it too? Or was he simply brushing off Lucien's comment because he didn't want a near-stranger poking around?

"Let's see what we can find, secret or not," I said, and took Lucien's hand. His small fingers wrapped around mine without hesitation. I couldn't remember what it was like to trust people like that. Perhaps I never had.

He took me to all the places I'd seen before. The library and the hall where we'd played hide-and-seek. This was his home and by showing it to me, Lucien was revealing little bits of himself. He spent a lot of time in the library. I could tell by the way he knew the locations of all his favorite books on the shelves, including the one we'd read together the other day.

"Look at how they drew this cat. He's wearing boots," Lucien said, finger on the illustration on the title page of another one of the stories in Perrault's book.

He didn't lead me to the kitchen, even though I was curious to see which village women were working in there. Lucien skirted it just as Sebastian had asked him to. Another peek into who he was. Lucien loved his brother, and that was normal for a small child. Obeying was usually less so. Siblings are connected to one another just as parents should be to their children—by this thick cord woven of love and obligation. I suspected it would be terrifying for Lucien to have Sebastian angry with him, the little boy wondering if the rope tying them together could fray.

There were few opportunities this time to get away and search the house on my own. After last time, there was no chance I could convince Lucien to play hide-and-seek again. Instead, I followed my small charge around and let him talk to me and tell me all about his world until the light fell away from the windows and the candles were lit around the big staircase.

"Do you think we should go in and see if the party is ready?" I asked him.

Lucien hung off my arm, pulling at me. "Do you think there will be cake?"

I laughed. "I hope so."

I wondered briefly if I was dressed well enough for such

an occasion. My dark green dress was the best one I had, but there was no adornment. It was made of wool and wrapped around my body in such a way to give me more of a woman's shape than I'd otherwise have, and I liked how the skirt and petticoat poured out from my nipped-in waist.

"Come on, Marie!" Lucien let go of my arm and darted ahead toward the dining room.

It shouldn't have mattered to me what I was wearing. Who was there to see, anyway? I wiped my clammy hands on the skirt and didn't even look down to see if they left wet marks on the wool.

The food served here was always more than I'd ever had before—meat pies or soup for dinner and roasted meat and salad for supper. Really nice, fluffy bread for breakfast with thick yellow butter and blackberry jam. Sebastian insisted I join him and Lucien for meals, and usually Madame Écrue served the supper and then sat down to eat with us. I hoped Sebastian had asked whoever cooked the supper tonight to also bring it to the table, but the party would be the same people I saw every day. No need to be nervous.

Sebastian stood in front of the long, deep fireplace with a glass of red wine in his hand. Lucien squealed at the sight of a caramel-colored cake topped with nuts in the middle of the table.

"An apple cake!" he said.

There was also a fish laid out on a serving platter, silver scales catching the firelight and slices of lemons on its eyes. Lemons would be very expensive this time of year. Sebastian had spent money I wasn't really sure he had on this party for his housekeeper. That fact lit a little flame of warmth in my chest that I didn't immediately try to extinguish.

"Come, sit. Madame will be down in a moment," he said with a smile.

As I pulled out one of the chairs and sank into it, I wondered which of the village women had been in the kitchen all day preparing the meal. Was one of them Maurice's mother? I tried not to think often of his cold, still face, but sometimes I couldn't help it.

"Have you had chicken pie before?" Lucien asked me. He pointed to a golden-brown pastry. "Or carrots cooked in honey?"

"Of course she's had carrots before, Lucien. We had them two nights ago."

"But not with honey!" he said with a little pout.

"No, not with honey," I agreed. "I can't wait to taste them."

Lucien's smile lit up his eyes. He was happy to share this meal too. Just like his house.

Madame Écrue came into the room then and Sebastian went to her, passing her the glass of wine. She *had* made an effort, with a clean dress of light blue cotton and a crisp starched cap. No apron tonight. She was the center of the party, not a housekeeper.

"Happy birthday, Madame," Sebastian said, and kissed her on her papery cheek.

"Happy birthday," Lucien and I echoed.

Once Madame Écrue took the wine from Sebastian's

hand, he pulled the vial of perfume from his pocket and presented it to her.

"Lavender water, for you. I thought you might like to have something nice."

Madame Écrue's eyes shone, even the white one, but I couldn't tell in the low light if it was from tears or happiness. Likely both.

A shimmer of excitement went through me. My sister would have loved this. The elegant table. The warm, fragrant pastry and the decadence of the fish. She would have taken a glass of the ruby-red wine without hesitation and sipped slowly, to savor it.

But she wasn't here. I didn't even know how she was doing since she hadn't written me back yet. She might be cold if she hadn't chopped enough wood. Or hungry if she hadn't been careful with our stores. And here I was, enjoying myself. Warm, fed, and taking way too long to find the spell book. How could I have done this? Lost my sense of time? Forget even for a moment about what I was really here to do?

"I'm so sorry," I said. "Suddenly I don't feel well."

My chair screeched against the wood floor when I pushed it back, but I didn't stay long enough to see if there were looks of disappointment on Sebastian's and Lucien's faces.

CHAPTER TWENTY

'd been a bad sister. Ama needed me to do this, or else she'd spend the rest of her life turning into a beast. Eventually, something terrible would happen to her. Awful things were already happening to the people around her, and I wouldn't be able to contain anything for much longer. I needed that book.

I went back to my room, Madame LaClaire's room, and pushed my hands under the mattress. I got down on my hands and knees and tapped each floorboard with my knuckles. I felt the wall behind the secretary for any hidden seams. This wasn't the first time I'd done it, but perhaps I'd missed something. The blankets came off the bed in a heap. I pressed myself into the mattress, feeling for any lumps that shouldn't be there. Nothing. Nothing. Nothing.

That couldn't be the end of it. The book existed; I was sure of it. Madame LaClaire used some kind of spell to curse my sister, and that spell was in that book she always carried with her, whether she'd ever revealed what it really was to Sebastian or not. I just needed it in my hands.

The foxglove sat heavy in my pocket. I hadn't even thought of it all day, but it might be the only way to get what I needed. That realization and the idea for using it wracked me with guilt.

I fell back on the bed, feet throbbing in my boots. Madame Écrue had left me this green wool dress my second morning here, but I only had my old boots that were a touch too small for me. I should have searched the boot room for an extra pair when I rescued Lucien from there.

I took off my boots and my toes ached as I rubbed them through my stockings. I glanced up at the big wardrobe on the other side of the room. I'd searched it quickly my first night. No book—and no boots that I remembered. The whole thing had made my stomach wobble. Perhaps it was knowing all those clothes belonged to a dead woman—then again, I slept in her bed each night.

The lines of the armoire curved and dipped, and the wood shone as though Madame Écrue continued to polish it. And maybe she did when I wasn't in here.

A month ago, I'd have been in awe of the richness of the wardrobe. Now I'd become unsettlingly numb to the grandeur of this house. I'd been here too long.

The gold inlay of the wardrobe's edges was rough under my finger and the handles shone in the golden light of dusk. Shimmering colors twinkled when I pulled open the double doors. Glittering blue sleeves and skirts hung beside embroidered green ones and yellow brocade. I hadn't paid much attention to them the first time I'd searched through—just pinching the skirts in my hands to look for the shape of a book.

I pulled out the blue dress. The full skirt swished against my legs and the sequins running down the sleeves and across the bodice caught the rich light of the setting sun. The line of sequins swirled into a pattern of flowers and cascaded down the skirt. I'd never seen such an entrancing dress before, and in that moment, I wanted nothing more than to put it on my body.

Shrugging out of my own dress was easy. I pulled at the laces at the back and tugged it down over my shoulders. Then I stepped into the beautiful blue confection.

The silk rustled with each of my movements and I sighed when I felt the tightness of the bodice around my waist. It fit. I couldn't do it up all the way by myself, but I swayed on the spot and pretended I danced at some great ball in a castle far from here.

"Do you need a partner?"

I jumped. My face flushed as I met Sebastian's eyes.

"I'm sorry, I was just looking around and I found this." I gestured inelegantly at the dress I wore. His mother's dress. I shouldn't have touched it.

Sweat gathered under my arms and behind my knees. Soon it would be running down my legs. *Please don't let him notice.*

"Here, let me." Sebastian stepped around me so he could reach my laces. Each time his fingers brushed my back through the thin fabric of my chemise, my heart beat a little faster. *What am I doing? Why am I letting him get to me like this?*

"There. Lovely," he said when he finished.

I wasn't sure if he meant the dress or me, but I couldn't meet his eyes.

"What are you doing here? You should be at the party."

"I wanted to check on you. You seemed a little green when you left the table."

My anger at myself must have showed in my features. At least Sebastian had mistaken it for illness.

"It's all right. I just felt a little sick all of a sudden, but I'm better now."

He nodded but continued to stare at me. I couldn't forget the way I'd felt watching him play with his brother, or how there'd been this simple happiness to seeing him hand Madame Écrue the perfume we'd made together. In the library, I'd imagined him as my husband, for heaven's sake, and the image wouldn't dislodge itself from my mind.

Now he stood in front of me with his curls tumbling around his face. His long, black eyelashes curled up at the ends. One had fallen onto his cheek. I almost reached up to wipe it away but checked myself and squeezed my hands into fists at my sides.

"Was this your mother's dress?" I asked to make the moment seem more normal. I should have just gone straight to bed—then Sebastian wouldn't have found me playing dress-up in his mother's closet.

"Must have been, but I don't ever remember her wearing it."

"Oh."

My tongue suddenly felt like a great sausage in my mouth and I was utterly incapable of speech. We stood there in a long moment of agonizing silence before Sebastian held out his hand to me.

"A dress like that deserves to dance. Will you do me the honor?"

I'd never danced with anyone before, but I was so relieved he wasn't angry that I simply nodded.

"I don't really know any steps," I said.

"Well, we don't have music either, so I suppose we can just make it up. What if I start by taking your hand?"

He tugged me close and laid one of my hands on his shoulder. I didn't know how rich people danced in ballrooms, but I guessed it wasn't like this—not with their bodies this close together. That would be scandalous, wouldn't it? Maybe Sebastian had never done this either.

I'd expected my hand to go all damp in his, but it didn't. My stomach fluttered, but I didn't mind. The hard knot of anxiety that often twisted my insides seemed to release. I was comfortable with Sebastian. He rested his chin on the top of my head and I leaned into him. He smelled of lavender and the particular musk of young men. I took a deep breath.

He hummed a slow, winding tune and I tried to move

without stepping on his feet. My dress glittered when we swept through the last rays of sunlight shining in from the window. A cold burst of wind hit my skin when Sebastian turned me.

"You shouldn't leave this open." He broke free of me and went to latch the window. "Anyone, or anything, could climb in."

I'd thought the same thing that first night, but I kept opening the window anyway. I liked sleeping with the fresh air after years of spending my nights in a cramped, stuffy cottage. I hadn't found myself outside again in the morning after that first time, so I thought there was nothing to be worried about.

I shrugged. "I like the air."

"It's dangerous, Marie," he said, sinking onto the edge of the bed. "Think of the animals roaming out there."

The most wild and dangerous of them all was my sister, and I wasn't scared of her. But the night air was starting to get too cold to leave it open anyway, so it was an easy thing to do to make Sebastian happy.

"I'll close it if you really want me to," I said.

"Please do, Marie. I'd be an awful host if I let you get hurt here."

You let Ama get hurt here. I wanted to tell him so much my skin itched. But he'd say I'd lost my mind, kick me out, and I'd lose my chance to find the spell book.

I stared into Sebastian's eyes, all soft with concern, and tried to harden myself. I'd need to lie to him, trick him, to make my plan work. Ama was going to turn soon, and it didn't look like I was going to find the spell book before she did. I'd have to go home, choose and mark a victim, then come back.

"You'll excuse me. I'm suddenly tired," I said.

He stood and the bed creaked from the release of his weight.

"Do you need me to help you?" he pointed at my dress.

"Oh, yes." I'd forgotten about the intricate laces tying me into the glittering thing. Sebastian tugged and loosened them until the dress gave around my shoulders and belly.

"Promise to keep it closed," he said, pointing to the window.

I gave him a little smile and nodded. "I will."

His face grew serious and my cheeks warmed again. "Good."

Sebastian closed the door gently behind him and I pulled his mother's dress from my body, then my petticoat and stays. Now in only my thin chemise, I crawled under the bed sheets and plotted how to trick the only man I'd ever danced with.

CHAPTER TWENTY-ONE

Madame Écrue wasn't in the kitchen yet—perhaps resting past dawn was part of her present. The girl who did the fires and lit the candles had already been and gone. I took a little knife and used the flat edge to crush the foxglove flowers until they bled, then I sopped up the juice with a twist of paper. These little drops of liquid would make Lucien bed-ridden all day. I felt sick myself at the thought of doing it, but I'd make sure there wasn't enough poison in his porridge to have a lasting effect. I could live with that if it got me what I needed to save Ama.

The path leading from the kitchen to the dining room was familiar now. Sebastian stood in his regular place before the fire, basking in the heat. The air was crisp, the snow still blindingly white outside the window.

I gave Sebastian the briefest hint of a smile, too nervous to do anything else. "Where's Lucien?"

"I'm sure he'll be down in a minute."

I almost wished he wouldn't come down to breakfast at all, that I wouldn't have to do what I was planning. Nothing in me wanted Lucien to suffer for even a moment, but this was the only way I could see to help Ama right now. I conjured up her face in my mind and held it there. I wished I had a miniature of her like Madame LaClaire's locket so I could squeeze it in my palm the same way the old ladies at church folded their bony hands around little wooden crucifixes.

I fumbled my fingers over the high back of one of the dining chairs. Sebastian turned stiffly to gaze back out the snow-covered window until the kitchen girl bustled into the dining room with a tray of white bowls filled with steaming porridge. She set a little jug of cream on the table with a small bowl filled with tawny brown powder before departing.

"Cinnamon," Sebastian said, and pinched some between his fingers. He extended his hand toward me. "Smell it."

His loose sleeve fell back to reveal a freckled wrist and I let my eyes linger a beat too long on his skin. He cleared his throat and I flushed, my underarms prickling with sweat. I clamped my elbows close to my body so he wouldn't see and leaned toward him to sniff the spicy powder. I hated how my own body betrayed me like this. No matter how hard I tried to mask it, my emotions were writ large by the sheen of sweat on my skin.

"It smells of heat," I said.

Sebastian smirked and wiped his ruddy fingers against

his blue trousers, leaving a smear behind. "Put some in your porridge. It tastes good."

"Does Lucien like it?"

Sebastian nodded and I took a bit in my fingers. While he watched, I sprinkled some in two of the bowls. When he blinked, I let the little twist of paper fall in Lucien's. If luck were with me, he wouldn't notice it in his porridge before the foxglove took effect.

The little boy came in then, with his eyes flitting like a bird. He walked over and took my fingers loosely in his hand. I liked how he did that so easily now, but it made everything so much harder. I was supposed to be there for his comfort, not for what I was about to do.

I took a deep breath, the cinnamon I'd inhaled still tickling my nose. *This won't hurt him much.* I had to hold that in my mind. The effects would wear off pretty quickly considering how small the dose was.

"I'd like to see the garden under the snow," I said, and gestured out the window. Sebastian took two steps toward me instead of watching Lucien.

"It's buried," Sebastian said. "But my mother loved it in the winter."

A jagged edge caught his voice and the last word came out as a half-whisper. He coughed and looked away from me, out into the trees so weighed down with snow it seemed their branches would break.

From the corner of my eye, I saw Lucien scrape the cinnamon off the top of his porridge and lick it from his spoon. My heart beat a little faster and my palms grew sweaty again. I clasped my hands, threaded my fingers together so Sebastian couldn't see the wetness there. I didn't want him to suspect anything. I held myself tightly together, my arms pressed to my sides and my legs pinched together under my skirt.

The sound of the silver spoon clattering against the porcelain bowl filled the room like a thunderclap. Sebastian and I both turned, but he stumbled for the table and I stayed where I was. For a moment. For a beat. Then I reacted.

Lucien shook in Sebastian's arms, the whites of his eyes too bright against his smooth brown skin.

"What do I do?" Sebastian cried. "Help me."

"Hold his head," I said.

He tried to hold Lucien, to stop his writhing body, but he could no more calm his brother than he could a roiling wave in a stormy sea. I pulled the shaking child onto my lap and he stilled, as I knew he would. The fits lasted only a couple minutes at most. Now, he would sleep.

"Lucien?" Sebastian bent his head to his brother's mouth. "He's breathing."

"Yes." I put my hand over his heart and felt the thud of life through his shirt. "He lives, but we need to put him to bed."

"He's been doing so well."

It wasn't a question, but Sebastian's eyes searched mine anyway. I didn't lower my gaze as I said, "Everyone's fine until they aren't."

Sebastian ran his hands through his hair, making it go wild.

I opened my knees a little and eased Lucien's head down my skirt onto the fading red carpet. The fire had gone out and a chill stiffened the air. With Lucien settled, I pulled myself up with a hand on the edge of the table. His bowl sat there with glutinous porridge sticking to the sides. Bile rose in my throat and I pushed the bowl away. It was done. There was no taking it back now.

Sebastian sat on his knees and brushed something from his brother's cheek. He loved him. It was as clear and as pure as the untouched snow outside—and it made him much more vulnerable. He pulled his hand back from Lucien and stared up at me.

"Can you save him?"

"Yes, I think so."

"What do you need?"

"I don't know . . . I . . . I need that book, Sebastian! Madame Écrue told me it has cures in it, remedies that would work."

He swiveled his head around as if he'd find it sitting out on the sideboard. "But I don't know where it is!"

"Think, Sebastian!"

"All right, all right . . . it might be in my mother's parlor, but this better save him, Marie! You have to be able to do something!"

"He's in my heart now, Sebastian. Of course I'll try to save him."

It wasn't a lie. I'd grown to care about Lucien—it was impossible not to. He was sweet and adventurous and refused to let his illness stomp out his light. I hated that he might have felt some pain while the poison set in, but now he slept soundly and I knew he'd be fine once the poison filtered from his body.

"No, Marie. You can't *try*. You have to succeed."

He said it without heat—just a fact—but I heard the undercurrent of the threat there. Surprise rippled through me, leaving a trail of something else in its wake. A small spark of recognition. We were the same, Sebastian and I. We'd both do anything for the ones we loved. He didn't have to verbalize what he might do to me if I failed.

Madame Écrue and a tall man with a dirty cravat picked Lucien up by his arms and legs. He hung between them like a rag doll and I fought the urge to help cradle his head. He couldn't feel this—any of it. He'd be fine, I knew that, and yet guilt made me ill.

Sebastian hovered close, moving in rhythm with the two servants, his hands just under Lucien's back. He resembled a bird taking teetering steps—scared and hopeful at the same time. Finally, they reached the stairs and Sebastian fell back. He let the servants carry his brother over the stairs and his shoulders dropped almost imperceptibly.

I wasn't only causing Lucien pain, but Sebastian too. It *must* all be worth it. I had to find the book and the cure for Ama's transformations. I'd be saving my sister, but there was more to it than that. Breaking her curse was the best way to save us all. Sebastian's estate would be safer, more prosperous maybe. Lucien wouldn't have anything to be afraid of.

"He'll be all right, Sebastian," I whispered.

Sebastian turned to me and sagged, his knees buckling as a sob crashed over him.

I caught him, held him, and he let me. I held up both of us, but my own heart was so heavy.

"Let's go get the book and we'll make him feel better," I said. "It's the best thing we can do right now."

Sebastian wiped at his eyes, took a deep breath, and looked away. I wanted to tell him I liked him more for all of it but couldn't bring myself to say the words.

I trailed a few paces behind as he led me through a hall so narrow that I could reach out my arms and touch the frail paper lining the walls on both sides. The wood-paneled ceiling hung low over our heads and the whole space made me want to run outside and take in gulping breaths of fresh air.

The musky scent of mildew lingered in my nose, so I brought my hand up to shield my face. Sebastian turned down a branching hall opening up into a long-forgotten sitting room. White sheets hung over pictures on the walls like a child's imagining of a ghost. A thin layer of dust dulled the color of the furniture—a settee and matching upholstered footrest; an inlaid card table on thin, tooled legs; two straight-backed armchairs by the cold fireplace.

The family would have gathered here, perhaps after supper, with Sebastian sitting at his father's feet by the fire while his mother played Quinze and laughed at her son's games.

Lucien had never brought me here. I hadn't even known it existed.

I could almost hear the faint sound of a woman's tinkling laughter whispering around the room.

Sebastian swung around and pushed the candle into my face. "I hate coming here."

"Because it reminds you of your parents?"

Sebastian tightened his jaw. "It reminds me of what I couldn't do for them."

Which was far worse, of course. The option of saving them was gone. He'd either had his chance and failed or he'd never had any chance and his parents had simply been stolen from him.

"Did you see how they died?" I asked.

My stomach twisted while I waited for his answer, while he pulled in a breath and wet his lips with his tongue. He probably hadn't seen Ama in any clarity or he'd have been much more determined a year ago to have Emméline catch the beast, but still. I squirmed.

"There was nothing to see except their bodies, and I tried not to look very hard at the details of what happened to them."

His face paled and flushed, like he was terrified just from the memory. I shouldn't have asked.

"I'm sorry, that's awful."

"Yes, well." He gave a half-hearted shrug and reached for a cloth on the card table. It was stark white and looked clean and out of place in this museum of memories. When he unfolded it, the fresh scent of rose petals drifted toward me. He pressed the cloth to his nose and took a deep breath. Then he carefully folded it again and placed it gently next to an ivory comb. Perhaps these were his tributes to the mother he'd never see again.

Sebastian made his way to the bookshelf and walked slowly along it, searching the tomes until he stopped and pulled out a thin blue volume—inconspicuous among other spines of emerald tooled leather. My heart thumped in my chest, hard and fast. I took it from his hands slowly, with the reverence it deserved.

I'd thought of it so often—imagined holding it in my hands—that it felt surreal to do so now. It was heavier than expected. Black splotches marred the gilded edges of the pages. The cover was deep blue leather with no title or words at all. It looked like a very expensive prayer book.

"Open it," Sebastian said. He was so close to me, his breath stirred my hair.

I turned the cover and flipped forward a few pages. The yellowing paper crinkled under my fingers.

Nothing. No words, no spells. Not even the scribbles Lucien said he'd seen his mother draw in this book, just brown mold edging the pages. My stomach contracted.

Every page in the book was utterly blank.

CHAPTER TWENTY-TWO

Sebastian slammed the book down on the polished wood table in the dining room, as mad as I was but for completely different reasons. He might not know it, but it wasn't a real blow to him that the book was blank—we'd never really needed it to save Lucien. The foxglove effects would wear off soon and Lucien would wake, a bit groggy and with a sour tummy. I'd been counting on the book, and it had let me down. All I saw over and over again was the blankness of the white paper. It didn't feel real, couldn't be real. I wouldn't let it. Everything I'd done, all that I'd come here for, all my hope, smashed in the time it took me to flip to the front page.

There was no other clue to what had happened to Ama. All I had were the villagers' whispers and superstitions and my own assumptions about the book, and all that was slipping through my fingers like wisps of smoke. *Now what? How could I help my sister? All of us? What could I do?*

"I don't understand, I've seen Maman's writing on these pages before!" Sebastian said.

"Perhaps you were mistaken," I said.

I was numb. I slumped against the table, no longer wanting to hold myself up.

"Marie?" Sebastian cupped his hand around my shoulder. "We'll find another way."

"There is no other way." Nothing else, no other direction to turn.

"There is, of course there is. We'll use your poultices and teas."

Sebastian wasn't making sense. There was no tea in the world that could stop Ama from becoming a beast.

"It won't work."

"Why are you saying that? You told me before you could save him! Marie!"

Sebastian's face snapped into focus. Lucien. *Lucien.* Not Ama. He didn't know anything about Ama.

"We . . . we will. I'll just need to think, just combine a poultice for phlegm and one for clear breathing and—" I pushed my hair out of my face.

"Marie, stop." He took my hand in his and rubbed my palm with one of his fingers.

My tongue stuck to the roof of my dry mouth. I had to swallow twice before I could speak again.

"I'm just trying to figure out what to do."

"I know, but you're breathing too quickly."

"Oh."

This always happened to me when there was just too much in my mind. When I was little, Papa taught me to count out my breaths to slow them down. *One, two, three, four, five.* It was one of the few things he'd ever given me—a way to manage through the chaos and the pain.

"Master Sebastian."

Madame Écrue came through the dining room door holding a silver tray piled with letters. I tried to spot Ama's handwriting on the front of one of them, but I was too far away to recognize any familiar spiky letters.

"I don't want the mail now, Madame. Did Lucien settle when you brought him to bed? Is he sleeping?"

The woman nodded her head. "He's sleeping yes, no coughing, or bringing up, or anything right now."

Sebastian ran a hand over his face before dropping into one of the dining chairs. "Thank God."

"He's not out of the woods yet," said Madame Écrue.

"I know. I'm not getting ahead of myself; I'm just happy for this moment," Sebastian said.

He surprised me with how he reasoned while his brother was, as far as he knew, ailing in bed. I wanted to be able to find the little slivers of good lodged with the bad like that, but I wasn't really that kind of person.

"You should read this." Madame Écrue reached for the top letter on the pile and passed it to Sebastian. A little whiff of lavender reached my nose. She was wearing the perfume we'd made.

"The courier told me what's in it," she went on. "But I didn't want to open it for you."

Sebastian took the letter from her with a question in his eyes. "What—"

"Just open it."

He did. His eyes flicked across the page of script, and the color drained from his cheeks.

"No," he whispered, and let the letter fall out of his hand onto the floor. "There's been another killing. The beast is roaming the forest . . . it's not safe to let people . . . children . . . go in there."

"Another killing?" I whispered.

A chill wound through my body. I'd thought I had more time. There was always at least a month between Ama's transformations, so there should have been a few days left. If this was her, if my sister was really killing people I didn't mark for her, she was changing much more often. The thought of that was terrifying. How could I mark enough victims for her then? I had nothing here, no spells, no hope of a cure. How was I supposed to help her?

"Who died?" I asked him.

"The Carters' boy," Sebastian said.

I searched my memory—he was twelve, thirteen maybe. All the promises of life stripped away by Ama's sharp teeth. This was my fault. I had to get home and mark her victims again, stop her from killing children. But that would only be a temporary fix. I'd need to come back and find the spell so I could cure her for good. I still needed Sebastian on my side.

"How terrible," I said.

"Two young boys in as many months." Sebastian ran a hand over his face again. "I'll have to go into town and talk to Père Danil. The parents don't have the coin for a burial."

I nodded with a knot in my stomach.

"Marie, are you all right?" Sebastian took hold of my hand and eased me into a chair. My mouth worked but I couldn't scrape the words out against my dry tongue.

The other letters were splayed on the silver platter and I could see none of them were for me. Ama hadn't written back even though I'd begged her. Maybe she wasn't answering me because she couldn't. She might be turning when she shouldn't be, killing people—children—who should have been out of reach.

"I'm coming with you, into town."

"What? But Lucien needs you here; you need to nurse him!"

I gripped Sebastian's chair and looked into his eyes so he could see the determination in mine.

"My sister is out there alone in a cottage at the edge of the woods and something is killing people. I need to make sure she's safe. Then I'll come back and take care of Lucien."

He reached up and cupped my chin. I almost flinched from surprise, but it only took a moment for me to sink into the warmth of his hand. He didn't know everything, but he knew I was worried for my sister and he cared, even though his own brother was sick in bed.

"All right, you can come with me."

Madame Écrue tutted from where she stood near the hearth. "She should stay here and help with Lucien."

"We'll both be back soon," Sebastian said, letting go of my chin.

"You're bringing trouble on yourselves by going out there, you know. It's safer in here," she said.

"I'm not supposed to stay safe, Madame. I'm supposed to protect the estate."

"Nobles," Madame Écrue said after a moment, turning to leave. "Such ideals you all have."

Her words may have been flippant, but her voice gave her away, and her tears.

Sebastian watched her go, then turned to face me. "What will you wear out there?"

I pulled my wool shawl tighter around my shoulders. "This is all I have."

Sebastian stared at me a beat and shook his head. "Come with me."

CHAPTER TWENTY-THREE

He ducked under a small doorframe set into the side of the stairs. A wooden chest creaked, opening on hinges in need of a good oiling. Sebastian emerged with two hunting coats in his arms.

"Here." He tossed one at me.

It was heavy, thick, something only the rich could own. It was supposed to be used on occasion to keep some lord warm while he play-acted at catching his own food. Others, those whose livelihoods depended on them standing outside while the icy air blackened their fingers and withered their toes, would never find themselves in possession of a coat so fine.

I shrugged it on and wrapped the soft fur collar around my neck, luxuriating in it. I might never wear something like this again.

"Does it fit?"

The coat was much too large for my frame, the hem

hitting my knees, but I didn't care about that. It would keep me warm.

"It's good. Thank you."

Sebastian nodded, not meeting my eyes.

"Since there's two of us, we'll have to walk instead of taking my horse. She's too old to carry us both."

"I'm perfectly happy to walk."

I'd never ridden a horse before and wasn't eager to try. The thought of it made me queasy.

"Are you all right? You've gone a bit pale," Sebastian said. "Lucien is sleeping. We have time to go and come back."

"It's not just that."

"I'm sure your sister is fine as well, safe in your cottage." He offered me a smile, even though it seemed like an effort for him.

Sebastian was trying to reassure me, but I couldn't help thinking what he said was unlikely to be true. Ama probably wasn't tucked up inside the cottage, warm by the hearth while the snow blurred the world outside. She could very well be the shadow in the snow, a creature peeled straight from children's nightmares.

I was too warm all of a sudden, the heavy coat making it hard to breathe.

"We should go," I said, because I wanted out, needed the sharp feeling of cold air in my lungs.

Sebastian pulled open one of the heavy double doors. Outside was another world entirely. The snow blanketed the ground, the trees. It muffled the air until not a sound met my ears. The only confirmation that I was still here, still real, was the tingling of my nose as the cold wrapped its brittle arms around me.

Sebastian marred the effect by crunching down the path from his house.

We walked down the hill and wound around the village, skirting the main street. I didn't need prying eyes wondering why I was escorting the young lord anywhere. There were already enough whispers about Ama and me—and whispers were easily turned to weapons in a place like this.

Tall trees drooped like tired sentries at the edge of the woods, weighed down by the snow. Frost scented the air crisp and clean. I took big, greedy breaths that tickled my nose. Then I froze, because I tasted it on the back of my tongue. Blood.

Ama.

Drops the color of garnets stained the glittering snow. I lurched forward, tripped up by the deep collection of flakes that had appeared beautiful a moment ago. Just inside the tree line, where the snow thinned and brambles snaked greedily over the ground, lay a girl. Her stillness made goose-flesh rise all over my skin.

"Sebastian!" I called out for him as I hurried to her side. The wind fluttered the dead girl's hair over her gray face.

He ran toward me, eyes wide and disbelieving. As if he'd see something else if he just looked a little harder.

"Who?" he gasped, falling to his knees.

"Vivienne. A young seamstress in the village."

I recognized the ebony of her hair and purple ribbon tied around her throat. She often wore it when she hurried from the baker's to her mistress's shop in the morning. It had brought out her green eyes. Now, pale eyelids hid them from view. Her dress hung in ribbons from her torso, much in need of a good seamstress. Vivienne would have been appalled.

Being coarse won't make this less unsettling, said a little voice in my head. It was something Ama would say.

Sebastian pressed his hand to her stomach and pulled it away coated in blood as thick as paint. He paled, screwed up his mouth, and tried to use a handful of snow to wipe the stuff away.

"Is she dead?" he asked.

"Of course."

I picked up a little tuft of fur from the ground. Russet red. Ama's was mostly golden, but maybe she had darker fur under her knees or near her feet.

"Why does this keep happening? Why here?" He pulled at his curls and then pressed his hands onto the side of his head. Wild and bare, without his manners.

I knew the answer, but I kept my mouth shut. Better to let him wonder at his village's misfortune than to reveal my own. Instead, I reached for his hand and moved it away from his face. He shivered at my touch but didn't pull away. I barely felt his skin against mine—we were both frozen through—but I liked the weight of his fingers. They were solid, here, alive.

"There's a monster in these woods," I said. I wasn't telling him something he didn't already know—everybody knew we were being hunted. They just didn't know the creature lived in the body of my sister most of the time.

The wind whipped and curled around us, blowing dustings of snow from the branches above.

"I have to go home and see my sister. I want to make sure she's safe."

Sebastian nodded. "I'll tell Père Danil about Vivienne and see what I can do for her and the Carter family. Then I'll go back to Lucien."

He didn't have to do anything for the Carter family. Not all lords would have, and I liked that he chose to care. It wasn't always the easier path. I hadn't necessarily made a choice to let Lucien worm his way into my heart, but he had. And I hated the thought of him trapped in bed while the poison slowly let go of his body.

"I'll come back soon, promise. Just let me make sure Ama's safe, and then I'll come see Lucien is too. Give him some of the tea in the kitchen to tide him over."

We faced each other, and Sebastian gripped my sleeves. The cold stained his hands pink and red. Mine looked the same. I was happy he held me though. His touch steadied me and made it a little easier to do what I had to do next.

"Don't be long. Lucien needs you," Sebastian said.

"I won't."

I dragged myself away from him and tried to brush thoughts of Lucien from my mind with a flick of my fingers over my eyes. He'd be fine with a little time. And I had other things to worry about. If all these killings were Ama's doing, if she had already turned, she was losing control. It was so much easier to get caught when you lost control. I made solid, purposeful steps toward home and never once looked back at Sebastian even though I wanted to.

As I approached, I could see the wooden door of our cottage stood closed, but I knew the thick gap between the door and the stone floor let in the cold like an unwelcome stranger. I wrapped my hand around the door handle, skin stinging against the icy metal, and took a deep breath.

Thoughts tumbled through my mind like scattered beads. I had to confront Ama. She'd lie, of course, but I'd smell it on her—the blood. She couldn't kill like this. It had to be planned, scripted, merciful. When the beast killed vagrants or drunks, no one fussed. It was explained away by the victim's own foolishness at getting too close to the woods. But a child was different. A young seamstress, a beautiful girl with a blush in her cheeks, would be different. Those deaths wouldn't be brushed off.

They'd be avenged.

I pulled open the door.

Silence filled the space, heavy and deafening. I tiptoed inside, not wanting to break the quiet. There was no one here to break it for. Ashes piled soft and deep in the grate of the fireplace. I ran my hands along the scrubbed table, digging my fingernails into the claw marks running the length of it. A tuft of fur fluttered lightly from a nail sticking out from the stone awning of the hearth. I snatched up the fur and wetness slicked my fingers. I shuddered and turned the patch over. It was still attached to a torn piece of bloody skin.

Ama had been alone and scared and hurt. And now she was gone.

Her absence echoed in my bones, just like it did when Papa had sent her away. The loss of her was a solid thing, a weight in the pit of my stomach, an anchor tying me to my sister.

I ran to the door, trying to pull in the imaginary rope, trying to feel for her on the other side. Wind twisted around the cottage and whipped through the trees, dusting the snow like finely milled flour, covering any tracks or footprints that might show me where she was.

The emptiness of the cottage enveloped me. Heavy and thick. My skin prickled with it. But no, it wasn't just that. It was the sudden feeling of not being alone when I thought I was.

A howl pierced the air—painful and raw. It ripped from the trees and shot like an arrow into my heart. I knew it in the same way I knew her smell. *Ama.* She'd turned again, and during daylight too. She was the beast. The beast was her. No space existed between them anymore.

This was the moment I could turn away. I could leave her to the woods and the trees and the blood on her teeth. The beast had swallowed her, and so Ama would never know I'd abandoned her. I could bolt the door and shut out my guilt and shake my head like any other villager the next time a body was found. I could leave the whispers in the square and come home to the safety of my empty cottage. I could scrimp and save until I had a dowry and keep my head down long enough that the villagers would eventually find me respectable enough to marry. I could find someone who wouldn't want to own his wife.

I felt the edges of a normal life with my fingertips. It was mine for the taking.

But of course, I couldn't take it.

I'd never be able to push Ama from my mind. She lived in my blood and bones. Even if I achieved a good life, it would taste like ashes without her to share it with.

So, I pushed back out into the snow and let the flakes melt on my face and against my sleeves until my skin ached with cold. I trudged back to the big house like I said I would. Sebastian had reason to want to destroy the creature who'd killed his parents, and I wanted her back. He could help me catch her. We might be able to destroy the beast together—and save my sister.

CHAPTER TWENTY-FOUR

My fingers stung when I knocked them against the thick wood of the front doors. Swirls and stars dipped and curled in the doorframe—carved inelegantly with rough, splintered edges. Fear had kept me from noticing them the first time I came here. Now, I ran my fingers along the frantic planes of a star and shivered when a sliver of wood slipped under my skin.

Whoever had scratched them into the wood had done so hastily. Perhaps the markings were part of a panicked protection spell—something to keep evil out. Or maybe to keep it in. Perhaps Sebastian's mother had realized what she'd done to Ama and what Ama might do to her. This house guarded its own secrets.

A cold tingle crept up my spine at the thought of Madame LaClaire and what she'd been able to do without anyone else knowing.

Witches and magic were supposed to be nothing more than superstition, egged on by Père Danil to keep people turning to the church for protection. When I first came here, I'd thought—hoped—Sebastian's mother had been a witch who cursed Ama because that might mean I'd find the cure within these walls. Now I truly *believed* she was a witch.

One of the double doors opened with a slow creak, and the afternoon light fell on half of Madame Écrue's face.

"You came back."

I nodded. "I told Sebastian I would."

The old woman stared at me with her one good eye. I always thought her somewhat blind, but it was clear from the certainty of her gaze she could see.

"You came back for Sebastian or Lucien?"

Heat flared in my cheeks, but I answered honestly. "Both."

"You helped him make my perfume, didn't you?"

"Yes, but it was all his idea."

The heart of the gift was all Sebastian, and I didn't want to take any credit for it.

"Lucien's not getting any better, you know," she said.

I knew she meant he wasn't getting better at all, not just from my dose of poison, but I chose to ignore that.

"He will."

The woman's sudden sadness, the tears in the corner of her eyes and the crumpling of her chin, was catching. My own eyes blurred with the promise of tears. I didn't want Lucien to live like he was either.

"It's harder, this slow weakening. With Mademoiselle, it

was quick. She was here and then she was gone, and I didn't have time to think about it."

"Sebastian and Lucien's mother?"

Madame Écrue nodded and waved me into the house. The door closed, blocking out some of the cold, but I still shivered.

"She left too soon. She had so much work to do." Madame Écrue pushed her fingers into her lips like she wanted to stuff the words back into her mouth. Tears slid down her cheeks.

"What kind of work?" I asked.

"She wouldn't ever tell me enough to understand. Never. She told me to look after the children and keep myself safe."

She looked up at me then, as a child looks up at their mother—wide, pleading eyes. Asking for something. Forgiveness maybe.

"You did look after them."

Her tears fell over the rims of her eyes and she wiped them away with the back of her hand. Powder smeared from her cheeks.

"Yes, but I didn't look after her. She was tangled up with that woman and then she was gone."

"What woman?"

Madame LaClaire's elusive friend. She was important to all this; she had to be.

Madame Écrue pinched her apron in her fingers. "Mademoiselle never told me her name; she said it was better that way. She just called the woman 'mon étoile.'"

My star. The woman in the portrait was someone very

special to Madame LaClaire. If only I could figure out who she was.

"Did you ever wonder where she came from, Madame LaClaire's friend?" I asked.

"I did, but it didn't really matter. The boys had all my attention then."

Lucien. I needed to make sure the poison was leaving his system as I expected it to.

"Let me see if I can make Lucien feel better now," I said.

"I hope you can," Madame Écrue said.

A few candles' flames bobbed lazily in the hall, their glowing light reflecting back in the little round mirrors behind them. The now-familiar smell of dust and disuse rose from the patterned carpet with each step I took. Madame Écrue led the way up the stairs with slow, measured steps. At the landing, we turned left down a narrow corridor with dark paneled walls. One small window revealed a faint yellow glow as the clouds swallowed up the weak winter sun.

"Here," the old woman said, and twisted a brass doorknob in her gnarled fingers. The door opened with a pop of swollen wood and I stepped inside.

Heavy, blue velvet curtains hung over windows that stretched from floor to ceiling, blocking the light and muffling the air. A wardrobe, swollen in the middle with gilded trim, stood proud against one wall. Pushed up along another wall was a four-poster bed with blue velvet hangings caught up by twisting ropes of gold. Sebastian leaned over Lucien, so I couldn't see the boy's face, but my palms were slicked with sweat. Lucien should have been sitting up by now, a little weak, maybe, but awake. *Is the poison affecting him more strongly because he's already ill?*

As I walked in, Sebastian looked over his shoulder and I finally glimpsed Lucien's face, white as the moon against the blackest night. He shouldn't have looked that ill. Then someone else stepped out from around the bed curtains. Emméline.

My shock at seeing her here robbed me of my voice. She wasn't supposed to be in Sebastian's house, in Lucien's room. Her braid fell over her shoulder as she bent closer to Sebastian and put a hand on his arm with an easy familiarity that caused a spike of jealousy to shoot down into my fingertips.

"He won't wake up," Sebastian said.

"Poor boy," Emméline said. "What in the world happened to him?"

She looked up at me, staring daggers. She couldn't know what I'd done, but still, she challenged me with her large, dark eyes. Even though I wanted her out of here, away from Sebastian and Lucien, I couldn't help studying her. Hair plaited in an intricate design, slim-cut dress, flushed cheeks, broad shoulders. She fascinated me and I hated it.

How did she manage to look so in control? It seemed like nothing could break the shell she'd hardened around herself. I wished I could be like that. My insecurities were laid bare to the world every time my palms dampened or my expression revealed too much. I had to really try to hide it.

Emméline squeezed Sebastian's shoulder and he spoke.

"You said you knew how to fix him, but he's not getting any better," he said.

He kept his back to me, which was worse than if he'd stared me down. I wanted his rage at least, anything but this cold indifference.

Lucien *would* get better. I'd put just the right amount of poison into the porridge. He was never supposed to be in any real danger.

"Did you make the chamomile tea I left in the kitchen?"

Not that the tea would make any real difference. Time was all that was needed here. Once the poison left his system, Lucien would be back to normal—well, his normal.

Sebastian gripped Lucien's limp hand. "I did it just like you said and tipped the liquid down his throat an hour ago. He stirred for a moment, then fell back into sleep."

"He'll wake," I said, but my certainty started to slip away. He should have been awake already. My sister always asked me things when we were little—why does the river flow that way, can birds understand each other when they sing, why did the blood drain from Maman's body after they took the dead baby out? I wanted to have the answers for her, so I made things up. Maybe over time I'd come to believe my own fables. Maybe I didn't always have the answers.

Sebastian stood with a creak of the ropes holding the mattress in place. Lucien's smooth face gave away nothing—the only hint of life was a thin sheen of sweat on his forehead, shining in the wavering candlelight.

Emméline barely moved out of the way. She positioned

her body so her skirt pressed against Sebastian's legs. He reached out absently for her hand.

"You should go, Emméline. Everything's more urgent now and my offer still stands."

"Good, because I intend to take you up on it," Emméline said.

They were talking about the prize for killing my sister that Sebastian had been dangling in front of her. The whole exchange curdled my stomach. Even if I thought Ama could hold her own against Emméline—and I did—having a determined hunter after her scared me.

Sebastian gave her a smile but dropped her hand.

"I hope you do. I think you're the only one who can help us."

Emméline bowed her head, but she couldn't completely hide her twisted smile from me. I watched her too closely. My eyes followed her until she stepped out of Lucien's room and closed the door behind her. She'd never even greeted me, and that hurt—even though I shouldn't care.

Now Sebastian finally met my eyes, and anger rolled off him like heat.

"You said he would be fine, and I believed you. I thought he'd be awake when I got home. I told you, you have to make him better!"

I swallowed my sadness and fear, and they burned down my throat, but I didn't even blink under Sebastian's gaze. I needed to regain his trust, so I'd have to tell him another lie.

"My sister is dead."

Surprise flickered across his face and drew his eyebrows together. "What? But it was that seamstress ... Vivienne, not your sister."

"When I went home, there was fur and blood and Ama was gone." That was true enough. The beast hadn't killed Ama, but it *had* taken her. The only difference was, I could still get her back.

Sebastian's hand never left Lucien's. He gripped it as if he'd tether his brother to this world with his touch. *It's not that simple. Their spirits can still slip through your fingers,* I wanted to say, but I didn't.

I tried not to look at Lucien and his pale face lying against that white silk pillow. I didn't like the sharp pang of guilt or the heavy sadness.

"Help me kill the beast," I said. "I know how to do it."

I laid the prize before him like bait—revenge on a silver platter. Once he snatched it, I'd rope him in. Only he didn't know I'd never let him kill my sister. But I did need to catch her and strip the beast from her skin. For that, Sebastian and his mother's spell book were essential. There was something more to the book than blank pages. There had to be. Lucien had seen writing on them. It was waiting for me to figure it out, to call up the letters and let them form themselves into spells. I wanted him to see the beast, scare him into action.

"The beast has ravaged our village long enough. I'm supposed to be the protector, right?" Sebastian said.

The protector. The innocent hero. *The innocent.* I

understood, then, what Sebastian was after. He wanted the whispers that he'd killed his parents to end. He wanted the villagers to look him in the eye again without shuddering.

"You want to clear your name," I said.

A grimace bared his teeth—sharp and a little yellowed from good wine. "I don't enjoy being thought of as a murderer."

"And do you think you'll prove anything by having Emméline kill the beast? The villagers will still think what they want, and you won't even get your revenge."

The thought of Emméline stalking the woods, determined to kill, twisted my gut and put fire in my belly. If it came down to it, I wouldn't let her hurt my sister—but what would I do to stop her from pulling the trigger? The answer flowed through my veins with every beat of my heart. *Anything. Anything.*

"It has to be us, Sebastian," I said. "We've lost people to the monster's teeth. We should be the ones to kill it."

Sebastian brought Lucien's limp hand to his cheek, eyes fluttering closed as a sob escaped his lips. I knew his pain, intimately. I wanted to throw my arms around him and hold him as he shook. I wanted to smooth Lucien's hot cheeks with the back of my cool hand. But I could do neither. It wouldn't be fair. I'd done this to them. I had no right to comfort.

"I can't do anything while Lucien's so sick," Sebastian whispered.

"There's nothing more you can do for him right now. Let him rest. He'll come out of it."

It was the truest thing I could say about Lucien's poison-induced illness. He'd get better; it might just take more time than I thought. I could use that time wisely—get Sebastian to help me lure my sister out of the woods and lock her in the cellar until she turned back.

"You think if I'm the one who brings the beast's body into town, the villagers will absolve me of my parents' death?" Sebastian said. "That won't be enough."

I couldn't let anyone kill Ama. I hardened my voice and spat out more lies like stones.

"I think they'll see the beast for themselves and know you've had your revenge. You can tell them it was the thing that took your parents' lives, just like it stole Maurice and Vivienne and the Carter boy from the world."

He stared at me, his gaze hard. "And your sister."

I dropped my eyes and willed them to glow with tears. It wasn't hard. Everything was too heavy, too awful, and my eyes filled before I lifted them to Sebastian again.

"Yes, and Ama. You'll prove to them you can protect them after all."

"You want to kill it too, don't you?" Sebastian leaned over Lucien and gripped my arms. Spittle flew from his lips. "You want to feel hot revenge pour from its throat onto your hands?"

The image sprang unbidden into my mind—the pool of deep red marring the lacy white snow. The grunts and yelps from the beast's throat. The sheen of terror in its eyes . . . my sister's eyes. My gorge rose and I swallowed sour bile.

I spat the word out. "Yes."

His eyes softened a little. "I want that too. I want to kill the monster that murdered my parents."

Ama was out there, somewhere, being hunted by Emméline. I had to protect her, but I also needed to cure her. I couldn't accomplish one without the other. If I didn't stop Emméline from killing my sister, there wouldn't be anyone left to save. If I didn't find the cure, my sister would always be hunted. These dizzying thoughts swirled in my head and I put the back of my hand to my warm temple. *One step at a time. Find Ama, keep her safe for now. Then, find the cure and keep her safe for good.*

I took Sebastian's hand, pulling it from Lucien's chest, not caring for once that my palms were damp. Sebastian's eyes lingered on his brother before shifting to me. When they did, I took in a sharp breath because they shocked me. Filled with hunger and need. He wanted a chance to prove himself—to show the town he wasn't his parents' murderer and to take his own revenge. I forced myself to speak.

"All right, Sebastian. Let's go monster hunting."

CHAPTER TWENTY-FIVE

Cold air hit me like a wall, freezing the sweat on my palms and the damp fabric under my arms. I knew how to call the beast. I did it all the time. All it took was some honeysuckle mixed with a little lavender or rose oil. But I couldn't tell Sebastian *why* I knew how to do it.

"You don't know it'll work," he said as we trudged toward the village.

"I know some animals are drawn to the sweetness of honeysuckle. It's not a big leap to think the beast will be too. I know I have some in my stores at home that I use for poultices."

I couldn't tell him the real reason I kept honeysuckle on hand.

"If you say so. And once the beast is near?"

Sebastian turned to look at me as we left the road and crunched through the stiff snow at the edge of the forest.

"We kill it," I said with a dry throat.

Sebastian took a deep breath and nodded, clenching the musket he'd brought with us in his hands. I reached down, scooped up a bit of snow, and put it on my tongue to let it melt.

I wondered how important it was to Sebastian to be the one to kill the beast—if his hunger for revenge would be enough to keep him with me. It seemed it was. For now, at least.

The door to our cottage gave easily without a bolt to seal it. The emptiness of the place got under my skin and made me shiver. It wasn't right. Ama should be here, filling the space.

"So, this is your home?" Sebastian said.

I nodded. *What does he think of it?* Sebastian may have never even set foot in a cottage like this before. He might really understand our differences now. Unbidden, I remembered the feel of his broad shoulders under my hands while we danced in front of his mother's wardrobe. Though I couldn't ignore the valley between us, between our lives here, I didn't really want Sebastian to feel it too.

"Do you have a tinder box?" he asked.

I started and leaned heavily against the table. "Near the window."

The cottage was dark in the pale, late afternoon light, but I knew it well enough to not need bright candles.

Sebastian fumbled with the flint and struck it against the fire steel. He then took a little stick from the fireplace and prodded it into the flames. The end caught and shimmered as Sebastian manipulated it in the dark. A clever puppeteer on a dark stage.

The low light made shallow shadows along the walls.

"We need to find the beast before anyone else does," I said, opening the cabinet that held my tinctures. "Or anyone else dies."

"Why do you think we'll be able to find it just like that?"

"We'll lure it to us ... and then poison it."

"And what will we use as bait?"

"Vivienne, the girl we found in the woods today ... she wasn't in as bad a state as Maurice was."

"She was lucky."

A shiver rippled over Sebastian's body after he spoke, and he wrapped his coat around himself. I stepped closer to him because the cold began to nip at my fingers too, and I wanted to feel the solidity of his arm against mine. Sebastian returned the pressure when I leaned into him.

"I think the beast didn't finish what it started," I said, keeping my eyes on the gouged wood of the table in front of us. "It got interrupted. We take the body, lace it with honey-suckle and stuff it with poison, and leave it out for the mon-ster to find. When it comes for the girl, it'll eat the poison with her flesh."

He took my mortar from the table and rolled it across the top. "And what if the beast prefers living flesh? We'll be an easy meal."

Something deep inside me still believed Ama would never

hurt me—even when transformed into a monster. But that didn't mean she wouldn't go after the warm, thudding pulse in Sebastian's neck.

I pushed the thought away and took the mortar from him.

"It'll be too distracted with the girl and then it will be sick with poison," I insisted.

"And then I shoot it?"

"Yes."

We stared at each other. The heat of his gaze made me want to drop mine, but I didn't. I couldn't—he'd see the lie in the shift of my eyes.

"And you just have this poison on hand? Why?"

"Rats," I said. "We're always trying to get rid of the rats."

Two cut glass bottles, one with honeysuckle and one with foxglove, sat snug in the basket Ama and I had taken to market the day Maurice was found. I slipped them both into the deep pocket of my skirt and let the door bang shut behind us just to hear the noise.

"What if she already stinks?" Sebastian asked.

I placed my boot into a footprint left in the hard-packed snow between my cottage and the edge of town. The hard edges of the print crumbled under my weight.

"It's cold. She'll still be fresh."

Sebastian's lips pulled down into a grimace and I couldn't

blame him. I didn't relish seeing the body again or feeling the sticky blood under my fingers.

Someone had draped a white canvas tarp over the wagon that had brought the body back from the woods so only the girl's feet were visible. The streets had emptied near the church as the villagers rushed to evade the moonlit night and all the threats darkness might bring.

I climbed into the wagon and yanked the tarp back, trying to ignore the girl's blank eyes.

"Grab her legs," I said.

Sebastian clapped his hands on the dead girl's ankles and pulled. I tried to catch the shoulders, but he was too quick and the body fell from the wagon with a sickening thud.

"Marie!"

"What? You pulled too hard!"

"Just hurry and help me turn her around. She's stiff."

I jumped down from the wagon and grabbed the dead girl's shoulder. It was like rolling a log. Her blood-stained dress was still sticky—the blood not yet frozen.

"Here." I handed Sebastian one of the delicate glass bottles. "Hold it steady while I pull out the stopper. Don't let any of the poison touch you."

I didn't want Sebastian to become the bait himself.

He did as I asked and held the vial carefully. I pulled the cork from the mouth of the bottle and then took it from him. A little sprinkled into the ruined skin at her stomach should be enough to weaken Ama.

"It won't be enough to kill it?"

"I don't think there's any poison that could kill something like that."

"Good. I want to strike the blow myself, like you said." His eyes shifted to the gore in front of him as he said it, and his mouth settled into a firm line.

He may want the revenge, but I wasn't sure he'd really be able to shoot the beast when the time came—he didn't seem like a person who'd ever actually felt the blood of an animal under his hands—and that suited me just fine. I wasn't going to actually let him kill my sister. I just needed him to see her, to spark his fear so he'd try harder to remember whatever detail would be the key to the book. And I wanted to weaken the beast enough to be able to take her away from the town and lock her up before Emméline found her. She'd be safe in the cellar, chained up so she couldn't kill anyone else. It would only be until I figured out how to make Sebastian's mother's spell book work.

Once I could make Ama fully human again, she'd be safe for good and everything could go back to normal.

A faint hint of lavender and sweet honey rose from the corpse where I'd laced it with honeysuckle. I hoped it would be enough to get Ama to come.

A handcart leaned against the church wall. I grabbed the handles and hauled it over to Sebastian. A chorus of voices rose from inside the nearby tavern in drunken song, and I prayed no one would get the urge to stumble outside to pee.

"Hurry! Let's put her in this cart. We won't be able to carry her all the way to the woods."

Sebastian eyed the corpse and shifted on the balls of his feet. "We should be leaving her to her rest."

His voice, laced with unexpected tenderness, softened the sharp reply that sprang to the tip of my tongue.

"She's helping to catch her killer. Don't you think she would want to save the others from the beast?"

Sebastian's eyes filled. He didn't even try to hide or wipe away the tears. He let them fall, fat drops that rolled down his cheeks and fell from his chin.

I stood still, not sure what to do. Part of me wanted to comfort him, to reach out and lace my fingers through his. The other part wanted to become invisible and leave him to his private grief.

It wasn't just Vivienne. It was his parents. No one had saved them. We were too late—he was too late. And there was nothing we could do about it now. Even if he had his revenge, it wouldn't bring them back.

He shook his head to clear the tears and reached to pick up the dead girl's arms. Together, we lifted her into the handcart—but we couldn't get her to sit naturally. Her body's odd angles were just another reminder that whatever had made her *her*, the part that had made her human, was gone.

The song inside the tavern grew deeper and stronger and then stopped, leaving behind an eerie lull. I let go of the cart and pressed my ear to the tavern door. A familiar command-ing voice rose out of the silence. *Père Danil.*

"We must prevail over this beast of the devil!"

"Kill it!"

"God will help us!"

Fear slid over me like a dark veil. We didn't have much time before Père Danil whipped up the crowd enough to con-vince them to go out into the darkening night. I picked up the cart handles again as Sebastian stepped forward to take one side, panic brightening his wide eyes. We hurried away, trying to stay ahead of whoever was about to spill out of the tavern with the priest. The cart wobbled dangerously as we tripped over exposed roots and black patches of ice. At the mouth of the forest, we put it down and lifted the body from it. I chose a tree, wide and rutted with age, and we set the dead girl down at its base.

"Now what?" asked Sebastian.

The woods spoke to us, with the murmur of the wind and the rustling of a squirrel. Most children in the village were scared to come in here alone. I'd never been.

"We wait for the beast."

CHAPTER TWENTY-SIX

crack of twig, the hoot of a far-off owl, the flitter of a moth at the corner of my vision. The sights and sounds of a forest in its primal hours. The dark, moonless night draped us in its cowl. Three bobbing lights marched toward us from the village, and I prayed the glow of their flames wouldn't reveal our hiding place.

My hand slipped to Sebastian's knee and he shifted beside me. We crouched behind a wide oak where we could still see the outline of the girl's body lying in the snow.

I thought I might feel Ama first—the vibrations of her footsteps, the pounding of her wild heart. But I didn't.

She twined around the trees with her long, elegant body. Her steps never faltered nor made a sound. Her black nose was bent low to the ground and the beautiful crest of fur stood thick and proud around her neck. I knew it to be golden—even if the night now stole its color.

Sebastian followed my gaze and tensed beside me. His chest rose and fell frantically with quick, silent breaths. I gripped his knee again, urging him to stay still.

Ama nuzzled the dead girl's hair. She licked her cheek with a long, pink tongue. Then she softly, gently, nipped at the bloody skin at the girl's stomach. There was no wildness here—instead, a precision I'd never seen before.

"Eat," Sebastian whispered. His eyes darkened with anticipation.

I untangled my legs and stood. Sebastian pulled at my coat and tried to bring me back down to him.

"What are you doing?"

I ignored him and kept my eyes trained on Ama. Her black nose and shining eyes. The teeth curving from her top lip. The long, strong legs with the tufts of golden fur at the back of each hock. She looked like the lions in the church's painting, Daniel in the lion pit, but she was more than that. More human. She didn't completely lose her normal shape when she transformed. She wasn't like any kind of animal I'd ever seen before. She was like an artist's imagining. The sense of awe never went away—no matter how many times I saw her like this.

"Ama," I breathed.

Her head dipped delicately, and she sniffed as if smelling my voice on the breeze.

"Ama, it's me."

My sister padded one large foot in front of the other and

turned toward me. She lifted her nose and stepped closer. The light in her eyes gleamed and her white teeth shone even without moonlight. I stumbled toward her and she ran for me. I opened my arms to her, but she kept going. She leapt through the air toward Sebastian.

His hands shot up over his head and he crouched into a ball. It wouldn't matter once Ama was on him. Her teeth were like razors. And all Sebastian had to protect himself was a musket he couldn't fire from close range.

I slipped the knife from my belt and aimed. I might hit him, but if I didn't do this, there would be no uncertainty— Ama would tear him to shreds. The cold hilt slipped through my fingers, the weight of the knife suddenly gone.

Ama shrieked as the blade split her shoulder, and my stomach clenched at the sound. I hated hurting her.

Sebastian scrambled over to my feet.

"You got some of the tincture on your clothes, didn't you?" I called.

"A little dribbled down the side of the bottle when you drew out the cork. I didn't touch my hand to my mouth, though. The poison isn't inside me."

No, but you're marked.

Ama was still under control. She wasn't feverishly killing—gorging on any warm body in her path. Here, now, she went straight for Sebastian. Straight for the cloying scent of honeysuckle laced with lavender. My sister was still under my power.

I drank in my relief. Ama could still be controlled.

She might have lost control once or twice, but she wasn't completely wild. Not quite yet. I could still cure her with the right spell.

"Get up," I yelled to Sebastian. If she tried to attack again, I didn't have another knife to throw at her.

He scrambled to his feet and picked up the musket, aiming it at my sister. My blood froze in my veins.

"No, don't! Ama!" I realized my mistake too late to stop myself.

Sebastian whipped his head around to look at me. "Why do you keep calling it Ama?"

"Sebastian, please!"

The sound of footsteps crunched in the snow and broke the charged intensity of our little circle. Dark blood trailed through Ama's fur but she didn't limp as she followed the sound of voices coming closer—the priest and whoever he could convince to come with him. They would have makeshift weapons, pitchforks and shovels. No real match for Ama. She moved away from us, winding around the trees as she closed the space between her and the villagers.

"Let's go. Now!" I said.

We didn't want to be found here in the woods at night—a girl unaccepted by the town and the lord thought of as a murderer.

I picked my way forward through dead brambles and over fallen logs. The clouds overhead drifted apart and the moon finally shone its pale light into the forest. Broken spiderwebs glistened like silver thread. The trees, tall with thick branches breaking open the earth at their feet, stood in silhouette against the sky. A deep vibration, a steady hum, rose through my feet and trilled through my stomach, chest, arms, fingertips.

Magic stirred in the forest. Somehow, I felt it tingling through my veins. It didn't make sense—*I* wasn't the magic one, *I* hadn't been cursed. Maybe I'd just been around whatever magic had cursed Ama for so long now, I could recognize it.

"Marie."

I felt a light tap between my shoulder blades and I spun around. Sebastian stood there with the barrel of the musket pointed at my face.

Sweat prickled under my arms, and my dress stuck to me under my coat, shockingly cold when I pressed my arms to my sides.

"What do you think you're doing?" I asked.

Sebastian ignored my question, but his lips curled into the imitation of a smile. "Tell me about the beast."

I wouldn't. Not even with a gun in my face.

"You know as much as I do. And now we've seen it, we have to do more, anything to stop it."

Like wake up a magic book.

The smile grew too big, showing too many of Sebastian's teeth. "You're lying."

I searched the trees behind Sebastian for Ama. I heard her, the snarls rumbling from her throat, threatening the people approaching.

"Remember, Sebastian...you still want me to make Lucien better."

His hold on the musket shifted ever so slightly and it dropped a breath lower.

"You called the beast your sister's name. Why? You told me Ama was dead."

A movement behind Sebastian's shoulder drew my gaze. The shadows stirred. Emméline stepped from between two pine trees, the brittle needles brushing against her leather breeches and falling to the snow-dusted ground.

"What are you two doing out here, and why do you have a musket pointed at Marie's face, Sebastian?"

He lowered it immediately and looked to me as if I could offer some explanation to Emméline.

"We were just...we gathered with Père Danil and the other men," Sebastian said.

"But they're all way back there. They've had too much ale to cover any ground," Emméline said.

I wanted her to go away. Ama was here somewhere in between the trees, and though I wasn't scared of her encountering a few drunken villagers wielding pitchforks and shovels, Emméline's well-strung bow was another story. Most villagers weren't allowed to own weapons, by the king's law, but Emméline and her family had never counted themselves rule-followers. She'd grown up with a bow in her hand and she knew how to use it.

"We got ahead of the group," I explained. "We're looking for the beast."

"But you said you wanted me to kill it, Sebastian. You know what you promised me."

Sebastian took a step toward her. "I do. I haven't forgotten, but . . . the thing killed my parents."

"That's what you say," Emméline said.

I couldn't tell if she believed him or not. She was using that ambiguity against him though, and I didn't like her playing games like that.

"The beast went that way," I said, pointing in the opposite direction from where Ama had actually gone.

Emméline looked me up and down, her cold gaze sending shivers along my arms and legs.

"I don't need your help, witch," she said.

The word slithered from her mouth, and old fear washed over me like frigid river water. I hadn't cared about the sharpness of Ama's teeth or even the musket's barrel in my face. But this was different. *Witch* was the most frightening word we possessed. Once it slipped from the lips of some accusing face, it could never be called back. It would feed on whispers and fear until it was too big to ignore.

"I'm not a witch."

I knew people thought badly of us in the village. We were poor and unwelcome in many circumstances, but no one had ever flung that accusation at us. We weren't taunted, not until the dolls first started arriving on our doorstep. *The dolls... could they have been from Emméline? Has she guessed? Does she somehow know about Ama's curse? Does she think I'm the witch who did it?*

She tossed her long braid over one shoulder and pulled an arrow from the quiver on her back. She notched it smoothly in the bow and I couldn't help admiring how skilled she was, how easy and natural the movement was for her.

She pointed the iron tip of the arrow at me and a growl ripped from the earth behind me. Ama sprang forward from the trees, landing between Emméline and me.

"Sebastian." I reached for him, afraid Ama would smell the honeysuckle again. He hesitated but eventually gripped my fingers. Ama pawed the ground, scratching at it with long, white claws. I couldn't stop my feet from moving backward. Sebastian followed. Emméline trained her bow on Ama and my heart contracted.

"Run!" I yelled, but I didn't know to who—Ama, Sebastian, myself?

The zip of an arrow cut the air beside my ear and I dove into Sebastian, pushing him to the snow. Then we both scrambled onto our knees and half crawled, half ran toward the edge of the trees with Ama and Emméline behind us.

CHAPTER TWENTY-SEVEN

Houses loomed in the dark, like teeth in the mouth of the valley. I ran until my lungs burned and pulled Sebastian behind me. I couldn't let go of his hand—I needed to feel the flesh and bones of it. I couldn't be alone.

"Up the hill," Sebastian shouted.

We tried to find purchase in the snow, but the road was so hard-packed it was like ice. We scrambled, digging our boots in and pulling each other as we went until the big house crested into view. A light flickered in one of the upstairs windows—Lucien's window.

Ama surged toward us, faster than we could run.

"Come on!"

Sebastian pulled me toward his house where the great double doors stood sentinel before us. He turned the knob.

"It's stuck."

I glanced behind us. Ama's golden coat gleamed in the moonlight, her movements smooth and strong as she ran up the hill. Emméline stopped and notched an arrow, pulled the string taut, released. It landed in the earth in front of Ama's left paw.

"Hurry up!" I shouted.

"I'm trying." Sebastian jiggled the knob and we both rammed our shoulders against the unforgiving wood.

"Again," I said. "On the count of three. One, two, three."

We threw our bodies against the door but it still didn't yield. Then I remembered the markings carved into the frame as Sebastian banged on the doors and shouted for Madame Écrue. I pressed my hands and forehead against the doors and traced the whirls and stars carved crudely and splintering into the wood. *Please let us in.*

One of the double doors gave way beneath Sebastian's hammering fists and he tumbled into the hall. I ran over the threshold and slammed the door shut behind us. Sebastian let out a heavy breath and pushed himself to his feet. He stared at me, and I thought I saw a trace of fear in his eyes.

"Somehow, your sister is the beast, isn't she?"

I pressed my lips together. *What's left to protect? He knows what Ama is.* I gave him a tiny nod.

"But she came after us!"

If only I understood as much as he thought I did. Sebastian marked himself, but Ama had jumped out when she thought I was in danger, like she knew me.

"She didn't come after us. She was running away from Emméline just like we were."

"She attacked me!"

"I think she thought she was protecting me."

"And now Emméline's out there with her."

My heart contracted. Ama could outrun Emméline. *She could.*

"You gave her the task of killing the beast, didn't you? Why would you worry about her now?"

Sebastian ran a hand over his eyes and through his hair.

"No more of this. Tell me everything."

The request lost its edge without a musket between us. Sebastian's face settled into indifference that didn't quite hide the sadness underneath. I couldn't swallow the lump in my throat when I looked into his careful, blank eyes. My sister had killed his parents, but I couldn't tell him that, couldn't sever the only line to another human being I had right now. So, I lied.

"I don't know if she killed your parents, Sebastian."

He titled his head a little and his black, curling hair fell over his shoulder. Sebastian came undone before me, wilting a little where he stood before falling to his knees and running his palms over his cheeks again and again. The mask broke and his eyes shone with wild agony. He bared his teeth and opened his mouth to let a growling scream tear through his throat. I flinched at the inescapable pain of the sound. I wanted to reach for him, but I didn't think he'd want my touch right now.

"Listen," I said after a moment. "I don't know who...or what...killed your parents, but something happened to my sister here."

He blinked away the wetness in his eyes and stared at me. "What?"

"This all happened when she worked here...she came home cursed. Someone did that to her."

"Someone in this house?" he said.

"It had to be. She came here a girl and came back a beast."

Sebastian's hands rested on his knees and I reached for them slowly because I couldn't stop myself anymore. I had to touch him. His palms burned as if he had a fever, but I closed my own cool hands over them. Sebastian didn't flinch or try to pull away. We sat on the embroidered rug in silence until he slipped his hands from mine. To my surprise, disappointment prickled through me.

"Does this have to do with what people said about my mother?" he asked. "She hated it here. The whispers followed her everywhere. *Witch.* People were awful because they said her own maman had been enslaved on Martinique. They thought she didn't belong here."

It was cold and brutal in this town. Judgmental. Small.

"She belonged here if she wanted to be here," I said. "Your papa owned this valley, didn't he? And now you do. You can say who belongs."

"He didn't own it and neither do I, not really. The king is the ultimate ruler of the land, and he's the one who made it all right for Maman's mother to be enslaved by someone.

People don't forget that that's a possibility, and the color of my skin reminds them even though I'm their lord. They don't treat me the same as they treated my white father. You don't think the color of my skin is one of the reasons they think I killed my parents, that I'd be capable of something like that?"

"You're right, of course. I'm sorry, but I know that's not enough," I said.

It was clear that Sebastian felt like he was on the edges of the village too. We were outsiders—for very different reasons, and I knew I'd never truly understand how he felt. He couldn't—and shouldn't have to—hide his skin color. I'd once thought I could move from the outskirts of the village into the heart of it, become accepted as the sister of a respectfully married woman. I didn't know if I wanted that life anymore, but at least it was possible. Sebastian didn't have that same opportunity. It made me even more angry at Père Danil and all the people who crowded into church on Sundays but refused to look outside of their own experiences to understand anyone else's.

"My father brought Maman here because he loved her, but he didn't know what he was doing," Sebastian whispered. "Maman told me the mountains suffocated her. She felt like the valley might as well be at the bottom of the ocean. She wanted to leave and go somewhere bigger where we wouldn't be the only ones with brown skin ... but she died before she could." He sighed, finally looking at me again. "Marie, I don't know what happened to Ama here. I don't even remember her...and I know how awful that sounds. But Maman wasn't like that. She was warm and kind."

I knew it wasn't going to be easy to convince him his mother might have been someone he might not recognize. She could have loved him and Lucien tenderly and still been the witch who turned my sister into a beast. People always treat those they love differently.

I stood and looked out the window, past the bubbles and imperfections in the glass. No Ama. No Emméline. I pictured the arrows gliding past the crest of fur on Ama's back. I wanted to go back out and make sure she was safe, but I couldn't know she wouldn't come after me too. Not after what just happened. Capturing her and locking her in the cellar wasn't a good plan anymore. She was injured, but her beast body would probably heal quickly.

Sebastian glanced up the stairs. "We need to check on Lucien."

The trust between us stretched taut like a gossamer thread, and I wouldn't test its strength by telling him Lucien just needed time for his body to expel the poison I'd given him. Sebastian wouldn't forgive me that.

But I *would* ask for what I needed most.

"Sebastian, the book I asked you to help me find. It's not a book of remedies. I think it's a spell book."

"What?"

He stood and stared down at me. I didn't like looking up at him, so I stood too.

"The book! I think it's a spell book and in it is the curse

that made my sister into a monster. You and Lucien saw her write in it! The words were used to curse her, so the curse's undoing could be in there too. It's a place to start at least."

"Why did Emméline call *you* a witch?" he asked suddenly.

I dropped back from him. "You just finished telling me how everyone made your mother miserable by calling her a witch and now you're asking why Emméline called me one?"

"You're saying Maman *was* a witch, or at least someone who could cast curses! How do I know you're not someone like that too?"

I reached up to put my hands on Sebastian's shoulders, squaring him to me, looking into his eyes.

"If I were a witch, Sebastian, I would have cured my sister a long time ago."

"But you want me to believe my maman was one and that she did something horrible to your sister. How can you ask that of me?"

"She could have been a witch and still good in many ways, Sebastian. I don't think all witches are always evil."

"Even if she was what you say she was, she wouldn't have cursed a young girl."

"Well, she did."

Sebastian glared at me. "She didn't, because she wasn't a witch!"

"Something happened here! Every month, my sister's body breaks and builds itself again into a strange imitation of a lion. I just want to undo the curse with your mother's book."

"The book is blank!"

A creak on the stairs made me turn. Madame Écrue stood there with her stiff white cap perfectly in place.

"How is he?" Sebastian asked her.

"You should come, my lord. Master Lucien's fever has worsened."

So, she'd been nursing Lucien and that's why she hadn't answered our banging on the door—perhaps she hadn't wanted to leave his side even when she heard us come in.

Sebastian seemed to absorb her words before whirling and grabbing my shoulders. He shook me hard. "You said he'd live!"

I wrenched away. "He will if you listen to me."

Sebastian took a deep, shuddering breath as if trying to tame his rage. Still, he shook with it and it leapt into his eyes. He didn't know the news about Lucien's fever filled me with a similar fire. It shouldn't have been happening. The foxglove poison should have worn off by now.

"If Lucien dies of this fever, it will be your fault!" Sebastian said.

Whatever heat had been left in my body fled through my fingertips.

"No. I'm trying to help him!"

Sebastian nodded slowly. "Oh yes? He's sicker now than he was when you arrived. If he dies, you'll have to leave and I'll let the villagers decide if you're a witch or not."

I wouldn't let my face betray me, but fear washed over me like a gust of frigid air.

"The book of spells, the one that looks blank ... maybe it can cure Lucien too, from the consumption ... from all of it."

"You don't know that!"

He was right, I didn't. In fact, if Madame LaClaire could have cured consumption with her magic, she would have done so as soon as the doctors told her that was what Lucien had. But I wanted to get the spell book to reveal its secrets, and maybe there *was* something in there that could help Lucien. The book might hold all the answers—I just needed to find the key.

CHAPTER TWENTY-EIGHT

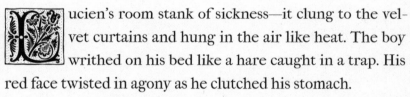ucien's room stank of sickness—it clung to the velvet curtains and hung in the air like heat. The boy writhed on his bed like a hare caught in a trap. His red face twisted in agony as he clutched his stomach.

What have I done? Regret and guilt hit me like twin arrows in the stomach. I buckled over and frantically swallowed the bile rising in my throat. It was never supposed to be like this. The foxglove was supposed to make Lucien drowsy and give him a mild fever—noticeable enough symptoms to draw Sebastian's concern and convince him to give me the book. This was something else.

"Lucien." Sebastian's coarse whisper rose faintly above the low treble of moaning. He dropped the slim blue book he'd retrieved on our way to the room on the foot of the bed and it fell open, revealing stubbornly blank pages. Sebastian fell to his knees beside his brother. He wrapped a hand around Lucien's small wrist and rubbed the skin with his thumb. "Hush. It's all right. I'm here."

The break in Sebastian's voice made me stumble over and put a hand on Lucien's squirming leg. Sorrow etched its lines on Sebastian's face as he watched his brother fight the invisible demons.

I gripped the leather edge of the book's cover and flipped it open. We could help Lucien win the battle. He'd seen his mother write in this book. We just had to get it to show us what we were looking for. Dull brown splotches sprinkled the edges of the pages like dried raindrops. When we first opened the book, I'd thought the splotches were mold, but that wasn't it—it was blood. Dried blood on each page.

"Sebastian," I whispered.

"What?"

"Look." I turned and flipped the book in my hand so he could see the gilt edges of the pages. "See these dark marks? I think they're blood."

I grabbed Sebastian's hand without asking and he let out a little noise of surprise but didn't pull away. Setting the book on my knees, I opened it to the blank title page.

"What are you doing?" Sebastian asked.

"Just wait. Hold the book. I want to try something."

I passed it to him, and he balanced it open on his free hand. Then I took a pin from my hair.

"Are you going to stab me with that?" he asked.

"The book might like your blood better than mine. It did belong to your mother, after all."

He pulled his hand away from me.

"Oh, come on, this could work!"

"I don't like this," Sebastian said.

I took hold of his finger. "You said your maman was good, right? In her heart? So, her book must have some good in it too."

Lucien moaned and Sebastian looked desperately at his brother's fevered face.

There was no mask now, no princely severity or cold distance. Sebastian sloughed off any pretense there had been and revealed the crumbling human beneath.

Seeing it made me want to collect the pieces of him and press them back together.

"We have to try," I said. "It's that or watch him suffer. I don't want to do that, Sebastian."

"Are you sure about that?" Sebastian tore his gaze away from his brother. "You were supposed to ease his suffering, but he's worse than he ever was."

Sebastian didn't know how close to the truth he was—that I might have done this to Lucien. I'd made him so much worse. He'd never forgive me if he knew. But this seemed like more than just the foxglove.

"I'm trying as hard as I can! That's why I want to use your mother's book."

"And if it doesn't work?"

He stared at me, daring me to tell him the worst thing he could hear. His flinty eyes shimmered with the tears pooling around their rims.

I backed away from him, but I couldn't escape the thin warbling moans or the cloying sweet scent of fever and sweat-soaked linen.

When I selected victims for the beast, I rarely saw the effect—the *after*. We marked outsiders and vagrants and criminals. When their bodies, or whatever was left of their bodies, turned up in the woods, they were buried in the pau- pers' yard without ceremony. I never heard their screams or watched the blood draining from their bodies. I never had to watch them defend themselves.

Now, Lucien's pain burrowed into my bones with an ache I'd never be able to get rid of.

"Does it matter whether it's magic or not if it saves Lucien?"

Sebastian scraped his lips between his teeth and sucked in a slow breath. "No, it doesn't."

"So give me your finger."

He extended his index finger and I gripped it again. The pin wasn't very sharp, so I pressed down hard until a little red bead formed. He flinched.

"Sorry," I said. "Now smear it."

"What, just there on the page?"

I wasn't really sure how to feed a book blood, but it seemed like a good place to start. I prayed it would work—then real- ized Père Danil would call that blasphemy. I wondered if Sebastian's mother had to do this every time she wanted to use her book.

"Press the blood into the page."

Sebastian raised his eyebrows but brought his hand down on the blank paper, pressed it, and lifted it away. He left a smudge of red with the imprints of the whorls of his fingertip.

"Now what?"

A thrill of excitement went through me. I didn't know what would happen or when. "We wait."

Every muscle in my body clenched with anticipation. If nothing happened, I had no idea how to save Lucien from this mad fever. The only thing left to do would be to call the priest.

Please.

The words faded in like rivulets of water. Ink trickled over the page—pooling, curving, forming curling letters in soft sepia tones.

I almost dropped the book. I'd hoped it would happen, but as the book of spells filled its pages, shock numbed my elation. Sebastian stared at the pages and then at me, his mouth falling open.

The scroll of the letters formed into words on the first page of the book—*Chansons pour la santé.* Songs for health.

"I always thought *she* wasn't one. Maman. Is this really a spell book?" Sebastian asked.

I answered him by flipping the page. A fine-lined illustration of a rose bloomed over a short inscription. It read, *Élever votre voix et tant pis pour tout les autres. Pour vous faites la magique.* Raise your voice and too bad for the others. For you make magic.

Sebastian reached out and traced the letters with his finger. "She wouldn't have done that to your sister. She was kind, always protecting everyone."

I couldn't ignore the catch in his voice—even if I wanted to. I needed him whole now, present. He couldn't help Lucien if his mind was in the past.

"I'm sure she was." I nodded. "She was probably protecting you by keeping this from you. It's dangerous to be what she was."

"It was always so hard for her," Sebastian said. "No one had ever seen someone like her when she came from the islands. By the time I was small, the people were more used to it, but they still gaped at me whenever we went into the village. Children even asked to touch my hair."

I wasn't sure what to say. Apologizing for the town's behavior seemed futile and inadequate. The villagers' view extended only so far as the mountains bordering our valley. We knew what the priest and our own eyes told us, and so many were content to never ask for more. It wasn't an excuse or even an explanation, though. It didn't erase Sebastian's pain.

"I'm sorry she had to endure that. And you too."

His face was like stone, but he nodded.

"These are her words." I smoothed my hand over the paper. "We can give them power now."

Lucien twisted between us and gritted his teeth. His eyes moved beneath his lids.

"These are spells?" Sebastian asked.

"I think so."

"So, which one do we use?"

The inky calligraphy slid down the page. I fingered the looping curl of an *s* where it trailed off the side. The thin paper felt as though it might crumble beneath my fingertips as I turned it over.

Little drawings decorated each page—figures of ladies, flowers, a fat spider in its web. Scrawled around the pictures were songs like half-formed recipes.

My eyes fell to a line drawing of a woman sitting slumped against the thick trunk of a tree. Her eyelashes formed crescent moons where they rested against her cheeks. A title inked thickly near the top said, *Pour la santé.* For health.

It seemed as good a spell to try as any. But I needed help. I had no magic in my veins to fuel the songs. The book had wanted Sebastian's blood—maybe it wanted his voice too.

I gripped his hand. His palm was dry beneath my fingers and I wondered how, with his brother sick in bed and his dead mother's spell book suddenly brought to life, Sebastian could be so calm. But maybe he wasn't. Maybe his nerves screamed inside his body and he was just better at hiding it than I was.

"Say it with me," I said.

"I don't know my mother's secrets."

"You're her son. Her secrets run through your veins. Please, just do this."

He scraped his teeth over his bottom lip again—drawing a little bead of blood. Lucien stirred and raised his own voice.

"Fine, I'll try," Sebastian said.

I took a deep breath and tried to wiggle my toes in my boots to shake out the tension in my legs. This was it—we'd see if the book was real and if Sebastian and I could make it work. If the spell drained the sickness from Lucien's body, it might work for Ama too. Hope glowed in me like a solitary candle flame. It shone bright in the dark, but it'd burn out if we didn't hurry.

I chose to ignore its fragility and hold the light in my gaze. This could be the solution to this madness, right here in my hands.

"This one, here, with the picture of the woman," I said, and laid a finger under the first word of the song. We didn't have a tune or even a rhythm, but we spoke together and the solidity of our voices seemed to soothe Lucien. He calmed bit by bit—his legs falling still and then his fingers and arms. Finally, his face settled into a smooth portrait of sleep.

I didn't believe it would be that easy for a second.

"Don't stop," I whispered in a stolen breath between words of the song. Sebastian looked at me with a question in his eyes, but I only repeated the spell, keeping him in time with the strength of my gaze.

All at once, Lucien came alive. His eyes flew open and his muscles jerked. Sebastian slipped off the side of the bed and let the spell fall from his lips.

"Keep going!"

He mumbled a few words, but they died before they even reached my ears. I ripped my gaze from his flushed face and found my place in the book.

L'automne s'abandonne a l'hiver.

I filled my belly with a breath and pushed it out, swelling the words in my throat and releasing them, coating them over Lucien.

He wrenched and whimpered and stared at me with wide, red-rimmed eyes. Somewhere under the fever, a little boy was scared, and I wanted so very much to help him.

Les feuilles tombent avec la neige.

Sebastian's eyes filled and tears fell silently down his face. They ran into his open mouth and dripped from his chin. Still, he did nothing. Still, he stayed silent.

The magic dimmed. It fell away like settling dust. The book needed Sebastian. Alone, I wasn't enough. His mother's magic wanted him.

"Come on!" I screamed at him. "Help me, Sebastian."

He tore the book from my hands and wet spots bloomed on the page from where his tears rolled off his cheeks and chin. Sebastian found the thread of the song and joined his voice to mine again.

Nothing happened. Lucien didn't sit up. He wasn't suddenly cured of whatever was happening to him. He'd slipped back into sleep as we sang over him.

"The spell didn't work." Sebastian's words fell like stones between us as he dropped the book to the floor.

Did it not work because we don't hold enough magic within us? Because it's the wrong song? Because Lucien could not be cured at all?

The questions swirled in my head, dizzying. Nausea curdled my belly. If Lucien couldn't be cured, maybe Ama couldn't be either.

I picked the leather-bound book off the floor and turned the pages randomly. I didn't know what I was looking for, but I had to find it. The musty scent of old paper clung to the inside of my nose. *For the heart, For calm, For revenge, For quiet.* Why had Sebastian's mother written such vague titles? There was no *Use this spell if you find yourself or someone close to you cursed as a beast.*

Lucien's groans filled the room again. Sebastian fell to his knees and gripped his brother's left arm with both hands.

"It's all right, Lucien, I'm here. Hush now, I'm here."

Right at the very back of the book there was a little poem of sorts inscribed in a different hand from the scrolling script of the spells.

Laissez-faire les souhaits.
Let go of wishes.
Et laissez-faire les rêves.
Let go of dreams.
Pour la vie suffit.
For life is enough.

Life might have been enough for whoever wrote it, but just any kind of life wasn't enough for me. Suffering, watching others in pain, wasn't enough for me. I wanted more.

CHAPTER TWENTY-NINE

I pulled my knees up to my chest. Cold crept over me like an unwelcome pall. My arm tingled with disuse and my ear ached where it had been pressed against my own shoulder. I sat up and looked over at Sebastian, but he was gone.

After Lucien had quieted, we'd descended into Sebastian's mother's sitting room. He'd dragged the sheets from the furniture and we'd each taken a sofa, not saying anything but seemingly agreeing not to spend the night alone.

My sudden sense of loneliness shocked me. I shouldn't need Sebastian for comfort. I didn't need anyone but Ama for that.

"Sore?"

I started and drew a hand to my breast—like a woman in a playing troupe—and immediately dropped it, cheeks burning. But I hid my face from Sebastian and took a breath. It's not like he could know I'd missed him for the few moments I thought him gone. I waited a couple beats for the heat to fade from my cheeks before looking over at him again.

He sank into the settee with his legs crossed under him. His shoulders drooped and his eyes fell on me, but they didn't burn with anger or even glow with hope. Defeat settled over him.

"Madame brought us something to eat. She wouldn't come over the threshold though," he said, and gestured to the tray on the table beside the settee. Nuts clustered near a loaf of bread and a thick, yellow slice of cheese that was already sweating. My empty stomach rumbled despite the fact I didn't think I could actually swallow any of it.

"Do you think the room makes her sad?"

He nodded. "It reminds her too much of my mother. She cared for her in Martinique too, you know, since Maman was very small. I think Madame thought of her as her own daughter."

She must know something.

"Does this room make you sad?"

Sebastian seemed to consider this, eyes flitting from the bookshelves to the little card table in the corner.

"No, it doesn't. I need to let myself remember more, because my memories are where Maman is still full of life."

I peeled myself off the firm couch. Plump cushions welcomed me as I dropped down onto the settee beside Sebastian. If he was surprised at this, he didn't show it. Instead, he reached out and hesitantly touched the tips of my fingers with his. Comfort seemed such a small gift to give, so I offered my whole hand and he took it.

"I hoped it would work," he said.

"Me too. But it's not over, Sebastian. We'll make Lucien well again. What about Madame Écrue? She knew your mother very well, didn't she? She might have known about the magic and the spell book. Maybe she knows why the pages turn blank."

"No, I don't think so. She was our nurse then, always with me and then Lucien later. Maman had another confidante."

The woman in the portrait. "Who was it?"

"I never knew her name, actually. I saw her from afar a couple times when she and Maman walked in the gardens."

"But you must have known who she was if she came from the village?"

Sebastian shrugged. "I'm not sure she did. My parents did sometimes have visitors from outside the valley— friends, cousins."

The woman in the portrait wasn't just a friend—her picture was in a locket with Sebastian's mother's. A cousin, maybe. It was possible. But I still couldn't shake how much the woman looked like my own maman in her painting.

"*Think,* Sebastian. Anything you remember about this woman could help."

Sebastian's fingers played in mine. "He's not cursed, Marie. There's no magic involved. Just bad lungs and a weak heart. Those aren't so easy to fix."

And a little foxglove poison. I shuddered and Sebastian squeezed my hand.

"Do you believe in the magic now?" I asked.

"It's hard not to believe after I saw the spells bloom onto the blank pages of Maman's book with my own eyes. I'm not saying she was a witch though. That word sounds too harsh and I can't reconcile it with Maman...or you. I'm sorry about yesterday."

A little glow sparked in my chest and I liked its warmth. I wanted to kindle it.

"Well, I'm sorry I spoke about your maman like that. I understand...she was your mother and I wouldn't be happy if someone called mine a witch either.

"The church has made the word scary, hasn't it? But what if it's not like they say it is? What if being a witch is just harnessing some source of power that was already in you?"

He raised an eyebrow. "If everyone had magic, this would be a very different world."

"I'm not saying everyone...what if some people have magic and they just have to learn how to use it, but they're not evil like the church says?"

Sebastian squeezed my hand again. "I like that version of 'witch' better than Père Danil's. But magic hasn't hurt my brother, so it won't cure him either."

"You don't know what magic can do. Neither do I. Perhaps there *is* a way to treat Lucien with it."

It wasn't much, but it was a thin thread of hope to hang

on to. Sebastian needed that now, and I did too. Sebastian's mother was dead, but there must be someone else who knew about magic. Children in the village always talked of the Woods Witch—maybe there was something deeper there than gossip. And the woman in the locket, whoever she was, she might know something about magic if she was still alive.

People were still dying—young people, innocent people. Ama had gone for Sebastian because he smelled of honeysuckle. I didn't know if I believed she'd killed the little boy or the seamstress anymore. Somewhere in those glowing yellow eyes, my sister lived. She wasn't fully animal. Not yet. She could have torn me apart so many times, but she never did. Even chasing us back to the house, she could have gained on us easily, but she didn't really. It had been as if she'd just wanted us out of the forest.

I thought back to the strange way the little boy's skin split at his neck—shallow and cleaner than Ama's work. And the seamstress—her dress was clean. Of course, there was blood seeping into the material at her belly, but her skirt had been spotless. When my sister killed, she ravaged the bodies.

Something wasn't fitting.

"What are you thinking about?" Sebastian asked. "Your palm's gone damp."

My cheeks burned and I ripped my hand away from his. I hated the way my body betrayed me. My thoughts weren't my own—they were on display. When nerves twisted my stomach, they also dampened my dress and palms.

All of a sudden, Sebastian was too close. He'd be able to

smell the damp wool of my dress under my arms and legs where the sweat would soak through.

I started to rise from the settee, but Sebastian grabbed my arm. He slipped his hand down my skin and closed it around my own again.

"Don't go. Please. I want to hold your hand."

"Why?"

"Because it's the only thing that's made me feel safe in a long time."

His face held no malice. He met my eyes with his warm brown ones and pulled me back down next to him. My palm was still wet but he only held my hand tighter, and the nerves in my belly settled.

"So, what were you thinking?" Sebastian asked, and nudged my foot with his.

I wasn't sure I wanted to bring him down this road with me. Things were strange enough. Exhaustion sat heavily on Sebastian—his shoulders slouched and his eyes were glassy and red-rimmed. But I was exhausted too, and I didn't want to do this alone.

I took a piece of cheese off the plate beside us and broke it in half. Sebastian reached for one crumbling chunk and I bit into the other. The salty tang of the cheese coated my tongue and little pieces of salt crunched between my teeth as I chewed. My stomach suddenly seemed to remember how little I'd eaten over the last few days, and it rumbled loudly in protest. Sebastian laughed and handed me a piece of soft, white bread.

"I was thinking," I said at last, "about the corpses."

"Well, that's dark."

I smiled and knocked gently into his shoulder. Nothing should have been funny right now, and yet we both clung to the lighthearted bubble we'd created on the settee. It kept the horrible reality out.

"It's not like that. I was thinking about their wounds."

"Still sounds pretty dark to me."

"No!" I grinned. "Just listen...the wounds didn't look right. I've seen the way the beast kills...those two bodies, the boy and the seamstress, didn't look the same as the others."

Sebastian sat up a little straighter and leaned into me. "What do you mean?"

"The way their throats and bellies were torn looked almost...well, they were too precise and shallow. It wasn't like Ama. Not like the beast."

"Maybe she's getting better at killing."

I swallowed at that thought, the same thought I'd had while cleaning Maurice, and the little piece of bread I'd just eaten stuck in my throat.

"There was something else too," I said once I'd swallowed the bread. "Whatever killed them didn't eat them..."

"What are you talking about? There was blood everywhere."

"When the beast feeds, it digs in. It doesn't leave that much meat behind..."

Sebastian didn't ask how I knew what the beast's kills

looked like, but the lighthearted veil we'd created disintegrated in an instant.

"What are you saying, Marie? That something else killed those people?"

"Something else . . . or someone else."

Sebastian narrowed his eyes. "A person?"

"A murderer."

CHAPTER THIRTY

The word hung in the air between us, so heavy I could almost reach out and touch it. If there was a murderer, it meant Ama hadn't lost control. The beast hadn't yet consumed her, overtaken her. If a human had sliced through Maurice and the seamstress and the Carter boy with a knife, I wouldn't have to live with the fact that my sister had killed innocents.

And yet, that hope gleamed like a double-edged sword.

If someone else was responsible for these deaths, they were trying to make it look like the beast had done it. And that meant someone was trying to pin the killings on my sister.

She could never come home if the village was always waiting on pins and needles for the next body to turn up. The beast needed to eat, and people in that kind of frenzy would care even when a vagrant or a drunkard turned up dead.

I ran my hands over my face to smooth away these prickly thoughts, and Sebastian gripped my knee.

"Explain," he said, and I didn't like the easy way the command rolled off his tongue.

But I did explain, because I didn't want to be alone with my suspicions anymore.

"When I took Maurice's body home to clean, I noticed something odd. His wounds were too shallow and there was too much of him left."

An involuntary shiver ran up my spine as I remembered the body, ravaged but still quite intact.

Sebastian took his hand from my knee and rubbed it over his tired eyes. Perhaps this was too much for him—the tipping point. In the space of a day, he'd learned that my sister turned into an animal and his mother was a witch. A murderer on the loose in his village might have been the thing that pushed him over the edge. But I didn't want him to fall.

So, I pulled him back.

"All of this is even more reason to find the cure."

His eyes didn't focus on me as I said it but stared over my shoulder with a glazed indifference. I moved closer to him on the settee and pressed my leg against his. He startled a little and then leaned into me, pushing his face into my shoulder.

"We can undo what was done to her. If we can find the right spell...the cure. Then it won't matter who's killing people in the village...because we'll know it isn't Ama."

Abruptly, Sebastian sat back and unfolded his legs, stealing his warmth from me, and slipped off the settee. He stood in front of the fire, framed by the orange glow of the flames, his face pinched.

"It won't matter who's killing people in the village," he repeated.

My face went hot and my palms instantly dampened. I hadn't meant it quite like that, but I realized how horrible it sounded when he spoke the words back to me.

"No, it will matter, of course. It's just we won't be responsible—"

"*You* won't be responsible," Sebastian cut me off. "This is still my village, Marie."

He was right, of course. The villagers were *his* people, and I was one of the villagers. Suddenly it seemed completely absurd that I'd sat so close to him, held his hand. He was a lord, born to a name with meaning. I was just a villager, one of many, a grain of wheat easily ground. Alone, I was worthless—only together with many others did I become a golden loaf worthy of serving at a banquet.

Peasants were just that—food and fodder. We held meaning only in what we could produce. We were grain and wool, wine and coin collected quarterly. Sebastian didn't even record our names when we slid light bags across the wide parchment of his book. He ticked off a number and weighed the coin and made a neat little mark with a sharp quill. Then he nodded and waved forward the next villager.

One as interchangeable as the other.

Anger seethed through me—hot, heady. I stood in front of Sebastian and let the heat coil into my fingers and toes. I let it fill my limbs like molten iron so it would harden me against those soft brown eyes.

Because the space between us loomed too large. We'd never be able to bridge it, and I didn't want to break away pieces of my heart to try and fill it up. His mother's book of spells wasn't useful to me unless I knew how to read it. I needed to learn the language of magic to recognize the cure for the curse. The only thing I could think of doing was trying to find the Woods Witch, if she was even real, and seeing if she would help.

I knew what I had to do before I moved my feet, but that didn't make it any easier. Sebastian stared at me, seemingly bewildered by the intensity of my silence. He opened his lips, but I raised a hand before he could utter a sound.

"You might have a responsibility to the village, Sebastian, but in return you get so much. You've never felt the pangs of hunger or counted how many sprouting potatoes were left in your cellar for the winter, have you? You've never come home from collecting firewood at the edge of the trees and felt the searing pain as your frozen fingertips came back to life. You hold your responsibility over the village from up here in your grand house with its full pantry, where someone else builds the fires and makes the food. And what happens to you if someone dies in the village . . . from hunger or something else? Nothing. Guilt, maybe. But nothing more. If anyone accuses me of being a witch or Ama of being a monster, they could kill us."

"Marie . . . I didn't mean it like that. I meant exactly the opposite! I care who dies in the village."

He might care, but there were no consequences for him. Suddenly it became clear how very different everything was for us. Lucien might die from consumption, but that was always going to be the case eventually. My sister didn't have to die and neither did I.

"You take care of yours and I'll take care of mine."

Before I could fall under the weight of my heart, I fled the warm comfort of the room and followed the hallway back to the echoing entrance hall. Madame Écrue stood silently on the stairs, twisting her white apron in her hands.

I didn't pause for her or for the thread of regret that trailed after me from the sitting room. I had to keep going or I'd never get out of there. I flung myself down the stairs to the kitchens and found the secret door in the pantry with ease. Inside, the remaining foxglove sat on the shelf exactly where I'd left it, buds full of poison. I pocketed three; I had none at home and they were useful to have on hand. Then I turned and walked back out through the kitchen.

The door to the garden gave beneath my hands. The cold slapped my cheeks, stung my ears, but I ran into the frigid morning with my arms spread wide. Around the house, down the hill, and past the village, heading for home.

The snow slowed me down, but soon my cottage came

into view in its clearing bordered by trees. The little plume of smoke rising from my chimney gave me no surprise. My heart made no leap—I didn't expect Ama this time. I knew who was inside. He had nowhere else to go either.

Papa was home.

CHAPTER THIRTY-ONE

The bulk of him dwarfed the simple chair, his back stretching out on either side of the wooden ladder-back. His presence filled the room with memories and a longing I didn't want. I knew I didn't live in his heart, and yet I never stopped hoping I would. The scent of tobacco and sweat clinging to his long chestnut hair, the worn string of leather tying it back, the way his shoulders tilted to the left because his brother had once accidentally cut into his back with a scythe—they were all so achingly familiar. If I let myself close my eyes and just smell him, I'd become a child again, a girl barely out of short clothes, wanting to run and hide in his arms.

But my father's embrace hadn't welcomed me then, and it couldn't save me now.

"Papa."

He turned slowly, creaking the old chair.

"When I heard you at the door, I thought it might be that hunter girl. I saw her through the window earlier, running toward the trees."

"Emméline Poitres?"

Papa made a sound in his throat and shrugged.

I didn't like that Emméline had been around here, but Ama could be anywhere in the woods. She could still outrun the huntress. She had to hold on for a little longer.

"I'm not surprised you came back," Papa said. "Amabelle didn't last long in that house either."

"You were the one who sold her to them. I went there to try to find a cure for what happened to her."

He scoffed at this. "You were always a dreamer, Marie. Your sister doesn't live in that monster anymore. I always knew it was only a matter of time before she faded away."

"No." It wasn't true. She was still in there and I could save her. I had to. She was half of my heart, and more than that... she was the key to the future that I wanted back now. There was a moment where my heart warmed toward Sebastian and there was a glimmer, a possibility of something else, but no. Not anymore. I'd help her catch a wealthy man and then I'd live as the sister, and then the aunt, and she'd get to be the lady of means and I'd get to be free.

"She was cursed and curses can be undone," I continued. "I found the spell book."

I glanced over at my mother's portrait on the mantel. She looked so like the woman in the locket with Madame

LaClaire—I *had* been remembering right. It wasn't her, though. The resemblance was there, but there were differences. There was something going on here Papa hadn't told me, and for once I was glad he'd come home.

"Did Maman have a sister?"

Papa looked out the window toward the trees. "What?"

"I saw a painting in the big house and the woman looked like Maman but wasn't Maman. Did she have a sister who was friends with Madame LaClaire?"

"Your mother didn't have any sisters," Papa said.

I pulled the miniature painting from the mantel. Maman with a pink ribbon tied around her neck. Her powdered hair curled over her shoulders in a style much too natural for a formal portrait. I'd asked her once when she'd had it done and she'd laughed and told me she'd still been a girl then—when my father first courted her. When her smile had still been full of hope.

"You're lying to me, aren't you?" I said, shoving the painting in his face. "But why...why would you lie about my aunt unless she was something to hide? Someone the family wanted to forget about?"

"No."

"Madame LaClaire had magic or else she wouldn't have been able to turn Ama into a beast. I want to know more about it, and the person who could tell me about it was painted in a portrait in a locket that belonged to the lady. Maman would have wanted you to help me."

"Your mother wouldn't have wanted to see Amabelle like

this. Never. I'm glad she's dead so she doesn't have to know how badly everything went for both of you."

It was an odd turn of phrase for the situation—*how badly everything went*—as if there'd been a plan that hadn't quite come to fruition. I searched my father's face for guilt and found it in his wet eyes.

"What did you do?"

"It wasn't me, Marie. I didn't start this."

Shock shook me and I leaned against the table. A gust of wind whistled through the chimney and blew smoke back at us. Habit almost made me reach for the poker to turn the low-burning fire, but I forced myself to stay still and face my father.

"Who started this, Papa? Tell me!"

He hung his head and wiped at the tears now running down his cheeks.

"I can't."

"Why not?"

"Because I don't know why they did it, only that it's done now and I'm the one God will punish for having a wicked daughter. I have to fix the mess they made ... your mother and those women."

Maman? She died before any of this started. He was speaking in riddles now, spouting nonsense. He'd probably had too many cups of ale at the tavern before coming here. I leaned a bit closer to smell him and sure enough—he was a little sour around the edges.

"Stop lying to me!" I screamed.

"I'm not!" he said, and pounded toward the door in his heavy boots. He swung it open and stomped outside, ready to run away again. But I wouldn't let him go until I had my answers.

My mortar and pestle sat ready and waiting for me just where I'd left them after grinding up the honeysuckle to mark Vivienne's body. A few turns of the pestle and I had some foxglove juice. Carefully, I took a bit on the ends of my fingers and rubbed it into the blade of a sharp knife I used for cutting stalks and stems.

"Papa!"

The cold made it hard to open my mouth wide enough to scream his name, but he heard. He turned toward me, just before he reached the cover of the trees.

"Wait!"

I ran to him, the knife hiding in the folds of my skirt, blade pointed down to the earth. When I reached him, Papa cocked his head.

"What more do you want, Marie? I have nothing."

"You know something. You have that. Tell me."

He shook his head. "No good will come of it. Now, off with you. I want to be alone."

I focused my attention on Papa's watery, pale blue eyes and dug deep into the pit of my stomach for courage I wasn't sure was there. I brought the blade up and sliced it through the air, the edge running over his sleeve. He jerked then and grabbed at his ripped shirt and broken skin, but once he saw how shallow the cut was, a frown stretched his lips.

"It'll take more than that, Marie. Ama always said you were a good hunter, but she was exaggerating, wasn't she?"

I slipped the knife back into my pocket and flexed my fingers. It was over, I'd done it, and I could breathe again.

"No, Papa."

Slow seconds stretched between us before his eyes paled and his mouth went slack. He looked down at the weeping cut on his arm and back up at me with fear darkening his eyes.

"Marie…"

"Tell me what women you were talking about in the cottage and I'll give you the cure for the poison."

Papa squeezed his eyes shut and laughed. "At least I can say my daughter's resourceful."

Even as I hated myself for it, I took the compliment like a scrap—lapped it up, sucked on the dry bone. I stored it away for later when I needed a little nugget of warmth. Then I focused and coated my voice with honey so it dripped soft and sweet.

"Don't you want to know how to save yourself?"

My father peeled his hand from his bloodied arm and a few red drops landed in the snow.

He took a deep breath and let it out in a low whistle. "Your mother, Aurélie, and Madame LaClaire spent a lot of time together and dabbled in things they shouldn't have."

"Is Aurélie still alive?"

The words sounded weak in the wind, but I'd successfully kept the quaver from my voice. But I couldn't stop the flipping of my stomach or the racing of my pulse. After all, this man was my father and he owned me until I married.

He'd already sold one daughter without a backward glance. It would be a mistake to think he'd want me or Ama, need us in some way. He'd already proven he didn't.

"Sometimes, Marie," he said, "it's better not to know."

"Well it's not up to you this time, Papa. I hold your life in my hands, and I want to know."

I'd never said what I wanted so plainly to him before, and stillness settled over us in our shock. We both stared at each other, not daring to move.

He broke the silence like cracks splitting ice. "I never thought you'd live through your first winter."

"What?" It wasn't what I'd been expecting him to say, so it took a moment for the words to unfurl themselves into something that made sense.

"You were a small thing, barely sitting up when the first snow hit. Your mother suckled you, but we didn't have enough food in the stores to satisfy her hunger. I collected bowlfuls of snow and she drank them to make more milk. You surprised me though. You never cried or complained, and as winter thawed to spring, you hung on."

My cheeks burned. I didn't want to be pulled into his memories or hear about the placid baby I'd been. I didn't want reminders that I'd once had a mother who held me to her breast.

"Why are you telling me this?"

"Because I want you to understand. We loved you. We both did."

Wisps of memory surfaced—hard to hold on to. Settling

into big, strong arms. The hum of a half-forgotten song. But nothing strong enough to prove what he said.

"You always kept away from Ama and me. Don't pretend it was different now. You can try and soothe your conscience all you want, but it won't change what you did."

I thought of Ama out there alone, without me.

"More people will be hurt if I don't find the cure," I pressed on. "So, tell me if Aurélie is alive. If you don't, the poison will spread slowly. And I've heard it hurts."

Papa blanched a little and warm satisfaction hummed in my chest. He couldn't play games with me anymore.

"She'll come after me."

"So, she's alive. Where do I find her?"

"She'll kill me."

"So, choose . . . sure death now or possible death later."

To my surprise, he thought about it. Contemplation flickered across his eyes. Whoever the woman was, she must really be dangerous. My own fear sprang to life unbidden, but I forced it down with a deep breath.

"Aurélie," Papa whispered, "lives near the caves at the foot of the mountain. The children call her the Woods Witch."

So, it is *more than gossip. Well, sometimes even the foolish, fearful villagers would get things right.* The Woods Witch was a threat, someone who might take you away if you were naughty. Now I was planning to walk right into her path. The idea made me shiver, but I had to find her. If anyone knew about Madame LaClaire's spell book, she did. The woman from the locket. Aurélie.

I stared at his lined face—the pores dipping crudely into his cheeks. Broken veins feathered the tip of his nose. He'd grown older and different since he'd been gone, but his gray eyes pulled at me with aching familiarity. No matter how old I was or how much I didn't want it to be true, I couldn't escape the little girl inside who longed for her papa.

I think that's why I told him: "There's a box of charcoal powder in the cabinet by the window. Take two spoons quickly or it won't work. Wash it down with some ale."

Papa stalked off toward the cottage without a word. I trudged through the snow around the edge of the forest until the hem of my skirt was soaked through and my toes went numb in my boots. Only then could I find the strength to do what had to be done next—I had to visit the witch.

CHAPTER THIRTY-TWO

had nothing but the hunting coat I'd taken from the manor, my pouch of herbs, and the already damp boots on my feet, but I knew I couldn't go back to the village for supplies.

Shivers tore through my body—little uncontrollable tremors. But there was no helping it. I was cold and I was about to be colder, so I might as well just get on with it. The trees behind our cottage yawned an opening into the woods. A little way through the underbrush, I'd find the path leading away from our village.

I stepped quickly, hoping to pump warmth into my legs and toes. It worked a little, the blood flowing faster through my veins until a little sheen of sweat grew cold on my forehead and upper lip. The ground sloped unevenly and fell away to ice under my feet. I slipped and stumbled over a thick log with old, crumbling bark. My left hand landed on a branch, and the sharp wood dug into my skin with a stinging pinch. I drew my hand away and sucked on the little red bead welling against my palm. I always did that when I got a cut, even though Papa would swat my hand away from my mouth. He thought it was a disgusting habit, but it brought me some sense of comfort. And secretly, I liked the taste of the blood, even though I knew I shouldn't.

The path cut through the brush with well-worn edges. It wasn't traveled often. When Sebastian's parents were alive, they'd fill the track of dirt with the wide wheels of a carriage on their way to bigger cities and fashionable hosts. Now I walked it alone—with only the scurrying of squirrels and occasional lazy squawk of a bird for company.

Trees leaned into the path and their branches bent over it like an archway. Maybe they couldn't really let this track of earth go. I stared at them as I went—thick oaks with scaly bark and ash with a few strong-willed white petals clinging to the branches—and thanked them for keeping the snow at bay. My toes thawed as I walked the sheltered ground.

And then, because I'd been so acutely aware of being alone, I was suddenly sure I wasn't. The air tensed and cracked around me. Gray-and-white bodies whispered between the trees.

Wolves.

Fear cramped my muscles and locked my joints. Running wouldn't have helped anyway—I had only two legs to their four, and they knew this forest, their hunting ground. The biggest one loped forward and fixed me with its yellow eyes.

Slowly, I crouched down and fumbled in the dirt for the stick near my right boot. It felt thin and weak in my grasp, but it was better than nothing.

Hot breath burst through my gritted teeth. The cold of the winter's afternoon made my gums ache, but I couldn't close my lips—it was as if my body needed to imitate the wolves' feral snarls.

They padded forward slowly, knowing they could take their time. These animals were used to being powerful, privileged in their speed and the strong snap of their jaws. Most everything they encountered was at their mercy. Including me.

I planted my feet and bent my knees, holding the thin branch out like I imagined I'd hold a sword. I found the biggest wolf's eyes with my own and challenged with a stare. *Come. You might take me, but I won't make it easy for you.*

I could have sworn he nodded.

They leapt forward in unison, as one coordinated attack. A scream tore through my throat and forced my clenched teeth open. I swung the branch wildly, aiming for their eyes. They threw themselves forward, one at a time, snapping strong jaws and sharp teeth. I slipped backward, turned and twisted, always just a breath out of their reach.

A growling howl echoed through the trees. Bigger, deeper than these wolves could have made. *Ama.*

Her presence burned behind me. I turned and drank in every inch of her—the smooth golden head and matching eyes. The crest of fur at her neck. Her wide paws pressing into the hard earth. I'd missed her so much.

The wolves whined and cowered, backing away while keeping Ama in their sight. Once there was enough space between us, the wolves turned and fled into the trees.

"Ama," I breathed.

She stared at me and sniffed the hem of my dress. My heart beat quickly, thumping against my ribs. I stood perfectly still, barely breathing, waiting to see if my sister would recognize me. I counted to ten and still she hadn't leapt at me. Ama sat in the dirt and swept her thin tail along the ground, the puff at the end gathering dry leaves. I crouched slowly and put out a hand.

"I'm going to fix this. Papa told me who did this. I'm going to see the woman now...Aurélie...and she'll help me fix you. I won't leave you like this, Ama. I promise."

She tilted her head, bending her long ear toward my words. I reached out and stroked the golden hair on her head. She shivered at my touch and fear leapt into my throat for a moment, but I swallowed it down. Ama wouldn't hurt me.

My sister fixed me with molten eyes, and we stared at each other while I tried to make my breaths steady and even. I didn't want to frighten her away.

Then something flared in her golden irises, pluming out from the black pupils. Like a scream. The force of it pushed me away and I stumbled back, landing in the frozen dirt. Ama was in there, screaming behind the beast's eyes.

"Ama."

The beast bared its teeth and growled. All at once, it was as if Ama's control melted away. The beast reared up onto its powerful hind legs, and I skittered back in my crouch, pulling my fingernails through the hard earth, trying to gain purchase.

A musket blast scattered the birds from the trees. The beast whipped its head around and sniffed at the air. Then it shifted back toward me and paused. It seemed like the animal was making a decision. As a second shot cracked the cold air, the beast turned and ran through the trees.

I knew I'd been spared, but I couldn't help the loss hollowing out my belly. My sister was gone again.

Sebastian rounded the bend with panic brightening his eyes. He ran a little when he saw me, bobbed along the path with steps too light for the moment. I stared up at him while he dropped to his knees beside me and set the musket down. The handle of a leather bag slid off his shoulder.

"Are you all right?" he asked.

It was too simple a question. I hadn't been eaten by wolves or by Ama, so I supposed I would be considered all right by most. I thought about saying *yes*, hissing out the word, but I didn't want to be alone in my pain.

"No."

Sebastian scanned my face, my arms and legs. He slowly reached for my hands and felt the bones of my fingers with his own.

"What happened?"

I stood and slipped from his grip. "Wolves first and then Ama . . . well, you saw."

"She attacked you."

A dark, dry laugh escaped me. "She considered it this time."

"I thought she was keen on protecting you?"

I closed my eyelids over wet, tired eyes. The trees blurred, a bright green mixed like streaks of paint with a too-blue sky. It hurt to look at. I rubbed the heels of my hands over my face. I'd figured out how to live with the curse—how to make it through the day with the scent of blood in my nostrils, but I didn't know how to make the pain of it stop.

"What are you doing out here, Sebastian?"

It couldn't be a coincidence that he'd found me on exactly the path my Papa had set me on.

"You're going to see someone who might have answers, aren't you? About my mother and magic."

"How do you know?"

"Your father. I went to your cottage," Sebastian said.

Of course. A few coins might have been enough to persuade Papa to tell Sebastian where I'd gone. My heart warmed a little to think he'd gone there in the first place—likely to see me. Or at least I hoped that was why. I was still angry at him for what he said about owning the village, but I was tired of being alone.

"How much did you pay him?" I asked, and let my mouth turn up in a smile.

Sebastian's cheeks flushed as I expected them to. "A few deniers."

My face fell. "That's it?"

"He didn't seem eager to keep it a secret. He was sitting

down with a big cup of something dark to drink when I got there. All I had to do was slip two deniers across the table and he told me where you'd gone."

Irritation coiled inside me like a spring. I'd had to poison Papa for the same information he'd given to Sebastian for the price of a few pints. My anger flared again.

"It's easy for you to just throw money around, isn't it?"

Anger etched deeper lines around Sebastian's eyes and mouth. "Well, if I hadn't, we'd be burying what was left of you next to the Carter boy and the young seamstress."

"Well, thank you for this short reprieve."

"What do you mean?"

"If the wolves don't get me, it'll be the beast. If not the beast, Emméline and her accusations of 'witch.' There's always a new threat lurking behind the last," I said.

"That's life. You just need to stay ahead of it."

Sebastian's stony stare weighed on me and ground his words into my mind. Yes, this was life—for me and for everyone else. Hunger and desperation lurked in the icy crags of winter. Summer brought sweating and sickness. Danger always nipped at our heels. We trudged on through bad harvests—through stubbed, rocky fields and thin cows and the ache of hungry bellies—because we had to. The only other choice was to give yourself up to the darkness.

And I wouldn't do that.

"I'm going to find out how to help my sister and hopefully your brother," I said, pushing myself to my feet. "Come if you want to, but I can't promise you'll leave again."

"I don't have much left to lose," Sebastian said. "The worst thing has already happened."

"Don't say that. You'll challenge the devil."

"You don't think he's here already?"

Was the devil here? I wasn't even sure I believed in him like Père Danil said we should. Believe in him, fear him—the same instructions he gave for God. Both were too abstract for me to care about when my sister had just nearly attacked me as a beast.

"We're losing light." I picked up the musket and propped it against my shoulder. The solid weight of it warmed me with an empty kind of reassurance—a false sense of safety because I didn't really know how to use it. And a bullet wouldn't hold back these woods or the monsters in it forever.

Sebastian adjusted his bag on his shoulder and fell into step behind me. We let silence become our third companion. The path twisted deeper into the trees. Branches encroached on our space, brushing my hair with their thin fingers when I got too close. Broken spiderwebs glinted from bushes spilling into our path. Soon the track fell away into the dry moss and thick roots of the wood.

It seemed the forest had reclaimed its land. Nature was quick to do that without our interference. We had to be diligent if we wanted to cut away a piece for ourselves.

"Do you know where you're going?" Sebastian called as the light faded to gray around us.

"Papa told me she lives near the caves. Look how thin the trees are here. It was a path once."

I stopped and turned toward him. Pale blue tinted his lips and his ears burned bright red. Any warmth from the sun had drained away with the day. Dusk offered nothing but the sharp edge of wind that stirred the dead leaves at my feet and blew my hair around my face. I pulled the strands from my eyes and mouth.

My fingers couldn't feel the cold anymore and that was dangerous. We had to keep moving and reach the witch's hearth before our skin blackened with cold.

"Walk, Sebastian, or you might lose your ears."

He pursed his lips but said nothing and picked his way around me.

"I'll lead," he said.

"But you don't know where you're going."

"Neither do you."

But I did. It felt like I was being pulled on a taut string, that I was being tugged toward Aurélie. I followed the string through the slick, hardened dirt and the brown mulch and the fallen limbs of trees because I needed to know more.

"Trust me, Sebastian, and we'll find her."

"Fine."

He fell back again but I slowed my pace, so we walked side by side while the sun continued its journey across the sky. I held on to the feeling of the witch's call and followed it until the cottage finally broke free from the shadows.

It was made of stones haphazardly stacked against each other and bound with dark mortar. Moss ran through the cracks of the rocks and made the whole thing look like something left out for too long, veined with mold. The low door hung crooked from rusted hinges. There were no windows, but a chimney burst from the roof and released a steady stream of smoke.

Sebastian moved ahead of me and stared at the little house so intently he tripped over a fallen log. I didn't try to catch him; he was too far ahead. The pull of the string urged me on, but my own trepidation slowed my steps. I wanted to know what she knew and was scared of that knowledge. Right now, I lived in questions and possibilities. If Aurélie gave me answers, those possibilities would solidify into hard realities, and reality wasn't always to my taste.

"Do we knock?" Sebastian asked, standing in front of the lopsided door. The slats of broken and splintered wood didn't even fit together—cold wind would whisper through. The witch must always have a fire burning in the winter.

I raised my clenched fist and tapped it against the door. Banging would have been too much noise for the quiet of the woods around us. And anyway, she knew I was coming. She'd pulled me here.

An iron bolt slid free from its cradle with a low-pitched keening. The door scraped against the stone threshold and swung back into the cottage, and my mother stood before us.

CHAPTER THIRTY-THREE

All the blood seemed to drain from my body into my feet, making them heavy like stones. I tripped over them, swayed, and fell into the dry leaves and twigs cluttering the doorway. She couldn't be here. She couldn't. I'd watched the midwife clean her body. I'd sat on her burial mound in the churchyard and whispered news to her. My mother was dead, but she was right here. She'd pulled me toward this cottage with a string of magic.

Sadness, confusion, and sharp, hot anger filled my heart to bursting. I couldn't decide which feeling to feel first.

"Maman?"

Sebastian pulled in a little gasp of air and bent to pull me up. Leaves clung to my dress, and my palms stung where the little twigs and rocks had pressed into my skin. This moment would leave its mark on me no matter how many times I tried to wipe it away. She'd abandoned me, left me, let me think she was dead. I'd cried for her until my skin had grown raw from the salt in my tears.

Yet she stared at me now with a sadness in her eyes she wasn't entitled to. *How dare she be sad when she's the one who'd done this to us. To me.*

"How . . ."

I couldn't push the words out before my throat closed around my tears. But I wanted her to know they were tears of anger, not happiness.

"You!" I tried again. "You're dead. Gone. You left me!"

Tears beaded at the corners of my mother's eyes and she shook her head.

"You did!"

She caught my hand as it flew out and I pointed a finger in her face. Her skin touched mine. I expected a jolt of aching recognition, that sudden sense of familiarity that comes with a mother's touch.

But there was nothing.

"I'm not *her*, Marie," my mother said. "I'm her sister."

Her words slid off me soundlessly as I stared into her dark eyes.

"Marie." Sebastian took my arm and pulled me a little closer to his side. "Are you all right? Did you hear her?"

I nodded, never taking my eyes off my mother's face. I drank it in like spring water.

She sighed and shook her head. Then she reached out and gripped my shoulders with strong fingers.

"I'm your aunt, Marie. Your mother is dead. I'm alive."

This time, I listened to the strong, smooth voice and let the words in. It made sense. The woman in the locket had looked like my mother but also a little different. I'd asked Papa if Maman had a sister and he lied to me, left that part out when he told me about Aurélie. My chest tightened and my breathing hitched. Shock and disappointment chased through my body like waves.

Of course it wasn't her. When pieces of your heart are chipped away, you don't get them back.

My mother's twin bent her head, and her dark hair spilled over her shoulder.

"Come in, mon chou. Let's have some tea."

✿

My boots clicked faintly on flagstones. The cottage surrounded us, dark and ageless. It could have been hundreds of years old with the musty scent of time clinging to the moss in the walls. The fireplace was cut into the stones to make a place large enough to hang a heavy iron pot. A table flanked by two chairs ate up the space between the hearth and the back of the cottage. On the opposite end, a small pallet bed was pushed up against the wall.

Every time I looked at my aunt's face, a shiver crept up my spine. She was my mother but not my mother—just like the portrait in the locket. I'd never seen anything like it. We had no twins in our village. Père Danil said twins were unnatural, abominations, devils. If any were born, they were killed immediately.

But here was my mother's near-replica, sweeping around us. Her dark hair shone in the glow of stubbed candles and her features settled themselves into soft planes and smooth lines. Her calm belied my gripping unease.

I had no idea what she might do to us. She might make us forget how to breathe—or worse—make us forget ourselves. But I bit back my fear because this woman, my mother's own sister, was the only person left alive in the valley who might be able to teach me to read the book of spells and pick the right spell to strip away Ama's curse.

Sebastian's hand had never left my wrist and now I was thankful for his dry touch. It was selfish, I knew that, but if something horrible was about to happen . . . at least I wasn't alone.

My mother's sister ladled water from a barrel into a kettle and set it on the fire to heat. She reached behind a little striped curtain hanging in front of a small cupboard and pulled out a jar of blackened leaves.

"Can I help?" I asked, because it was something to say into the silence, and I also wanted to see what they were, what plant they came from. We wouldn't drink the tea until I could be sure it wasn't poison.

She flicked a grin at me. "Do you know the leaves?"

I studied the leaves for a moment before replying. "Daisy."

"So, you know plants."

"Yes, no thanks to you."

It slipped out before I could stop it, resentment sharpening my words. She could have helped me, taught me, been there for me. Instead, she hid herself from me. *How could that fact hurt so much? I don't even know this woman.*

She gave a quick laugh. "You have a barbed tongue like your mother."

Maman's tongue had rarely been sharp with me. I still remembered how she pulled me on her lap and hummed soft, sweet melodies into my hair.

"She wasn't like that," I said. "She was kind."

My aunt leveled a steady gaze at me. "Calm, child. I didn't mean all the time."

I broke eye contact and looked around the room. There must be something here I could use to our advantage. Herbs hung stiff and dry from the exposed rafters of the ceiling. The muted tones of old lavender mingled with fresh green leaves of mint. These plants were pieces of a puzzle—to be sliced and milked and mixed together. Nothing to work with on its own.

But something else hanging from the ceiling caught my eye: sheets of worn paper twirling on strings. They drifted between the herbs like white snowflakes.

Before I could reach out for one, my aunt slammed three chipped, cream-colored mugs on the table between us. The kettle hissed and steamed over the fire, dampening the air around us.

"Amélie and Aurélie. Our maman thought the similar names would connect us," she said.

"Why didn't you come when my mother died? Why haven't I ever seen you before?"

The questions were simple, predictable, but still they begged asking. Why hadn't my mother's sister come for us when Maman passed? If she had been there, Papa might not have sent Ama away.

Aurélie wrapped her hand in a thick cloth to retrieve the steaming kettle from the fire. She poured water over the pinch of leaves at the bottom of our cups and the sheer scent of daisy drifted under my nose.

"I was raised out here, Marie. When we were born, my parents separated us and sent me out to this old cottage with a nurse. The villagers would have killed us both if they knew we were twins. My parents and your mother came to visit often, but no one could know about it."

Instead, rumors had crept through the streets. A Woods Witch living out in the trees, working magic against the laws of the church. A friend for Sebastian's mother, another witch. And my mother, what was she? What was I?

Sebastian reached for one of the mugs, took a sip, and gasped. He touched the tip of his finger to his burnt tongue and winced.

"Too hasty," Aurélie said.

Sebastian dropped his hand and stared at the witch—my aunt. A frisson seemed to pass between them, something almost tangible. I shifted on my stool and watched the two of them. Sebastian kept his eyes on Aurélie with such intensity

I almost wondered if he was trying to communicate with her without talking.

"Why you?" Sebastian finally asked out loud. "Why did your parents keep Marie's mother instead of you?"

A shadow darkened Aurélie's eyes. Hurt lingered there. She tried to shrug, but it came off more like a twitch. "They chose somehow. Perhaps they flipped a coin."

"That's cruel," Sebastian said.

"Crueler than killing us both as infants?"

Sebastian and I both sat back in our wooden chairs. The uneven ladder-back dug into my spine. The past was gone. My mother was gone. But Sebastian, Lucien, me, and Ama—we were here. And we needed Aurélie's help.

"Are you really a witch, or is that a silly fear of the villagers?" I asked.

Aurélie took a sip of tea and shrugged, her shawl slipping from her left shoulder.

"I have an herb garden and I make possets whenever someone brave enough finds me and asks for help. They get their remedy and I get to keep my secret because they're too afraid to tell anyone in the village they sought out the Woods Witch."

That didn't really answer my question, but I asked another anyway.

"Were you close with Sebastian's mother?"

Aurélie's lips pulled down and lines appeared in her forehead I hadn't seen before. I noticed threads of gray in her hair too. It was how Maman would have looked if she'd had the chance to grow old.

"Yes, we were close. I found her wandering the woods one day and brought her back here. I taught her about the herbs and things," Aurélie said, and wiped her eyes with the corner of her shawl.

So, it was Aurélie who showed Madame LaClaire how to be a witch?

"But did she have magic?" I asked. "Before you taught her about the plants and herbs?"

Aurélie pursed her thin lips together for a moment before responding. "She had magic, like me."

Sebastian gripped my fingers and I squeezed. Whatever doubt he'd been tending would be cut down now. He had to accept this, that his mother was a witch with the power to curse my sister, and I had to accept that I had an aunt and she had magic too and had done nothing to stop Ama from turning into a beast.

"So, can you help us? I'm your niece, aren't I? Your blood? My sister, Ama, needs your help."

"And my brother too," Sebastian cut through my words. "Lucien. He's ill."

Guilt flared under my ribs, and I couldn't look over to Sebastian beside me. "Yes, Lucien too. Can you come back with us and help us read Madame LaClaire's book of spells?"

"You're both young," she said, and took a sip of tea. "Your memory hasn't had time to become as solid as a stone yet.

The town would remember your mother, and they'd kill me as her ghost if I came back. And what makes you think I could read a book of spells?"

"We heard tales of you as children. The witch on the edge of the woods," Sebastian said.

Aurélie reached out a hand and slid her fingers around his palm. She traced the lines there and murmured under her breath, and Sebastian flinched away.

"Your heart hurts still, doesn't it? Even though I gave her to you? Even though she lingers on the cusp of time?"

"What are you talking about?" I asked. "Do you know Aurélie, Sebastian?"

He shook his head, brow furrowing. "No, not really. I've seen her once or twice from afar, walking in the gardens with Maman."

"More than that," Aurélie said. "The big house was far enough from the village to be safe for me. It helped that no one, not even the priest, would ever question the lord and his wife."

"What did Papa think?" Sebastian asked.

"He didn't know I couldn't go into the village. He was happy his wife was happy."

Aurélie blew on her tea and took another sip. "She was a fighter, your maman, wasn't she? What's wrong with your brother?"

The pain in Sebastian's face ached in my own belly. He didn't seem to want to say it out loud and I understood that—words held power. They made things real.

"Consumption, or it started as that anyway," I said. "It's worse now and I don't know how to stop it."

"And Marie's sister transforms into a beast, she kills people. What do you know about that?" Sebastian asked, matching my confession with his own.

Now my aunt knew about Ama, which was what I wanted. Aurélie closed her eyes and took a deep breath. She shook her head and her hair stirred at her shoulders.

"We're all trapped here in this valley with our sorrows, aren't we?"

I didn't have patience for riddles and nonsense. I wanted answers.

"Do you know what happened to my sister?"

Aurélie finally met my eyes and a shiver ran through me at her clear gaze.

"People were dying. Too many."

"What are you talking about?"

My aunt broke our eye contact and took another sip of tea. Her smooth, calm movements got under my skin.

"We tried to protect them ... you ... everyone. But we couldn't control it like we wanted to."

"What do you mean?" I slid my chair back and stood over the table. "What did you do?"

A breath of wind whispered through the cottage, and the herbs and slips of paper hanging from the ceiling shivered. Aurélie set her cup down quietly.

"We wanted to save everyone, but it hasn't worked," she said, her voice wavering. "I know what it is to watch someone you love torn apart by the beast. Don't think you're the only one who's suffered."

I rubbed the heels of my hands over my eyes. There was a history here I wasn't privy to. We were living the consequences of things that had happened when we were no more than children. How could I fight something so old and so woven into the fabric of the valley?

"I'm trying to end the suffering now. I don't want any more innocents to die! Tell me how to read the book of spells so I can save them."

A laugh gurgled to my aunt's lips and Sebastian startled beside me. He stared at Aurélie with hard eyes. I wondered whether he was trying to mask his fear. I certainly was. This woman, whether she was my blood or not, had lived out here on the edge of civility all her life. She shimmered with something I didn't understand—magic. I didn't know where it came from, but it was there, tugging at me. Was Aurélie a witch because she'd been born a twin? Touched by magic? And what about my mother? What about me—why could I *feel* her?

But the biggest question in that moment was: What might she do to us now if we made her angry?

CHAPTER THIRTY-FOUR

The cottage was stifling now, even though the cool early winter air blew outside. The fire in the hearth spat and hissed, the flames reaching too high. Pulling in a breath was a much bigger effort than it should have been. Aurélie sat across from us, a bead of sweat running down the side of her face. I wanted to get out of here, but we couldn't go without the answers we came for.

"Help us, please Aurélie," I said, hoping, praying, squeezing Sebastian's hand in mine. I was her sister's daughter. He was her friend's son. Aurélie had reason to care.

"You'll never be able to read her book of spells properly, mon chou. Never," she said.

"So, you know what we're talking about? It was my mother's?" Sebastian said.

"Yes." Aurélie dipped her head and fiddled with the cup in her hands in a way that made me think she was suddenly sad.

"You can't do her spells without her magic. You can read the words from the page, sing the songs, but it will never work without the voice of the one who wrote them."

"But we did make one work. We sang the song and Lucien started to get better!" I said.

Aurélie found my eyes with hers. "And then?"

I dropped my shoulders. "And then it stopped working. We couldn't heal Lucien."

Devastation sucked out all the energy I had been using to keep myself upright. This couldn't be it, the end of the journey. There *had* to be a way to save Ama and Lucien and all of Ama's would-be victims.

"You have magic, Aurélie," I said. "So, if you read the words, they'll work, won't they? We need to at least try!"

"I have my own magic, mon chou, but it's not the same as hers. Sebastian, though, he has her magic running through him."

"He sang the spell with me over Lucien and it still didn't work."

Aurélie took a sip of tea and eyed us both over the brim of her cup. The lavender and mint above us swayed against the strung-up pieces of paper, and the strips twisted in the breeze. Illustrations had been etched on them in a fading sepia ink—much like the ink used to inscribe the spells in Madame LaClaire's book. There were answers here and I wanted them. Aurélie was holding back, denying me the information I needed. One paper twirled on its string and I finally caught the picture clearly. A girl in a beautiful dress, a dark stain at her stomach and pooling below her prone body. The seamstress.

I couldn't pull any air into my lungs. *Had Aurélie planned the seamstress's death? Maurice—what about him? Had the Woods Witch killed him too?*

We had to get out of here. I had no idea how dangerous my aunt really was. She was toying with me, giving me more questions than answers, and who could say she wouldn't stop my asking with a spell to seal my mouth shut.

Sebastian sipped his tea, more cautious now as he sucked the liquid through his lips. The musket leaned against his leg between us. I had to grab for it before Aurélie saw me move.

"You've gone pale, Marie," my aunt said.

I pushed a breath out and dragged another one in even though it scraped against my throat. "Why didn't Maman tell us about you?"

Aurélie frowned and the deep lines of her mouth made her face sharp. "She was protecting me. And you, really."

I slid a little closer to Sebastian on my chair until the barrel of the musket dug into my leg. If I reached for it, I might have a few seconds before Aurélie saw. I'd have to trust that Sebastian had packed the barrel properly and it would fire instead of blowing up in my face.

The fireplace exhaled a gust of wind and the leaves of the dried plants whispered overhead. I glanced up at the dangling papers slipped between the lavender and mint. More echoed the first with soft, curling pictures of blood and bodies.

"Why stay in the valley after you'd grown up?" I asked,

picking up the thread of conversation again. "Why not go to a different town?"

"I had people here...your mother, Sebastian's mother. And anyway, where else could I go?"

Few ever left our village. Other villages didn't just accept newcomers with no family connection, and bigger cities—where one's lie about the past might get lost in the mud of the streets—were far away. People born in our village died in our village and were buried in the graveyard next to their parents' bodies.

"So, you stayed here and watched your niece become a monster?" I continued, trying to keep my voice calm. "Why didn't you stop it?"

It was so easy to ask the question of her, to push the blame over to someone else. I wanted someone to point my finger at her and say, *You! You did this. Fix it.*

But my aunt gave no reply.

"How do I save her?" I asked.

Aurélie sighed into her mug of tea. "Ama's not the most dangerous thing in these woods."

"So, what is?"

My aunt shook her head and leaned back against her chair, head tilted up, eyes closed. I grabbed the musket.

She must have heard the scrape of the gun against the flagstones, because her eyes flew open. I pointed the wide mouth of the barrel at her. Sebastian sprang up, tipping his chair over. The sound of it hitting the floor made us all jump and my finger wrapped just a little tighter around the trigger.

The crack tore through the air. There was a moment of utter stillness before the bullet hit. Then chaos. Crumbling dry leaves rained from the ceiling and caught in my hair. Aurélie stumbled against the hearth. No blood bloomed on her dress. The bullet hadn't hit her, but this was the moment to leave. I knew it—I even grabbed Sebastian's sleeve—but something held me back. I didn't have what I came here for.

I aimed the musket at my aunt's chest again and found her eyes with mine. "I'm asking one last time. How do I save her?"

Aurélie pulled her lips into a tight smile. "You already took the shot. You think you can load it faster than I can move?"

I was quite sure I couldn't, but I kept my lips closed tight.

"I'm quick," Sebastian said. "Light fingers." He held up his hands and splayed his long fingers before dipping them into his coat and pulling another cartridge from his pocket. He tore a piece of paper at the end with his teeth, slid the gun out of my hands, filled the pan, and loaded with quick, practiced movements. I kept my eyes on Aurélie the entire time. After he rammed down the cartridge, I grabbed the musket from him.

Aurélie frowned.

"You're digging into something neither one of you is old enough to understand. You might not like what you find."

"I can take it," I said. "If it means a cure for the curse."

"You keep calling it that. Why?"

Her question surprised me so much I almost lowered the musket. Sebastian must have seen, because he touched the bottom of the barrel to keep it lifted.

"It's awful…evil. What else do you call something like that?"

Aurélie smiled again, but this time her cheekbones rose and thin webs of lines threaded out from her eyes.

"Perhaps it's really a blessing."

"You're playing games with me, which is pretty senseless considering I've a gun pointed at your heart."

"No games, mon chou. I loved you once. Both of you… well, the idea of you, anyway. My nieces… my sister's girls. I wanted to see…"

"What?"

"I wanted to see if I could feel her in you."

"My mother?"

"Yes."

It was so strange to be connected to this woman through blood and history and yet know nothing about her. Strange to be threatening my mother's shadow with a musket.

"And can you?"

My mother's sister considered me with the small, pink nib of her tongue stuck out between white teeth. She examined me closely. I felt naked in my layers, exposed, laid bare. In some absurd twist of my own feelings, I didn't want to be found lacking. And yet, I was sure I would be.

"You're clouded with anger. Something dark. I can't see your heart at all."

"Good." I hissed. She had no right to measure me against a mother I'd barely had the chance to know.

"What do you want for it?" Sebastian asked.

Aurélie's eyes flicked toward him. "For what?"

"For magic. What will it take? I need it, and I must have something you want."

The dryness of his voice leeched any arrogance from the phrase. The objects in his house didn't mean anything to him except to buy him Lucien's salvation.

"The cure, as you call it, isn't mine to give."

Frustration seethed through me. We'd braved the frozen forest and the dark shimmer of magic to find this woman for nothing.

"Why bring me here then?" I cried. "I felt it. You pulled me with your magic!"

Aurélie splayed her long fingers and shrugged. "I've already told you. You were coming here anyway, and I was curious."

"That's it?"

My frustration fizzled into deep, aching disappointment. I'd thought the Woods Witch would have an answer, that I'd be closer to saving Ama by now. But I'd gotten no further—I still didn't know how to read the book of spells, and according to Aurélie I never would. This was another dead end.

"Stop looking for evil in your sister, girl," she said. "There's enough of that in the village without conjuring more."

She wasn't wrong, but her calm face goaded me. I almost pulled the trigger out of spite.

Sebastian stood beside me, his face strained. The silence

stretched taut between the three of us. It seemed we all held our breath, waiting to see who would make the first move.

Aurélie's threat was the unknown—her weapons veiled in magic. I didn't know what she could, or would, do to us. But I wasn't going to wait around to find out.

The last shot had been an accident, and I didn't really want to squeeze the trigger on purpose to try and shoot my mother's sister. But still, the musket was heavy. I swung it toward my aunt and smashed the yawning barrel into the side of her head. Sebastian let out a strangled sound, but I grabbed his arm and dragged him toward the door, the gun propped under my armpit.

We burst free into the ice-laced night and slipped over the frozen ground under frosted leaves. The invisible tether that had pulled me toward the cottage tightened and snapped as we fled. Aurélie's draw drained from my heart, leaving more room for the panic spreading through my veins like hoarfrost. Branches snagged my skirts, and owls called out with warnings and bright eyes that glowed in the dark. Sebastian sped ahead of me, glancing back with every few steps.

I silently urged him on and pounded my boots against the dirt and frozen brush. I slipped and landed hard. Twigs and rocks dug into my palms, leaving indents when I brushed them off against my skirt.

"Marie!" Sebastian stopped but didn't come back for me. *Good. At least he isn't stupid.*

We couldn't run through the forest all night. Wolves sung

their devotions to the moon and they sounded close. We needed shelter.

I turned on my heel and ran north toward the foothills cupping our valley. We'd be safer with stone at our backs. The sky sparkled with broken stars overhead, and iridescent flecks of blue floated down among the white flakes of snow. Magic tainted the air. *Aurélie.*

CHAPTER THIRTY-FIVE

he blow hadn't even knocked her out. I should have struck harder.

"A cave," I cried through the wind to Sebastian. "Find a cave."

The two of us raked our hands over the rock face, searching for an opening to swallow us up. In the dark, shadows played over the stone and tricked my eyes into seeing dips and crevices that weren't there. Finally, my fingers slipped into a triangular break in the rock. If we crouched, we'd be able to slip in.

"Sebastian!" The wind carried my voice to his ears and he turned with panic in his eyes. I held up my hands to show him I was all right and pointed to the opening in the stone.

"We can fit if we crawl," I said when he reached me.

"You don't know what's inside."

Fear crept over me like an insect running over my skin. We could get trapped in there, in the dark and the dirt.

"No, but I know what's out here. The cave is the better bet."

I went first, down on my hands and knees in the cold, flaking dirt. My skirt caught against the jagged ends of stone. I heard Sebastian behind me, but there wasn't enough room to turn my head. The walls of rock pushed in at me from both sides, squeezing the breath from my lungs. Darkness consumed all the shapes around me and I had to feel my way deeper into the pitch. My eyes ached with the effort of trying to see, but there was nothing at all. I pushed my hands against the cold rock on either side and stumbled along on my knees, trying very hard not to think of what might be scurrying away from my fingers unseen. The cave walls became farther and farther apart until I couldn't reach both sides at the same time anymore.

"Stop," I called back to Sebastian and heard his knees scrape against the earth.

I found the seam of the rock and dirt and felt my way up the side of the cave. Cold waves of apprehension rippled over me. If I found the ceiling only a little over my head, we wouldn't be able to sit up or stand. We might have to shimmy backward out toward the cries of the wolves and the threatening sting of magic.

My hands explored further and further—rough edges of cold rock biting into my fingers—but I didn't find an end to the wall. I crouched up on my haunches and placed my hands, palms up, over my head. Slowly, very slowly, I rose, ready for my hands to hit an unforgiving slab of stone.

But they didn't.

I stood on cramped, shaking legs, and a little laugh fell from my lips.

"Sebastian, we can stand here."

The rustling of his heavy coat told me he was unfolding his body and standing, but his movements sounded timid—as if he didn't wholly trust what I'd said.

I heard Sebastian shuffle toward me and stop when he reached out and found my arms, my hands. He held them with his own before dipping down to retrieve what must have been the musket.

"We need light," he said.

"And heat."

I'd been so cold for so long I'd forgotten how frozen my toes were. Now, out of the wind and with the exertion of crawling through the tunnel, they ached. We were in danger of our limbs turning black in temperatures like these.

Sebastian's hands, suddenly on me, roamed my torso and patted at my coat.

"Hey!" I twisted away from him without moving too far. I didn't want to smack my head against the rock wall.

"Stop moving. I'm trying to look in your pockets."

"Why?"

"That's my hunting coat."

"So?"

As I asked my question, Sebastian gave a little yelp and

dipped his hand into one of my pockets. He pulled something out and I heard the scrape of metal against stone.

A bright orb of flame lit up Sebastian's smiling face.

"My tinder box," he said, a laugh trailing his words.

I couldn't help it, I laughed with him. This was the first good thing to happen in days. This stub of lit candle was our first win. Something so small, but it would mean we could spend the night in this cave with the warmth and light of a little fire.

"What's in the bag then if not a tinder box?" I said.

"Food."

My stomach moaned with the promise of relief. My apprehension had pushed my hunger out of the way during the walk to Aurélie's cottage, but I couldn't ignore it anymore.

"Does Madame Écrue know where you are, then?" I said.

"Not really. Just that I went to find you and took a couple of cooked eggs and some bacon. She wrapped up some cheese too."

"Well, we might just last the night because of her."

"Here, you take the candle," Sebastian said, handing me the taper. "Lead the way."

I held it in front of me and the bobbing flame illuminated a diamond-shaped cavern with a dirt floor. Pale light fought with the shadows as I circled the small space. Gossamer threads woven by hidden spiders clung to the walls, and uneven rock formations cracked the dirt and climbed toward the ceiling.

I pulled lichen from the rocks and let the soft green

strands fall between my fingers. Sebastian grabbed a few stray stones and rolled them into a small circle. I threw in the lichen and other forest debris that had made its way inside. Then I lit a roll of bark and tossed it in the heap. The fire flared and I squinted at the sudden onslaught of light.

When I could open my eyes again, I glanced around the stone room with renewed curiosity. There didn't appear to be another way out. No one could sneak up from behind us. It wasn't easy to get in either, and we could guard the entrance until the safety of daybreak.

"Marie."

Sebastian knelt near the back wall. The stillness of his body—his back barely rising and falling in quiet breaths—made me rush to him with my throat tight and burning.

"What is it? What happened?"

I'd expected blood, torn skin, broken fingers. Instead, the empty eye sockets of a long-dead woman stared up at me—her blue silk hat faded but still beautiful atop a naked skull.

Her bones stuck out haphazardly from the dirt, a few broken ribs scattered near her skull. I picked one up and ran my fingers along the deep teeth marks running the length of the long, white bone. Ama might have been here. Killed her. Or perhaps it was Aurélie. Or even just a wolf. I didn't know anymore who'd done the killing, but this girl had still died here nonetheless.

I thought I'd had it all figured out. I thought I could control the beast. But these bones shone white and clean—this wasn't a recent kill. If it was Ama, it might have been one of her first. She might have dragged this girl out to this cave and eaten her fill.

My stomach soured. Hunched in the dirt beside me, Sebastian brought a hand to his mouth, as if trying to hold something in. Maybe bile climbed up his throat too.

The blue silk hat was beautiful but ordinary—trimmed with a wide ribbon and a single drooping flower. The milliner probably made it, which meant this woman had likely been a merchant or soldier's wife or daughter. She'd had a life not so far away.

I slipped a couple of the broken rib bones into my pocket.

"What are you doing?" Sebastian asked.

"Taking her home."

I'd bury them in the graveyard when we got back. My sister may have stolen this woman's life, but I'd give her some kind of peace in the ground of her ancestors instead of alone in this cold cave.

"Does the beast ever stop killing?"

My heart beat painfully in my chest. The wildness in Ama's eyes ate at my hopes of ever being able to pull her back. The beast had her so firmly in its jaws, I wasn't sure she even knew it was happening.

What does she see when she runs through the forest? Do the colors fade as she sniffs out blood or do they glow with her antici-pation? Does she know she isn't wholly human anymore?

"I don't know about the beast," I said. "But Ama will."

Sebastian shifted his weight. His sleeve brushed against mine and I didn't pull away. The wind whined through the tight opening at the mouth of the cave and it rang through my ears like a painful moan. I wanted Sebastian here beside me, wanted the heat of him and the blush under his skin and the crinkle of his eyes when he smiled. I wanted to press my hand to his chest and feel his life beating under my own cold fingertips.

"You still think you can change your sister back?" he asked.

"Yes," I lied, because I wanted it to be true. I wanted to ignore what Aurélie had said about the book of spells. "And we can make Lucien better too."

Sebastian swallowed and his throat bobbed. A shadow of dark hair had bloomed on his cheeks, chin, and neck—he hadn't shaved in at least a few days. I wondered if it was even something he did himself or if he trusted Madame Écrue to wield the blade so close to his throat.

"Aurélie didn't tell us anything useful. What can we do now?" he said.

I didn't know. He was right. We didn't have anywhere else to go for answers. I didn't want to believe what my aunt had said about the spell book, but I couldn't stop doubt from seeping into my skin. What would I do if I couldn't figure out how to read it? If I really needed magic that I didn't have to make it work, I'd lose Ama forever. I was already running out of time.

And now Sebastian and I might both freeze in this cave and lie here until our bones were as clean as the woman with the blue hat.

"There's an answer somewhere, Sebastian," I said without

really believing my own words. "We just have to find it. And we better make sure we live to see the morning . . . or we won't find anything."

"Here," he said, pulling his bag from his shoulder and bringing out two eggs and two parcels of folded cotton— cheese studded with sage and a small stack of thick slices of bacon. He even had a flask of ale.

I wasn't sure I could eat. The rib bones seemed heavy in my pocket. I hesitated.

"I don't really want it either, but we have to eat," Sebastian said.

"Yes, I know."

The egg seemed like the best thing for a queasy stomach, so I peeled one. Once I took a bite and the yolk hit my tongue, my hunger returned. It seemed the same for Sebastian, who broke off a piece of cheese, laid a slice of bacon on top, and took a big bite. We finished eating in silence. A little water fell from the ceiling onto a rock below with rhythmic drips. The wind continued its tirade on the trees outside, a faint whistle reaching us now.

When all the food was gone, Sebastian scooted closer to the small dancing flames of our fire. I stretched my fingers out to it, but the cold stone walls leeched the warmth from the air.

"That won't be enough," I said, gesturing to the fire.

"There's not much else to stoke it with. Unless we want to throw in that hat."

"No," I said. "But we should share our own warmth. Ama

and I used to do that when we were little and the cottage was cold."

It was purely for survival, but a flush rose in my cheeks at the thought of pressing close to each other again. I wondered what those hairs on his neck would feel like against my cheek.

"So, you want to cuddle?" he said.

"Actually, it will work better if it's skin against skin."

Sebastian's cheeks flushed red. "Oh, uh . . . well yes, all right if that's what we need to do."

I swallowed with a dry throat. Only Ama had ever seen the skin of my belly or the curve of my breasts. And I'd only ever seen hers. Boys were different—forbidden. Marriage and all that came with it was nothing more than a concept to me. It lurked in my periphery. I'd always thought Ama would be the one to marry and I'd just reap the benefits secondhand.

But I'd never actually imagined what it would be like to press my skin against someone else's. Sebastian sat here beside me in the flickering glow of the firelight. Shadows dappled his face and almost hid his set mouth.

I can be practical. This is survival and nothing else.

CHAPTER THIRTY-SIX

ebastian shrugged off his coat. He hissed as the cold air hit the thin sleeves of his shirt. I pulled my own arms from the hunting coat.

I wore more layers than he did. He stripped down quickly, efficiently, slipping his linen shirt from his body in one smooth movement. Dark hairs curled in the middle of his chest, and I wanted to both look away and stare at him. I settled for gazing at his smooth stomach while I loosened my laces. My fingers, numb and stiff from the cold, did a poor job of it.

"Here, let me help you," Sebastian said with a shivering stutter. The air must have felt like knives against his bare skin.

I let his deft fingers pull the strings free. My dress, once snug around my body, yawned at my chest and my hips. I pulled it off and faced Sebastian in my chemise. A glance down confirmed the thin fabric was little more than a veil—blurring the lines of my nakedness but not concealing it. I tried to let the sensibility of the situation settle over me. We needed to stay warm. Skin to skin—or close to it, because there was no way I was taking off my chemise—was the best way to do that.

But the heat in my belly wouldn't go away.

Sebastian picked up our coats and wrapped them around us. Facing each other, we lowered ourselves down beside the fire and I nestled easily into the crook of Sebastian's arm. He splayed his hands over the fabric of my chemise and rubbed circles with his thumb into my back. I breathed in the musky smell of him and my nerves quieted.

His nose and mouth rested on the top of my head and I hoped my hair still smelled of lavender.

"What will we do when the sun comes up?" Sebastian asked.

"Go home. Start again. Aurélie had a picture hanging from her roof of a girl torn open just like the seamstress . . . a spell or a recording of what happened. If she had something to do with it, someone in town might be helping her and making it look like the beast. So we have to find out why."

"What if it's just her?"

"It isn't."

"You said you thought someone might be using a knife," Sebastian said.

"Sometimes, maybe. The cuts on Maurice were shallow enough for that, but Vivienne . . . it looked like teeth, didn't it? And Aurélie doesn't have the teeth to tear anyone apart. There's something else going on, someone helping her."

"Or it's simply Ama doing the killing. Or wolves."

I hadn't forgotten that. "Yes, it could be. But the kills don't look like Ama's work. And wolves would eat more of their kill."

He nodded slowly. "So, who in the village would benefit from it?"

"Well, Père Danil would love to be the one to vanquish the devil made flesh. Did you see how people flocked to church after Maurice was found?"

"Yes, Père Danil would revel in being a savior of the church. But he doesn't have teeth that can tear flesh open either."

I pulled away from Sebastian a little so I could see into his eyes, gauge his reaction while I went on with my theory.

"Emméline," I said. "You gave her an incentive. What was it?"

Sebastian raised his brow and widened his eyes. "An introduction to the king, a recommendation to be one of his hunters at Versailles."

"She could make her name defeating the beast. Prestige is alluring, and there aren't many ways to earn it in a town like ours. The men don't always accept her as her father's heir. By creating more fear, she'd have an even bigger trophy to present if she finally destroyed the monster that everyone thought was doing the killing."

"I can't see it. I've known her since I was a child, and I can't picture her as a murderer. She hunts animals, yes, but killing people would be very different."

The possibilities swirled in my head, making me dizzy. A

blast of icy wind wound through the opening of the tunnel and broke over us. My muscles seized up, shivering relentlessly, and I settled closer to Sebastian again. His grip on me tightened and my belly tingled with what I could only describe as anticipation. Lying together there, in the low glow of a stuttering fire, I wanted something to happen. But I wasn't sure what. My own hands explored the soft skin of his back. He didn't react and the tingling twisted into sour embarrassment. I stopped moving my hands and lifted them from his skin so he couldn't feel the wetness on my palms.

"Even if we find the killer, we still don't have a way to break the curse," I said, to draw his attention away from my awkwardness. "We just have more questions than ever."

"And no cure for Lucien's illness."

The edge of accusation to his words made me bristle in defense.

"I *am* trying. I came out here, into the frozen woods, on my own to find out how to read the spell book."

"For your sister."

"What does that matter? Magic could still work for Lucien too."

"How do you know?"

I didn't, not really. I could only assume magic could claw back the consumption better than tea and poultices could. But I didn't know the rules of it any better than Sebastian did. We'd waded out into the unknown, and we had to hope we wouldn't fall into the deep.

"Do you have a better plan?"

He hesitated, taking a big breath and letting it out slowly. My head rose and fell with his chest. "No," he said.

"Then we go home and figure out who the killer is and buy ourselves time to figure out how to save Ama and Lucien."

"What if there are no answers for us in this valley?"

Everything seemed contained here. I'd never left the watchful eye of the jagged mountaintops. My parents had been born here, and my parents' parents. We were tied to this valley and the people in it.

Secrets festered in close quarters—among the boredom of tidy lives. We heard gossip, of course. Pamphlets and papers made their way here in the bags of travelers and pilgrims. Trinkets—a pair of paste jewel earrings, an embroidered handkerchief, a gilt fan *just* like the queen's—glittered in peddlers' packs. We weren't cut off from everything; we were just far away. By the time those things reached us, they were already out of date, so sometimes we had to make our own news.

In a town of our size, we knew each other intimately. And we knew our stations—where we were supposed to stay. Rumors slipped through town like silk ribbons through a lady's fingers and easily spun out of control. Blame was cast with the casual pointing of a finger—whether jeweled or browned and spotted from the sun.

It was easy to fall into the thrill of the mob. To belong to their passion. Sometimes I yearned for it, for the automatic acceptance that came with shared outrage.

But now their sour whispers were about Ama...and

me . . . and I hated them for pushing us to the outside when all I'd ever wanted was to be accepted by them. I remembered the little dolls on our doorstep, Emméline's knowing grin.

"What are you thinking?" Sebastian asked. He lifted a finger and ran it between my brows. "You've a line here from frowning."

I brushed his hand away and tried to smooth my expression, but the rancor couldn't be defused in a moment. Sebastian didn't understand. He wasn't part of the town—not like that. He belonged to a different world.

The politics of the town were beneath his notice because he held no stake in them. No matter what happened in the village nestled below his estate, he'd always be its ruler.

"My grandparents had to hide their baby away to keep the villagers from killing it," I said.

"Not the villagers. A priest."

I dragged my courage up from the bottom of my belly and said, "Père Danil was suspicious of your mother, wasn't he? As a witch? And he didn't chase her away."

The cold air hit my skin the instant he pulled away, the space where he'd been quickly draining of warmth. He stood, facing me. Pain veiled Sebastian's eyes and he stared at his feet, but I didn't miss the tears on his lashes.

"Papa would have protected her, yes. Her status helped with everything else, but it didn't stop the whispers. Didn't ease her pain at being an outsider."

"No, I imagine that pain lived deep inside. But she was safe from expulsion and that's something," I said.

"I don't think she ever really felt safe, Marie. She was always peering out our windows, looking toward the village or into the woods. She kept Lucien so close to her you'd think she was afraid of him dying if he was on his own."

"Well, he was sick, wasn't he? That's understandable."

"It was more than that. She was terrified even before that. She really loved us. Please don't try to take her away from me."

I wished I could take us back to a few moments ago, when I could still feel the steadiness of his warm breath against my forehead.

"I'm not, I'd never." I stumbled for the words. "Whatever she was, I'm sure it wouldn't have changed the way she loved you."

"It didn't." Sebastian wiped his eyes.

I hadn't wanted to upset him, and regret made me want to call my words back. But I couldn't, so I called Sebastian back instead.

"Please come here. It's cold," I said.

The fire burned low with glowing red embers and the black of the night wound round us like dark velvet. The howl of wolves rang through the trees outside the cavern and a tingle of fear ran down my spine.

He seemed to struggle with it for a moment, but then his shoulders dipped and he took a couple steps toward me. I stood and wrapped my arms around his waist. He pulled us back down to lie on his coat in front of the waning fire.

"We need to find out who ... or what ... is doing the killing," I said.

"How?"

"Bait them."

"Like we did with Vivienne's body?"

"Maybe..."

If we used honeysuckle, that would only attract Ama. And we didn't have another dead body to work with.

"I could be the bait," I said, a plan suddenly coming to me. "I could make myself vulnerable, sit outside on the church steps like a vagrant, all wrapped up in an old cloak, and see who comes."

"How do we know anyone, or anything, even would come? It would be taking a chance."

"What if we double the bait?" I'd already thought about it, but I hesitated to say the words out loud because the idea terrified me. "You could drag me back into town with my hands bound. I'll be your prisoner. Give in to the villagers... let them have their monster. And while they're all watching me, you'll dress as a vagrant and watch for the killer. If the killer is a person, they'll want to keep everyone scared of me, and killing again is the way to do that. If it's not a person"—I couldn't say Ama's name—"it will be drawn by the scent of blood."

"Blood?"

"You can smear some on yourself."

"And where will this blood come from?"

"Me or you."

Sebastian stared at me. "You know what the villagers can be like, Marie. What if I can't stop them from hurting you?"

I tried to smirk, but it couldn't have come out right, because Sebastian only frowned more deeply.

"You'll have to control them, *my lord*."

He huffed out a sigh. "This is dangerous, Marie."

"Everything is dangerous. How many will die this winter from cold and empty bellies? The pox could come for those who survive this spring. Safety is an illusion, Sebastian."

I meant everything I said, but I left out how much I wanted to believe in that illusion.

"I don't like this plan," Sebastian said.

"Neither do I, but it's our best chance at figuring out what's going on and heading off whoever's responsible."

"So, we control the situation?" Sebastian said.

"As much as we can."

We fell silent, and it was a warm, still, enveloping quiet. The smoke hung low—trapped by the cavern roof—and stung my nose, so I buried a little closer to Sebastian and breathed in the smooth scent of his skin. He tightened his grip on me, bringing me still closer. The bulk of him pressed against the length of me. Heat bloomed in my belly again and my breathing quickened, my breasts rising and falling against his chest.

He let out a little sigh into my hair, and I slowly tilted my head up so I could look at him. His blush, familiar to me now, reddened his cheeks, but his brown eyes shone with a spark I'd never seen in them before. Sebastian bent his head and his breath plumed against my lips.

I pulled back and dipped my head back down to his chest, all sweat and nerves and glowing embarrassment. I'd never been this close to a boy before, never seen anyone but my father without his shirt on. I shouldn't have, either, until the wedding night I didn't want. But here we were, his skin against my thin chemise, hiding in a cave to make it through the night, and the only thing occupying my mind was the gentle curve of his lips and the heat of his skin.

How much I wanted to kiss him was a problem. Because I'd never be allowed to keep him.

An invisible line separated us. We might have crossed it a few times because the threat of death was involved, but once we cured Ama and Lucien, things in our town would go back to normal. And normal meant Sebastian in his estate and me in my little cottage. Pretending it could be otherwise was foolish.

I dared a glance up at him, though, and found hurt in the set of his jaw. My own disappointment tightened my throat. Why were there so many rules? I didn't want to play by any of them.

CHAPTER THIRTY-SEVEN

y muscles ached, stiff and cold. Light glowed at the entrance to the cavern and I sat up abruptly, teasing a groan from Sebastian when I pulled my warmth away.

"It's morning," I said unnecessarily, because I couldn't think of anything else to say.

Sebastian avoided my eyes and pulled his shirt over his head. I stepped into my dress with trembling hands—though I couldn't say for sure if it was the cold causing me to shake.

"Where will we get rope?" he asked.

"What?" My mind turned sluggishly, thick with sleep and leftover desire.

Sebastian stared at me. "You wanted me to drag you back into town bound as my prisoner, right?"

The plan came flooding back. The idea of submitting myself to the townspeople, even falsely, rubbed me like a rough woolen dress. I'd have to stand like a dog before them—tethered and obedient.

"I don't suppose you have a length of rope in the pocket of your hunting jacket?" I asked.

The corner of Sebastian's mouth lifted in a grin. "No such luck."

Then we'd have to go back to my cottage. I kept coils of rope in the cellar, on a shelf near the chains I'd used to hold Ama. Our cottage sat near the edge of the woods, away from the crowded center of town, so we might be able to sneak there without anyone seeing—as long as Papa wasn't home.

"All right, well, let's go. I have rope at home," I said, and made my way to the cave's entrance. We silently crawled back out to the woods.

In the too-bright light of a fresh morning, the forest took on a mask of innocence. Sunlight shone through the trees and revealed the glitter in mounds of snow. Ice, beginning to melt at the edges, fell back from the path and took its threats with it. Suddenly, our flight the night before, my panic, seemed almost dramatic. Daylight laid bare the absurdity of it and embarrassment heated my face.

Is this what Sebastian thought too? I studied him, taking in the way he licked his chapped lips in the cool air and shrugged his jacket open. *Does he think me ridiculous to run from Aurélie and insist we hide in the side of a mountain?*

"Sebastian," I started without knowing how I planned to finish the sentence. I grasped for something intelligent to say, but really, I just wanted to know if the stark reality of the morning felled his fears too. "It all looks so normal, doesn't it?"

He glanced at me, brows furrowed, and shook his head. "It's a ploy. Don't fall for it. The woods hide their secrets well in the sunlight, but they're still here."

I nodded into the bulky collar of the oversized hunting jacket. *Did I want it to be true, want the threat of the witch and the beast to dissolve like the ice in the sun's warmth? Perhaps. It would have been easier.*

But nothing in my life had ever been easy. We scraped out a living, carved it from edges of the town, hoping one day to settle into—what? Enough money to hear news of the harvest with indifference, knowing it would not affect us? Enough of a position that no one would whisper after us when we walked in the street? A warm hearth and a clutch of nieces and nephews huddled around it, spinning tops and threading ribbons through their dolls' hair? Visions pushed themselves in front of my eyes—all the things I'd hoped for, dreamed of. The desires lighting my core.

Now my dreams faded into mist, leaving a residue of disappointment behind.

"Everything is still in front of us," I said. "Ama, Lucien, the townspeople, the witch. There's still so much to do."

Sebastian turned toward me, breaking a twig beneath his boot with a loud crack. My gaze instinctively flicked around, searching the spaces between the trees.

"Marie." Sebastian set his hands on my shoulders, but I barely felt them through my coat. "Is this worth it to you?"

"What do you mean?"

"Do you want to save your sister this badly?"

Anger, unfair but bitter, bubbled to the tip of my tongue. "You'd ask that of me? After everything I've done already?"

He smiled and I balled my hands into fists inside the sleeves of my coat to stop myself from hitting him.

"See?"

"What?"

"There's much to do, Marie. But you wouldn't even think of *not* doing it."

The truth of his words settled over me like the warm water of a yearned-for bath. *Of course I'd keep going.* This was exactly what I was meant to do.

I struck out in front of Sebastian and stepped nimbly over a fallen log blocking the path away from the cave.

"If we hurry, we'll get back around dusk. Papa will be away having supper at the tavern and we'll steal the rope," I called back to him.

"I knew you'd go through with it."

I slowed and took a deep breath. I was always moving forward, working toward the next thing. Figuring out how to make sure Ama only killed certain people, saving for her dowry, working on my perfumes and cordials, working toward acceptance and a steady life. I wasn't about to stop moving now.

"So did I."

We'd been walking for hours when darkness settled back over the forest, blurring the features of the strong oak branches and sharp ends of pine needles.

Sebastian and I stayed close together. Every few steps he reached out and touched the hem of my jacket as I led our way through the trees. I clung to the comfort of his presence as once again the woods fell into the realm of twisting shadows.

The tree line around our cottage had been defined generations ago by a great-grandfather who'd craved distinct borders and separation between himself and the forest. I broke through the line with one boot in frozen mud and the other slipping on snow and dead grass. Papa kept the property in order, and I suspected it was because pulling weeds and keeping the forest at bay were the few things in his life he could control. Everything else spun out—wild and untamable—around him.

The cottage itself stood dark and silent. It didn't look like Papa was home and I was grateful for his predictability. A loaf of bread sat on the table, probably stale. I took it, broke two big pieces off, and passed one to Sebastian.

"Your father will know you were here," he said.

I shrugged. "I could have come home before you caught me."

We ate quickly and I poured us both a measure of ale from the barrel.

"Where's the rope?" Sebastian asked when he finished drinking.

"The cellar, and we should be quick," I said, because my skin prickled with fear I couldn't place.

The cellar doors clung to each other and it took both me and Sebastian to tug them open. The hinges wailed in protest.

I hated this space. This was where I chained my sister to the dirt and watched her skin break and bones crack as the beast claimed her. The memories burned in my mind and slowed my steps on the narrow wooden stairs.

"Is this the right place?" Sebastian asked, pausing behind me.

"Yes, there's the rope." I pointed to the shelves lodged in the cracked earthen wall. Sebastian tried to step in front of me, but I stopped him with a hand. "I'll get it."

I had to keep him from going deeper into the room. The very air hung thick with pain I didn't want to share.

The rope turned in on itself like a heavy snake, and I coiled my hands around it tightly enough for the rough splinters to dig into my skin. Sebastian kicked at the chains behind me.

"What are these for?"

His question was much too simple, said with too light a voice, for the answer it demanded.

I told him anyway, quickly, crudely. "They're for Ama. I chain her up when we can't find a victim."

Sebastian's face fell and my heart dropped with it. I'd hoped he'd understand. I *had* to do this. It wasn't cruel—it was what was best for the townspeople and Ama.

"And this?" Sebastian asked, lifting a shred of thin cotton chemise from the dirt.

"Her clothes rip when she . . . changes. But she gets cold while she waits for it to happen."

He nodded and his face relaxed, as if he heard this kind of explanation every day.

"And these?" He scooped something from the dirt and shook it in his cupped hand. I couldn't see what it was.

"Stones?" I guessed from their rattling.

In response, Sebastian stretched out his hand and splayed his fingers, palm flat. Two small, white teeth gleamed up at me.

The shock of it made me stumble backward, hands still full of fraying rope.

"Where did you get those?"

Sebastian's face twisted into a frown. "Right here beside the chains. They look like milk teeth, don't they? Are you sure the simplest answer isn't the right one, Marie? That Ama isn't the one doing all this?"

I tried to say I was sure, but the words stuck like burs in my throat. I coughed and shook my head instead.

She'd promised—we both did. No children. It was the only way I could live with it, and I'd had to live with it. I'd had no choice. What else was I supposed to do the first time she transformed and Papa had turned his back to my screams? I couldn't run from her or kill her. I'd had to trust she wouldn't hurt me. And when she'd sniffed and snarled, she seemed to know me at least. It was then I was sure we could control it—this thing, this curse—because Ama was still in there somewhere.

"Why would there be teeth here, where she was always contained?" I asked, scrabbling for a thread of logic to hold on to. "She couldn't have killed a child in this cellar."

That was true, at least. She'd never escaped the chains, even with the strength of a monster.

"So, how'd they get here?"

I peered at them again, nestled together in the palm of Sebastian's hand. There was no way to know they were human. Not for sure.

"They must be from the rabbits I throw her sometimes when she's down here."

"Rabbits?" Sebastian closed his fist around the teeth.

"Yes, must be. And what are you, a surgeon now? An expert on teeth?"

My twisting nerves soured my words and Sebastian looked a little sad. But I couldn't worry about his feelings right now—I was about to let myself be dragged in front of a bunch of people who'd likely happily hang me for being a witch.

"Tie the rope around my wrists, Sebastian. Let's get on with this before I change my mind."

CHAPTER THIRTY-EIGHT

He pulled too hard and I stumbled and slipped along the slick cobblestones, but I silently begged him not to look back, not to show concern. Already people gathered on the street to watch their lord drag me toward the town center.

Night fell with alarming speed and obscured the tops of buildings in gloomy dark. The clang of the blacksmith's hammer still rung out interrupted by the burst of his bellows. Children clipped closer on their small-heeled boots until mothers grabbed their skinny arms to pull them back. A couple farmers, tossing empty grain sacks into the back of a wagon, stopped in their work to stare as we passed.

After a moment, the tavern door burst open and Emméline came out with a group of men and women. Papa stumbled out behind them. I peered at them all through my lashes until Sebastian pulled me away. I didn't want Papa to see this. He'd think I'd done something wrong, been too weak or not smart enough to stay safe.

"My lord." Père Danil swept forward with his black robes billowing and his big wooden crucifix bumping against his chest. "What is this?"

Sebastian hesitated and I willed him to say the words. He took a breath and did. "I've caught the witch who's killing children."

The priest pinched his lips into a grimace. "How do you know it's her?"

"I saw it, the most evil thing I've ever experienced. She . . . controls the animal."

I couldn't fault Sebastian for his acting. It was quite convincing—even I felt the passion in his words. In fact, it was unnerving.

The priest's cheeks lit with a self-righteous glow I wanted to slap away. He blinked slowly and nodded gravely, like every movement he made was so vastly important it needed to be savored. He thought he'd won and he wanted to make the moment last.

I gritted my teeth so I wouldn't spit on his boots.

"We'll take her and clean her," the priest said.

Sebastian pulled the rope and I stumbled a little closer to him.

"Lock her in the cell in the church," he said.

"No." Emméline stepped free from the crowd. Her

simple dress rustled against her legs as she rushed toward us. Her eyes shone with greed. She ran them over me and I flinched away.

"We should burn her now," she said. "Lay bare her evil so she can be saved."

The girl smiled at me, pleased, and all the confidence I'd felt in this plan drained away. Even Sebastian couldn't control the tide of anger. These people, thirsty for something, anything to call justice for their dead children—they'd satisfy themselves on my humiliation.

Emméline's eyes bore into mine with a flash of triumph that made me catch my breath. This is what she wanted—to pin the blame on someone else. If she was the killer, she'd likely strike again tonight to prove that the witch was angry and controlled the beast and that together they brought evil unto this town. Frenzy would fizz through my neighbors. They'd take me out, make me stand among them while they threw their accusations and fears at me like rotten cabbages. I'd become their effigy—the one to burn because they couldn't burn the beast.

Panic flared in my chest as the stares of the townspeople bore down on me. I ached for Papa to step forward, tell the people they couldn't do this, and take me home. Even though I knew he wouldn't. Even though it wasn't part of the plan.

He didn't step forward. He didn't say a word.

It shouldn't have hurt, not after years of him showing me he couldn't love me properly. But it did.

I swallowed and forced my face to settle into hard lines

against Emméline's unsettling stare. Fury rose like mist in the crowd, twisting, feeding, growing. They changed from watchers to crusaders in two beats of my heart.

Suddenly, it was clear how simple our plan had been. Too simple. We hadn't accounted for how wild fear could be. We'd thought they'd let Sebastian lead me out, wrists bound, by the authority of his position. I'd hoped they'd stew in their anger and whispers and encourage the killer to kill again—if only to prove the townspeople did indeed have something to be angry about.

But now their anger and fear swirled around me like an unstoppable current, and Emméline stood in their midst, arms raised like a Greek goddess, calling up a storm.

"Your curse leaks like poison through the streets, witch." She spat, but the little glob of spittle landed wide of my boot.

Cries of agreement rang out from the crowd. Men bobbed their heads up and down, risking their hats. Women pursed their lips and pushed their children behind their wide skirts. *If only that were enough to keep them safe.*

Sebastian raised his hands, pulling my wrists up with his, but the townspeople didn't fall silent. His command lacked the authority of his title. The odd nature of this, the capture of a witch, seemed to afford the people certain liberties.

"We can't let this evil live in our town," Père Danil said.

"A trial first," Sebastian cut in, "in case the king's magistrates come calling. We don't want them to find we did anything wrong."

"Yes, yes of course. A trial in the morning. Tonight we

shall keep her locked up so she can't spread her evil any further," Père Danil said.

Emméline stepped forward and grabbed for the rope binding my hands together.

"She can control the beast from anywhere, locked up or no. Witches have the magic to bend the rules."

I almost shook my head, ready to deny any magic, but this was exactly what we wanted. We needed the killer to come out tonight so Sebastian could see who it was.

Père Danil pinned me with a glassy black stare. A purple blush swept under his deep-set eyes.

"I see you, Marie Michaud," he hissed. "I see the chaos in your soul."

An unsettling heat licked my stomach. *Could he really see the questions in my heart? I'd guarded them so well. But maybe you could only wonder for so long whether evil lived in the one you loved most without it showing around your eyes.*

The heat fled my body and left a dreadful ache of exhaustion in its wake. I'd been holding myself *just so* for too long. It was taxing to pretend—to try and fade into them without them noticing. To put on the appearance of a life I didn't have in hopes one day I would. To smile and hand bottles of scent into silk-gloved hands and act like I wouldn't have to choose who my sister would kill that night.

My knees buckled under me and Sebastian put a steadying hand under my elbow. The others jeered, glad for my weakness. This was a spectacle to them, a show they'd write to their cousins about.

Well, fine. I'm used to pretending anyway.

"The devil walks these streets." I let the *s* slide off my tongue smooth as silk. "He calls to me and I answer. I unleash his servant into the night and someone else will die when the moon rises!"

It was a challenge for the real killer. If it *was* someone like Père Danil or Emméline behind all this, they would want to make sure to kill tonight so it looked like I'd fulfilled my threat. But if the killer did take the bait, they'd have Sebastian with his hunting knife and musket to contend with.

Sebastian dropped the rope and stared at me with his mouth open. I hadn't told him I'd start proclaiming myself a witch in the streets. His reaction lent a certain authenticity to the moment. I ran with it.

"I've tricked you. All of you. And it was easy."

Père Danil fumbled forward to pick up the fallen rope. "Sorceress, wife of darkness, why have you done this to our town?"

He stared up at me, reverent. What looked like a spark of pride lit up his eyes. The death of innocents, the unveiling of a witch made him special. In a moment, he'd been elevated to circles of God's most precious servants. He'd become a chosen one—a deliverer from evil. A savior. A saint.

He had all the benefits that came with prestige as reasons to want to draw attention to the killings of a ferocious beast and a sinister witch in his lonely little town. Without the horrible deaths, the king likely would never have even heard the name of it. Certainly, he'd never have heard of Père Danil.

I hoped Sebastian saw the gleam in the withering man's pink-rimmed eyes and realized what it might mean.

Shouts erupted from the crowd with the force of bullets from a musket.

"Kill her now!"

"Burn her! The beast will die without its master!"

"Enough debate, take her to the oubliette!"

The oubliette.

My whole body sank, folded in on itself, cowering, as my blood froze in my veins. The oubliette was a hole dug deep into the ground at the town's edge. A tunnel of damp earth with nothing but worms for company. Sometimes we forgot about the poor drifters thrown in, and we'd discover their bones, draped in rotting linen shirts, a year or so later.

The oubliette was one of the deepest punishments. Rumors rose like dust from peddlers' packs—the king had forbidden oubliettes. The queen was so afraid of the dark holes, she'd asked her husband to board them all up.

But it hardly mattered here. We were so far away from court, we could choose to interpret the king's laws as our priest and magistrate saw fit. Which meant they could throw me in the oubliette if they wanted and leave me there until my bones were clean.

"You can't take her to the oubliette," Sebastian shouted over the crowd.

"Why not?" the baker asked. A shiny burn on his cheek glinted in the light of the torch in his hand.

"She should be kept in the church; it would be safer. The devil hates sanctified ground."

I bit the end of my tongue and tried to focus on that pain instead of the possibility of what might really happen to me. *This is part of the plan.* I repeated those words inside my head over and over again, but I didn't really believe them. Nothing about this felt within my control anymore. These people—the ones I'd spent years wanting to be part of—were more than ready to sacrifice me for their own salvation.

I shouldn't have been surprised. But I was and I hated myself for it. Hadn't I learned this yet? With a father who preferred his ale to his children and a sister who swept in front of me whenever we entered a room, shouldn't I have realized this *was* normal? People's own lives were always more important to them than anyone else's.

There was no position to cling to, no sympathy to tug at. But I wouldn't let them stamp me out like the wavering flame of a cheap candle.

"The oubliette won't hold me," I said, trying to plant a seed of doubt. If they thought a witch could escape the oubliette, they might lock me in the church and I could handle that. Anything but a hole in the ground.

The crowd grumbled. Emméline's white teeth nipped at her lip. She quirked her mouth into the ghost of a smile and I couldn't stop a shiver from running down my spine. Papa watched me with the slack look I'd learned to associate with one too many pints.

"We will put her in the oubliette for the night and hold

the trial after matins," the priest said to Sebastian. "The magistrate will question her."

I whipped my head around to Sebastian, but he wouldn't meet my gaze.

"I want to be there," Sebastian said to Père Danil.

"Whatever you wish, my lord."

"Good."

Sebastian looked as though he didn't know whether to stay or turn away. The priest tugged on my rope and I stumbled on the cobbles beneath my boots.

"One more thing, my lord." Père Danil's voice simpered, rich but prim. "When you write a letter to the king about our vanquishing, I hope you will mention my key part in this discovery of the devil's servant. The eye of the king would be a great benefit to our little church."

Sour bile coated the back of my throat. I swallowed to rid myself of the taste as the image of pilgrims leaving their hard-earned coins at the foot of this priest's church pulsed in my mind. I would not be a part of this man's immortalization.

"I might remember," Sebastian said, and I wanted to kiss his cheek for the way his words wiped the smug look from the priest's face.

The night air fell even cooler. I was tired of standing there in the street with my wrists bound. It was time to get on with it.

"The beast calls to me," I whispered low so Père Danil had to lean in. When he was close enough, I slipped my tongue between my lips and touched the soft, curved flesh of his ear.

He jumped back as if scalded and I grinned at him, eyes wide and full of false desire.

"Mistress Poitres," the priest said. "Take her."

"Stand up." Emméline lifted my arm and I let her. She took the knife from her belt, wrapped herself around me so the whole side of her blade kissed the delicate skin of my neck.

"Walk."

I did because I had to. This was the plan. And because there was nowhere else to go. Papa wouldn't help me—if I somehow escaped, he'd probably hand me back over to Père Danil just to earn some goodwill. Sebastian wasn't going to fight harder to keep me out of the oubliette—it would seem too strange and foil our plan. I understood and yet . . . I couldn't help feeling like he was abandoning me too.

The woods on the side of the village never looked more welcoming. The trees and shadows tugged at my heart. Ama was in there somewhere. All I wanted to do now was go to her. She was the only comfort I'd ever known and I ached for her now.

"Keep moving." Emméline's voice shot into my ear.

We stumbled back through town, an awkward four-legged animal. When we approached the church, I paused but Emméline pushed me forward, the blade biting into my skin.

It was only then that panic truly licked at me like a flame.

CHAPTER THIRTY-NINE

I t was a peculiar kind of fear—the kind where you picture the thing you're afraid of over and over but it's still worse than you ever imagined. The oubliette was like that.

A gaping hole cut into the earth. A grave for people and memories. The oubliette—the forgetting place. This was where I'd disappear.

"In," Emméline said, her knife still at my throat.

"How?"

There was no ladder and no rope. A fall that far could break bones. Emméline twisted her head to stare at me. She lifted her knife away from my throat before cutting my ropes away. Then she used the full force of her body to push me in.

The weightlessness of falling lasted only a moment. The pain of the impact lasted much longer. I hit the ground with a solid squelch of mud, and my arms and the thick sleeves of

Sebastian's hunting coat were the only things that protected my face from the many stones littering the dirt.

Up above, Emméline smiled. Bile rose in my throat and I spat on the ground.

"I always knew there was something off about you," she called. "You're not like us; you're cursed, tainted, and now everyone knows it."

"Do you think this will make the men accept you as your father's heir? Because it won't."

"They won't be able to deny I'm this town's best hunter when I bring the beast back to Versailles on a platter," she said. "I'll never be left out of a hunt again."

"You think you can get them to accept you?" I rasped through my pain. "They might learn to fear you, but you'll never be one of them."

Her smile slipped, making the exertion of talking up at her worth it.

"You don't know anything about them," she hissed. "They all laugh at your father when he trips out of the tavern, did you know that? No one trusts him or you or that sister of yours. Where is she anyway? Someone must have told her where I've taken you."

I couldn't trust myself to answer. My tongue tapped at the back of my front teeth and I pulled in thick, noisy breaths through my nose.

Emméline bent down, hands hanging over the lip of the hole.

"Do you want to know something? My papa never wanted

a son. He was always happy with just me. Loved me so much he kept little bits of my hair and my baby teeth in a jar on the windowsill in the kitchen."

I cringed at the idea. Then something fell into place in my brain and I couldn't hold my tongue any longer.

"The milk teeth in the cellar . . . they were yours, weren't they? You put them there."

She grinned again. "I thought you might find them there and wonder what your sister's really been doing. I thought you'd come to suspect her. Hate her."

Did she know about Ama? Had she figured out exactly who the beast she was hunting really was?

"What do you mean suspect her? Suspect Ama of what?"

Emméline dipped her head lower over the lip of the hole. "The seamstress, the Carter boy, Maurice."

She drew out the soft sound at the end of Maurice's name and her spittle dropped down on me. I covered my face.

She knew. She'd worked it out about Ama, somehow. Maybe her time spent in the forest, maybe she watched us. None of it made sense. I'd only ever known her from afar. I wasn't one of the men who refused to let her join the hunt. I had nothing she could want.

"Why do you hate me so much?"

Her eyes darkened and the grin twisted into something else, something crueler. The points of her eye teeth pressed into her lips.

"You and her, always walking through town with linked arms, lost in a world none of the rest of us were invited to."

"What are you talking about?"

"It never mattered that no one in town wanted anything to do with you, did it? Because you had each other already. I tried and tried to be exactly what they wanted, what Papa wanted, but no one would have me the way I was. I was alone at home, at school, in town."

She might not have meant to reveal so much. Splotches of pink appeared on her cheeks and she sniffed furiously as if to ward off tears. I never imagined Emméline to be lonely.

"You're upset I have a sister and you don't?"

"A friend God gave you," she said, wrapping her arms around herself and standing back up. The movement loosened some dirt from the edge of the hole that fell down into my face. I covered my eyes to protect them, and when I opened them again, all hints of Emméline's sudden confession were gone. Her face was smooth and bright again, eyes level and strong.

"You're alone now though," she continued. "And you will be for the rest of your life."

"That doesn't mean you won't be. You haven't gained anything by throwing me in here."

I'd found her so interesting once, enviable. Now I knew she was nothing more than a child who thought hurting someone else would lessen her own pain.

Her lips lifted into a smile again. "Well, soon I'll forget you."

Then Emméline's face disappeared from the opening. Once I heard her walk away, I shifted my weight and tested my legs. Nothing seemed to be broken, but everything ached.

I balanced in a crouch until my ankles screamed and I had to admit defeat. There was nothing to sit on except the mud, and I couldn't avoid it. I fanned out my skirts a bit so it was almost like sitting on a blanket in a meadow—if the meadow wriggled with worms and beetles and the blanket was a stinking scrap of fabric.

Tears spilled from the corners of my eyes and left warm tracks down my cheeks. I wiped at my nose with my sleeve and hated that I still wore Sebastian's coat. I despised that it was the only thing keeping me from freezing. I was still, irrationally, angry at him for letting me go to the oubliette in the first place.

I didn't want his help—not even this way—but I wasn't about to surrender my skin to the winter air for the sake of my pride. I was too practical for that.

The sky faded into the gray-blue of dawn, but I didn't sleep. I stared up until the stars winked their good nights and the sun's rays chased away the final vestiges of night.

CHAPTER FORTY

Sometimes I was able to find hope in the beginning of a new day. Something about the sunrise spoke of possibility, and I often clung to it. *Today, Papa could decide to change. Today could mark his last drink. Today I could find the key to ridding Ama of the beast. Today I could save her.*

But today I knew I would languish in a hole in the ground. Today I would shiver until all my muscles ached. Today I might eat dirt to stop the shooting pains in my empty stomach.

The only thing I could hope was that the killer had tried to strike again and Sebastian hadn't gotten hurt when he confronted them. I hoped he did what we'd discussed—wrapped an old cloak around him to hide the knife and musket, then crouched down in front of the church after the streets emptied. If it worked, we could show the villagers who the *real* killer was and clear my and Ama's names. We'd try the book again, sing all the spells inside until one worked with Sebastian's blood. I could finally be free from all this, and all it might take was one day as a prisoner in the oubliette.

There might be hope after all.

❖

"Marie."

Papa's familiar voice woke me and I opened my eyes to find him peering over the edge of the oubliette. His long hair looked clean and he'd tied it back with a blue ribbon that looked ridiculous with his worn trousers and yellowed shirt. But at least he wasn't dressed for hunting.

He tossed me a small loaf of bread, but I wasn't awake enough to catch it and it landed in the mud. I picked it up and wiped it off with my skirt before tearing into the warmth of it with my teeth.

"I can't be seen to be helping you."

I swallowed, the bread sticky in my dry throat. I'd need something to drink soon.

"Are you helping me?"

Papa glanced around. He wasn't drunk—sleep had healed him and it was too early yet for him to have been able to drink enough ale or wine to unsettle him. Morning had always been my favorite time of the day with my father . . . it was a moment of clarity before the alcohol took him away from me again.

"You've tied yourself to this, Marie. What can I do now?"

"You can save Ama."

He shook his head. "Death is her only escape."

Tears welled again and I looked down at my boots so Papa wouldn't see. After a moment, I cleared my throat and said, "Did anything happen last night? An attack?"

I was desperate for news of Sebastian. The image of a monster, Emméline, pouncing on him while he squatted in front of the church kept tormenting me.

Papa pursed his lips under his ruddy mustache. "Nothing. You said there would be, but there was no attack."

That meant one of two things—Sebastian saw the killer, who I was almost certain was Emméline or Père Danil, and stopped her, or the killer didn't take the bait. I wanted to know but couldn't ask Papa. But he would have told me if Sebastian had been hurt, so I didn't have to worry now.

"Did you believe anything I said yesterday?"

He shook his head and gave me a long stare. "Of course not. I don't think you're a witch, not like that."

"But maybe like Aurélie?"

Papa flinched away from her name. "No, not like her either."

I stared up at my father's haggard face. His watery eyes peered down at me, and even in the gloom, the red lines of broken veins crept out like spiderwebs from his nose. He was too far away to know for sure, but I could imagine how he smelled—the musk of a worked-in shirt tinged with the sour notes of last night's ale. I knew that smell so intimately, and it hurt to think it had become comforting to me.

"What are you doing here, Papa?" I asked.

"You're still my daughter. I had to see this for myself."

"Why? So, you could make sure I can't get out?"

His features twisted with pain and I reveled in it—for once it was me hurting him and not the other way around.

"Marie, I never wanted this for you or Ama."

"So, help me."

"You know I can't without them throwing me in too."

I waited for the tingle of shock, for surprise to flutter through my heart, but it didn't. Somewhere deep inside, I'd expected this.

"You must understand, Marie— "

"No," I cut him off. "I don't have to do anything for you anymore. Why didn't you tell me about Aurélie before? I could have kept the secret. I'm good at secrets."

Papa bowed his head and the wind whipped around him, whistling over the top of the hole and pulling at his tied-back hair.

"Just leave me, Papa."

I wanted to be alone with the worms, and I buried my face in the bulk of my sleeves. I felt Papa's gaze on the top of my head for a time, but I refused to look up at him again. He might seek absolution from the priest, but he wouldn't get any from me.

After a time, I heard the rustling of his clothes as he stood and walked away. Only then did I peer up at the gaping mouth of the oubliette again. Soft puffs of white cloud whispered across a pale blue sky. It might have been a beautiful day if not for the frosted mud at my feet. My legs prickled and I had to shift my position and lean against the earthen wall. Roots stuck out and dug into the back of my head. I ground my skin against them, glad of the pain. It burned and I welcomed it over the frozen numbness of my toes. *Where is Sebastian?*

I closed my eyes and wished for Ama. I didn't care which form—the silken shag of her fur or the crisp crinkle of her eyes when she laughed—either would do. I just wanted to feel her close. To know someone loved me.

I wrapped my arms around myself and shoved my stiff fingers in my pockets. They ran into something smooth and hard—the rib bones. I'd forgotten my promise to bring the woman home. I could bury her here with me, in the oubliette, but she had already been forgotten, and leaving her here seemed especially cruel.

The bones shone white in the dark gloom of the hole. *Will mine look just like hers? If I'm left in here, will I wither until my skin falls away and reveals what is underneath? Will I become this—forgotten pieces of a once-upon-a-time girl?*

It didn't seem fair. Surely, she'd deserved more than this. This girl would have mattered to someone. She would have been missed. I dragged one rib bone through the mud to start a hole. Whoever she had been, she might deserve more than the oubliette, but it wasn't within my power to give her anything else. Not now that everything had been taken away from me.

I dug deeper, past stones and the odd scampering beetle. The warm scent of wet earth clung to my nostrils. Snow had fallen here and melted into frozen muck. This was all that was left to us, me and the dead girl. Dirt and bugs and endless shivering.

The mud parted way for the bone like butter for a hot knife. I took another one and scraped away at the earth with a rib bone in each fist. Deeper and deeper, harder and harder. I tore into the dirt as if it were everything I hated, everything I was angry at. My chest heaved with great, pulling breaths and my skin buzzed with something akin to desire.

Tears flowed unchecked down my cheeks and the salt stung my broken lips.

I won't forget you, I told the pieces of the dead girl.

With a great sob, I realized I was talking to myself and not the bones at all. *I* mattered. My wishes and dreams were solid things with as much importance as anyone else's. I couldn't rely on Papa or Ama or Sebastian to give them to me or shape them for me. That was something only I could do for myself.

I stopped digging. The bones rested heavily in my red, raw hands and I flung one into the side of the earthen wall. It stuck. I pulled it and tried to wrench it free. It didn't come easily. It might work. I didn't have to wait for Sebastian to pull me out of this hole. I could climb out myself.

I reached as high as I could and jammed one of the rib bones into the wall of the oubliette. Then I reached up with my other hand and stuck the second bone in. Gripping both, I pulled myself up and tried to find purchase with my boots. I had to balance my feet on a tiny protruding root, steadying my weight with one bone in the wall while I pulled the other one free. Then my boots slipped. My stomach swooped with sudden weightlessness. Sweat prickled all over my body. I pulled out one bone and dug it into a place a little further up the wall. Then again with the second. Found purchase with my feet. Climbed. I stabbed the first bone into the mud and the earth again and it hit against something—a stone or a root—and I lost my balance.

I plummeted toward the bottom of the hole. Pain split through me, hacking, relentless. All my bones were breaking. My skin was ripping apart. I squeezed my eyes closed but I heard everything—the whoosh of air, the scurrying of the bugs in the wall of dirt, the dead leaves rustling at the lip of the oubliette.

I landed hard, but the pain melted away. Opening my eyes, I stared down at my legs, ready to assess whether or not they were broken. But the bones weren't cracked. They'd been remade.

Where I'd expected to see my mangled skirt and pale calves above my boots, there was golden fur. Thick paws, claws extending down into the dirt. My jaw cracked as I opened it and flicked my tongue out to discover the sharp points of my teeth. I was like Ama. A beast. A monster.

I'd always thought it was just Ama. Yes, I'd woken with scratches on my body, nightgown shed in the night, but I thought I just walked in my sleep. Now I knew the truth: I'd been turning. And now that I was in this body, I remembered.

Wisps of memories floated in. The splitting pain of my bones cracking and reshaping, the heightened smell of pine and snow, and the warm scent of fur and flesh. The taste of blood on my tongue.

Did I kill those children?

The beast's body couldn't feel nausea like my human body could, because if I'd been human in that moment I would have vomited. I'd been trying to do the least amount of harm I could while still keeping Ama's secret, feeding her so she didn't fade away or die. I'd tried so hard.

But I couldn't have done those terrible things. I was in the beast's body now and my mind was still mine. I could think, feel. Make choices. Even if I hadn't wanted to remember after turning back, I wasn't as entwined with the beast as Ama said she was becoming. Relief rushed through me, making me want to move my new, more powerful muscles.

My human arms and legs couldn't climb up out of this hole, not even with the rib bones to help, but I had claws now. I squatted and launched myself, moving with an ease that proved to me I'd been in this body before. Dirt and mud fell away from the wall under my claws and I scrabbled to the top of the oubliette. I hauled myself over the side and fell back on my haunches, looking around and sniffing the frost-scented air. The warm smell of blood, the heady scent of fur, and the slip of small paws on frozen mud told me a fox was nearby. I tried to pull the scent of humans out from the tapestry of the forest, like a piece of string, but I wasn't sure. Papa had been here earlier, and it might have been him who left behind the tang of unwashed skin.

The top of Sebastian's house peeked over the jutting

edge of the forest, and I knew I had to go find him. I wanted to know if it had been worth it—if Sebastian knew who the killer was now.

I tasted freedom on the winter-sharp breeze. Wisps of fog shrouded the road leading up to the manor house—to Sebastian. I let them wash over me, hide me, like I'd called them up myself. My own soft, padded footsteps were the only sounds I heard and I counted them in my head to calm myself. *One, two, three, four.*

Something smelled strange on the air. Sweet. Warm. Not at all like the sour smell of Papa.

I stopped dead and turned around. There were the woods on the side of the road and the silhouette of the town in the distance. And Emméline.

She stood with her legs planted wide, hair streaming down her back, free from its usual braid.

"You're more beautiful than I thought you'd be." She smiled. "I like a challenging hunt."

I ran as fast as my four legs could carry me.

CHAPTER FORTY-ONE

Emméline's steps beat out against the dirt like the steady ticks of a clock. My new body fought against cold and hunger, but hers had recently been in a warm bed, and she probably had breakfast in her belly, meat. All that sat in my belly was dry oat bread and fear.

I pushed my numb legs, stamping out an unruly pattern as I swerved from one side of the road to the other. Pain ricocheted through my insides, burning, tearing. My bones bent underneath me and I fell, skidding to the side of the road. In the space of a breath, I was me again. Human and naked. Fragile and exposed. Emméline ran toward me, closing the gap my animal advantage had given me. The big house stood indifferent at the top of the hill. If I got there first, I could try and lock myself inside. I rolled to my feet and ran.

As I breached the drive, I pulled in a burning breath and took a precious second to look behind me. Emméline tore up the hill, dress flapping around her legs.

"It's you!" she screamed. "You!"

The gate to the garden jutted out from the side of the house at a haphazard angle. I pushed on the cold iron and forced it over the flagstones. Then I pulled the gate closed behind me and melted into the shadows.

The winter roses had closed in on themselves, sheltering their petals in the night. The garden blushed with their frost-tipped scent. The deep green leaves pillowed the red flowers and the bulk of the bushes cast shadows on the gravel path. I couldn't walk there—it would be too loud. I balanced my steps on the little strip of wood outlining the path instead and followed it to the lonely bench set under the weeping tree. A crackle of gravel under heavy boots almost made me fall.

I strained my ears, listening to every breath of the wind and rustle of a mouse. She was in here with me.

I jumped the expanse of the path and landed in the dirt of a flowerbed. Suddenly aware of my height, I dropped into a crouch and crawled deeper into the bed on my hands and knees, branches grabbing at my back. Two rosebushes branched out from their roots and mingled their leaves and flowers, leaving a little space between their lower branches. Another crack of gravel. She didn't even care if I heard her.

I pushed desperately through the rough branches of the

rosebushes, but my body wouldn't fit. I gripped two branches from the other side and pulled until my hips scraped against the wood and I tumbled into the tiny space. Thorns caught in my hair and tore my skin when I tried to slip free. I hoped they'd protect me as they protected the roses.

"You're in here, aren't you, Marie?" she called.

My whole body tensed and I held my breath—as if even that would betray me. I was like a rabbit, trapped, with nothing to do but wait for the wolf's yellow eyes to shine in my direction.

"You don't want more people to die, do you, Marie?"

I hated the way my name sounded in her mouth, too sweet. Sweat ran down my forehead and froze in the bite of winter air. I pressed my hands into the dirt again and peered through the leaves. Emméline's legs moved ever closer. If she found me here, I wouldn't be able to get free. I had to move now.

The space between the bushes looked even smaller from the inside, so I rolled out from under the other side in a tangle of leaves and branches pulling at my hair. But when I turned onto my stomach, a twig snapped under me.

"Got you."

I stood now, while sweat dripped down my spine and turned cold on my legs. Fear pressed in on me, making it hard to breathe, but Emméline already knew where I was and I'd be faster on my feet. I pumped my legs again and took off down a dark path hugging the side of the house. There was a door here I'd never seen before. I could only hope it wasn't locked.

Emméline approached behind me. She took her time now, assured in her victory. Like an animal closing in on easy prey.

But that was her mistake. I wasn't prey.

With a turn of a cold brass knob, I swung open the small wooden door and tumbled into a dark room. On the other side, I slid the bolt in place and fell to my knees. Musty air ripped my raw throat, but I couldn't stop gulping it in. I wiped the cold sweat from my upper lip and forehead on the back of my hand. I was safe for a moment and I'd take it. My heart slowly steadied as I closed my eyes and leaned against the solid door separating Emméline and me.

After a few steadying breaths, I looked around. I'd never seen this room before. It looked like some sort of antechamber. Empty wood-paneled walls surrounded me and I stood on quivering legs. A door set into one wall was slightly ajar. Candlelight flickered in whatever room it led to. I hoped there would be clothing inside.

I pushed open the door. Tall, slim white candles stood like sentinels from the many sconces lining the room. A long, rectangular wooden altar took up most of the space. The body of a woman was laid out on it, her hands folded neatly over her heart. Heaps of dried roses, cut from their stems, surrounded her, so no wood of the altar showed through. Her blue dress clung to the curves of her body. Her features were so familiar, mirroring those of a face I had gazed at so many times but without the deep blush that so often bloomed in his cheeks. Her skin looked as though it would be hard to the touch.

On a chair in the corner of the room, Sebastian stared at me, the spell book in his hands, my own shock reflected in his eyes.

I covered myself as best I could, not sure which emotion to give in to—embarrassment or fear. Sebastian stood and swept his cloak from the chair beside him in one smooth movement. He draped it over my shoulders while keeping his eyes on the ceiling. I pulled it tight around me.

"Marie," he whispered, and I flinched. Any sound in this strange room was too loud. This eerie place should be utterly silent.

I shook my head and tried again to make sense of what I saw. Now that I had something covering me, my mind was clearer. This was Sebastian's dead mother, I was sure of it, but she'd been gone for a year. How was it her skin hadn't fallen away from her bones? Why did Sebastian keep her here like a morbid ornament?

"What is this?"

He cupped his hands, the long fingers coming together. "You'll understand when I explain."

"No, I don't think I will."

"Marie..." he tried again, but I turned away from him, back to the living corpse of his mother.

"You said the beast killed your parents."

I'd thought they'd been Ama's first kill. I'd felt guilty

about it—knowing my sister had caused Sebastian such sadness. Even though his mother was the one to curse Ama in the first place, I'd actually felt sorry for the woman's son.

"The beast did kill them."

I gestured to the woman on the altar. "Not very thoroughly."

Sebastian sighed. "Papa was torn to bits and Maman was left barely breathing. I brought her back here."

"But that was a year ago! What is she now?"

Every one of my instincts wanted to get away from this woman. Nothing about this was right.

Sebastian closed his eyes and ran his fingers along his brow.

"It's not so simple, Marie."

"Your mother was here the whole time and you let me run around the forest searching for someone with an answer... a cure!"

"There's more than one witch in this valley, Marie."

"But it wasn't Aurélie. She wasn't the one who cursed Ama."

Sebastian shook his head. "No, I don't think so."

"It was your mother!"

He stood very still and wouldn't meet my eyes. My knees gave way and I slid down the wall behind me to sit on my haunches. Too much had happened since last night and I couldn't let it all in. If I did, it would tear me apart. Ama, the curse, me. The memory of how that body felt, how I moved inside it, wasn't far away.

Finally, Sebastian said, "If she did, she was trying to protect us."

"Did you know about the spell book the whole time?"

"No, I swear. I didn't know what it was or what it could do," he said.

Did I believe him? I wasn't sure. He could be lying.

My heart shattered into pieces. Sebastian's betrayal, the endlessness of the lies, rolled over me like waves on a lake. I couldn't get my bearings, couldn't breathe. It was easiest to slip into anger. Anger was mine to control. I could spit it at him like venom. Sebastian couldn't hurt me if I hated him.

"What happened last night? Did the plan work? Did the killer try to attack you?"

"Yes."

His single-word answer pricked my nerves. We were past games now.

"So, who was it? Emméline? Did she try to attack you?"

"It was the beast . . . Ama. I'm so sorry, Marie. It looked just like her and there was no one else around. Emméline wasn't there."

My mouth worked but nothing came out because I couldn't give the shattering of my heart the proper language. Pieces lodged themselves in my insides until pain wracked my whole body. My knees gave out, unwilling to hold my weight anymore, and I slid further down the wall, out of Sebastian's circle of light, back into the darkness.

Ama. I'd been so worried, but I hadn't ever really wanted

to believe it. I'd worked so hard to make sure she wouldn't fall to the nature of the beast. I'd sacrificed my soul to save hers—marking people like I was some kind of angel of death. And she'd thrown it all away. She'd let the beast win.

"Marie."

Sebastian's voice drifted to me as if through the waters of a rushing river. Ama and I used to bathe in the little stream in the woods behind our cottage. We'd play we were sea monsters and mermaids, dipping our heads under the shallow water and opening our eyes to a strange blurred world we didn't belong to. This felt like that. I couldn't belong to a world where Ama was a monster.

CHAPTER FORTY-TWO

I stared up at Sebastian. I could tell him what happened to me at the bottom of the oubliette, but I was sure it wasn't me who came to him last night. I only transformed *after* Papa visited in the morning. If Sebastian saw a monster, it had to have been my sister.

"We need to wake your mother, Sebastian. Bring her out of whatever state she's in."

He paled in the low light. "You can't."

"We have to. She's the only one who can read her book of spells . . . the only one with the cure to Ama's curse."

Sebastian shook his head, bit his lip. "She's frozen in the moment before death. If you wake her, she'll slip away."

"It's the only way, Sebastian," I said, wishing it weren't. "I need her to read the book of spells."

"Please don't take her from me."

"You don't have her now!"

His features broke into those of a child, a little boy looking for reassurance. But I couldn't give it to him.

"She's nothing more than a statue to you! You sit beside her the same way you'd sit beside her gravestone. Look at her! You haven't saved her, Sebastian. You've only delayed the inevitable. If we wake her now, at least her final moments could save Ama's and Lucien's lives!"

"Lucien isn't dying!"

"Not yet, but he will! Consumption will take him eventually. All you're doing is waiting for that day."

Tears ran unabashedly down Sebastian's freckled cheeks and I ached to pull him to me. His sadness sat heavy in my belly, fighting against my anger toward him. He'd lied to me the whole time, and I'd given him so much of my truth. He knew about Ama, knew my greatest secret, and yet he'd kept his own from me. I didn't want Lucien to die either, but I wouldn't comfort Sebastian now.

I couldn't know what went through his mind as he stared at me with wet, shimmering eyes. But after a shallow breath, he nodded.

"What do you think you're going to do, Marie? Shake her awake?"

That stung a little. I thought he knew me better than that by now.

"Foxglove could start her heart back up."

"Or it might kill her right away."

Guilt washed over me as a look of pain spread over his eyes. "I need to talk to her, need her to read the book of spells or tell me how. It all comes back to *her*."

The candles lighting the space flickered. *Who lights them,* I wondered. *Sebastian? Madame Écrue? Does she know her mistress is suspended in this half a life? Probably.*

Sebastian nodded and began walking toward the altar. He knew this room and the precise way to step around his mother without bumping any candles or accidentally touching her. He kept a space between them. I wondered if he was scared of touching her . . . of what he might, or might not, feel under her skin.

I pulled myself to my feet and followed him, finally really looking at the woman before us.

Her waxen skin had a gray tinge, as if the blood had drained from it. Her lips peeled and her dull curly hair spilled over her shoulders. Perhaps she had the same soft brown eyes as Sebastian, but veined eyelids covered them from view.

The same sense of the uncanny I'd had when washing Maurice's body nipped at me with its sharp teeth. She was like us, but she wasn't.

She was frozen, caught in a pocket of time while the rest of the world moved around her. Waking her wouldn't be without its risks. What if time came to claim the year she'd been lying here, shriveling her skin and robbing her heart of the final beats it should have taken? But it was a risk I had to take. Waking her was the only way to figure out how to read her book.

"How did you do it, Sebastian?" I asked.

Magic clouded the room. This frozen half life could only have been achieved with a spell, and Sebastian hadn't had the power necessary to stop the curse in Lucien when we'd tried. He couldn't have done this on his own.

Sebastian was very quiet, as if afraid to disturb his mother. He glanced at me but wouldn't meet my eyes, and I knew another secret was about to deepen the space between us.

"It was Aurélie."

Shock numbed me for a moment, but I shook it off and thought back to our meeting with my aunt. I'd wondered why they'd stared so fiercely at each other. Now I knew it was because they shared this secret. I remembered Aurélie's words to him: *Even though I gave her to you? Even though she lingers on the cusp of time?*

He'd kept it all from me.

"She helped you because she was your mother's friend?"

Sebastian finally slipped his hand under his mother's still fingers—touching her for the first time since I'd entered the room. A small ache thrummed in my heart for him, but I had to ignore it. He'd lied to me, more than once, and he could because he was a lord. There would be no consequences for him. Unless they came from me. I'd harden against Sebastian to show him he couldn't do just anything to *me*.

"Aurélie loved my mother and Maman loved her back," he said. "Papa knew, I think, but he ignored it every time Maman took the path into the woods. When Maman and Papa were hurt, I rode into the trees, down the same path I saw Maman take. I knew I'd find the friend I'd seen before . . . I wanted her help, someone to heal Maman, who cared for her . . . not with magic but with love. Aurélie came back with me and that was the first time I ever saw magic. She couldn't save Maman from her injuries, but she used a spell to freeze her before her death."

Aurélie and Madame LaClaire. When we were playing hide-and-seek, Lucien had said he used to hear and see things outside his windows. It couldn't have been Ama, because she was still at home with me then. Lucien was seeing things before she was turned into the beast for the first time. If Madame LaClaire cursed her, and maybe me, to protect her sons, there must have been a threat. People have always died in the woods, long before Ama became a monster. Maybe whoever was killing people now was responsible for threatening and scaring Lucien all those years ago.

But if Madame LaClaire chose Ama and me as protectors—monsters to fight a monster—Aurélie must have known. And she did nothing.

The betrayal was dulled by the time that had already passed. My aunt had never come to us anyway, never tried to be part of our lives after our mother died.

"Sebastian, did your mother ever tell you who she was protecting you from when she made the curse?"

He stared at me, eyes lighting up a little. He might have taken my talking to him as forgiveness, but it wasn't. We were so close and I wasn't going to give up now. I still needed him.

"These huge wolves would come out of the forests and

right up to our windows, especially the ones in Maman's bedroom. They'd paw at them and whine and scare Lucien. I always thought they were just animals and a musket blast would do away with them if we needed to protect ourselves. But Maman was terrified. She never let us outside alone and none of us could leave the house after dark. It was then she started spending more time with Aurélie."

"They came up with this curse together," I said. "Those two sacrificed my sister to protect you and your brother from a few animals?"

Sebastian rubbed the heels of his hands over his eyes. "I don't know, all right? She never told me what she was doing. All I have are guesses because she was dead before I could ask."

He bent his head and rested it on his mother's arm. I wondered if she still smelled the same to him.

"We need to do this, Sebastian. For the people we have left."

He nodded and pulled away with a sob. Pooled tears left shining spots on Madame LaClaire's dull skin. My heart ached again. I couldn't help it.

"What are you going to do?" Sebastian asked. "Will it hurt her?"

"I don't think so," I lied, and the familiar heat of guilt squirmed in my belly.

"There's some foxglove blossoms down in the kitchen," I went on, hoping he wouldn't ask how I knew that. "I can extract the nectar."

"All right." Sebastian nodded and stepped away from his mother's body. "Go get it."

I went quickly, opening the door from the chamber and propelling myself down the hallway, past the family room and grand staircase until I came to the servant's door. I hurried into the kitchen, into the hidden workroom. The stem of foxglove was right where I'd left it, and I squeezed out a few more drops of nectar with the flat edge of a knife. I collected them on the steel and ran the knife along the edge of the mouth of a little glass bottle. The nectar pooled inside, and I gripped the bottle in my fist so I could run all the way back to the chamber.

Sebastian sat with his back to me, head bent over his mother. He pulled in a deep, audible breath as I stood next to her and tipped the little bottle to her lips. Foxglove juice ran down the glass and slipped into the woman's barely open mouth.

Nothing happened.

I studied Sebastian's mother's chest. It didn't move up and down at all, but at the hollow of her throat, just above the square neckline of her dress, a pulse beat under her skin.

"It'll take more, I guess," I said.

Sebastian paled even further, a tinge of green shadowing his skin. I almost wanted to reach out to him, comfort him, but the sharp betrayal, his secrets and lies, kept my arms at my sides.

A shiver ran through me, and I had to suck a breath in through my teeth to keep myself steady. I couldn't help thinking this was magic I didn't want to be a part of. It was wrong. My teeth worked the inside of my lip, and I relished the pain when I bit too deep—the pain was real, understandable. Normal. I ached for normal. What we were doing here made my skin crawl.

"I'll try again," I said, unnecessarily, to give myself a moment before approaching the body for the second time. I tipped the bottle to the woman's lips again and held my breath.

CHAPTER FORTY-THREE

tiny flicker of her chest under her thin white chemise. A small beat of life. The poison had shocked her body and shaken off the spell.

A glow rose under her deathly pallor and returned the look of life to her cheeks, her chest, her hands. All at once, she trembled, and her chest rose up and down. She was breathing.

Sebastian threw himself at his mother, touching her hands, the pulse at her neck, the curve of her forehead and sweep of her hair.

"Maman!"

Pain broke his voice in two, and I couldn't keep the sadness from welling up in my chest and pushing a lump into my throat. Sebastian loved his mother so much he found a way to bind her to the earth when she'd been on the threshold of death. It must mean she loved him too. She had probably held him close when he cried. She might have taken his hand in church and played secret games with him while the priest droned on. Perhaps she saved him treats—his favorite petit fours or a pinch of special tea—just to see him smile. She had probably been a mother to him in all the ways mine never could be to me, and I tried to keep my jealousy from souring my stomach.

How could I think these things when he'd lost her? When she'd been as good as dead for a year?

I shook my head to clear it of these dark thoughts and bit the inside of my lip again. Sebastian's mother's mouth moved, and her hands shook as she tried to raise them. Sebastian soothed her, but her breathy grunts soon turned to a keening wail. Her fingers fluttered over her stomach and the fabric of her blue dress started to change. A deep red cloud devoured the pale blue silk, the spot starting in the middle and weeping to the sides of the embroidered stomacher.

"No, no!"

Sebastian looked to me, frantic, and I broke from my frozen stance. I ripped off a piece of fabric from my chemise, and used it to staunch the blood. I held it tight to Madame LaClaire's belly and pressed down while she gasped and sputtered.

"What's happening?" I asked.

Sebastian's stricken eyes flew to mine. "This is what I was afraid of. We did the spell after she and my father were attacked. She was injured then, but the magic froze her injuries too. Now she's awake and bleeding."

"She can't survive like this," I said as her blood ran between my fingers. "Get me a needle and thread, quick!"

Sebastian looked startled but he nodded and ran from the room. With him gone, I tried not to look at the eyes of this long-dying woman, but she drew my stare with a low moan.

"You," she whispered. "I feel you."

I dropped my pressure on Madame LaClaire's stomach and stepped away from her. Sebastian saved me from answering by flying back into the room holding a long needle and a spool of white thread, but her words lodged in my mind. Of course she could feel me. Her magic ran in my veins.

"Here." Sebastian thrust the sewing supplies into my empty hands and threw himself over his mother's belly once more. He pressed the cloth into her and tried to steady her quivering.

She stared at him now and her mouth opened again. "Bastian?"

His eyes lit up with such hope I couldn't help a little piece of my heart breaking off for them. They'd never truly be together again, but at least they had this stolen moment to say goodbye.

"We need to take the stomacher off," I said.

Sebastian looked up at me with a bloody streak across his cheek where he'd wiped away tears. "Will this save her?"

I thought about lying. I'd have done it before, just for the few moments of happiness it would have given him. But in the end, a lie would be much more painful than the truth.

"No. If I sew her up, I think it will buy us a little time, but she'll still die. She's hurt inside, Sebastian. No one can fix that."

He opened and closed his mouth a few times, as if tasting my words and deciding whether or not he could swallow them. Finally, he nodded, and I had to think that somewhere deep down he'd known her death had been inevitable from the moment the beast took a swipe across her belly.

We got to work. Sebastian held his mother's shaking body while I pulled her laces free and pried the blood-soaked stomacher away from her. Sebastian took the knife from his belt and tore her shift away from her stomach so we could see the damage. The gore brought bile into my throat, but I did my best to detach myself from all of it. I tried to think of it like I would a chicken or a pig that Papa had slaughtered. I'd butchered animals and cleaned bodies before. Seen others mauled. This didn't have to be so different.

Madame LaClaire's arm slipped from the altar. She pointed with a long finger at the little blue book tucked under Sebastian's arm.

"Pain," she rasped.

Sebastian seemed to understand at once because he picked up the book and turned to one of the first pages. The woman read the lines in blurred haste. Slowly, her brow smoothed and her lips lost their grimace. Sebastian breathed a sigh and closed the book.

"A spell against pain," he said.

"She might not feel it, but she's still dying." I didn't want him to raise any hopes to the contrary only to have them crushed when she finally left him for good.

But he nodded. "I know."

"Good, let's get on with it."

I threaded the needle while Madame LaClaire stared at her son and rubbed the skin of his hands over and over again with her thumbs. The pain spell had been incredibly effective.

"You've grown," she said to Sebastian. "I hardly know you. You're a man now, mon étoile."

He smiled, and the blush I'd come to know so well bloomed on his cheeks. I bent over my work so as not to intrude. Once I pushed everything back in, the skin was easy enough to pull together. My needlework was as good as any and I made neat little stiches across Madame LaClaire's belly while she gazed at the child she'd lost and would shortly lose again.

"What's happened?" she asked Sebastian.

"Lucien is sicker now."

"Nothing worked. I tried so many things," Sebastian's mother said. "I never had the right magic to save him."

"I know," Sebastian said. "We'll keep trying though, all right?"

"I never told you what I was . . . what Aurélie taught me to be. I'm sorry."

"A witch," Sebastian said.

His mother gave no acknowledgment to the word. Her eyes slid to me as I tied off the thread and cut it with my teeth.

"I feel you," she said, repeating her words from before.

"Yes, I imagine you do," I said, glancing up at Sebastian. He was going to find out somehow, and I didn't have time to be cryptic. "You cursed me and my sister."

"Cursed?" Her thinly plucked brows furrowed. "Is that what you think of it?"

I bit back a laugh. "Well, you turned us into beasts and now Ama is killing... children, so yes, I do think that."

"Not a beast. A savior."

"Us?" Sebastian cut in. "What are you talking about, Marie?"

He didn't deserve my honesty, but it was easiest to give it. "I turned while in the oubliette, into a beast like Ama. That's how I escaped."

"But you've never... you were here all this time," he said. His eyes glistened with fresh tears. This day had offered him so much pain, and I couldn't help feeling the hurt along with him. Caring for someone isn't an easy thing to stop doing.

"I woke up on the lawn once. I thought I'd just gone through the windows in my room in my sleep. Another time the windows were open and I woke naked with scratches all over my legs. Now I wonder if I went out to turn on both nights."

"But you don't remember it?"

"Some memories came back when I turned today, scents, sounds... but I'm not sure. I never knew I was doing it."

He stared into a candle flame, wrestling something inside. "It could have been you."

"It wasn't." I didn't need him to elaborate to know what he was talking about. If I'd been turning into a beast without knowing it, I might have killed those children, the seamstress. I might have attacked his parents. But it wasn't me.

"My thoughts were still my own while I was turned. Ama may have lost herself to the animal inside her, but I didn't. And if I'd turned and been the beast you saw last night, I would have stayed out of the oubliette. I wouldn't have climbed back in just to turn back into a girl."

He nodded quickly. I wasn't sure if he believed it like I did, but we didn't have time for him to mull it over, because Madame LaClaire was dying again.

CHAPTER FORTY-FOUR

Madame LaClaire tried to sit up, but Sebastian lunged forward and stopped her. It was probably for the best. She may not feel it, but her life was draining away and she'd quicken its leaving if she moved around too much.

"We picked you both. Aurélie and me. Your maman always talked of how strong you were before she died, and Aurélie said you'd be perfect. She was supposed to watch over you, guide you, teach you how to protect my boys and the village against the monsters."

"Aurélie didn't watch over Ama or me."

Madame LaClaire's face darkened. "She didn't?"

"No. *I* watched over my sister. *I* kept her from being suspected, killed. No one helped us."

Sebastian leaned into his mother as she ran her hands over her face. I didn't want to see the regret there, the pain. I didn't care what she felt. She and my aunt had worked magic on us, and *I'd* been the one left to deal with it.

"You left my sister to suffer," I said.

"Both of you," she whispered.

It was true. I'd suffered too.

"I made sure she only killed who I told her to. I protected her *and* the village."

Madame LaClaire narrowed her eyes at me. "But what about you?"

"What about me?"

"Who did you kill? Did you get rid of the dogs... the monsters?"

I didn't want to know who I'd killed, but I didn't think it was the dogs or monsters or whatever Madame LaClaire had made us to destroy. My memories seemed like a rosebush full of thorns. If I tried to work my way through them, I'd be shredded to pieces. It was better to let my memories of turning remain shrouded in mist, and trust myself, knowing I would never have killed innocents.

"I never knew I was turning too, not until this morning. I was at the bottom of the oubliette... desperate."

"So, the animal inside saved you."

She wasn't going to make it sound good now, not like she'd given me some kind of gift.

"No, I saved myself, and I would have whether as a girl or as a beast. You didn't protect Lucien or Sebastian or me or Ama or anyone else with what you did. You just made things awful for us."

Sebastian leaned out from his mother and she slumped against his shoulder. He stared at me. I returned his gaze and shook my head very slightly. His mother was waning. He didn't have long with her, but I was still so angry.

"We made you stronger than you know, child."

Sebastian looked from his mother to me. "But why, Maman? Children are dying. Why did you make these monsters?"

"No, no," Madame LaClaire wailed and closed her eyes. She rubbed at them with the backs of her hands. "That's what we were trying to stop."

"Who?" Sebastian asked.

"Aurélie and me. This was our plan. She recognized the magic I didn't know I had inside. She taught me, and we created two protectors to guard against those things that came to our windows and scared you and Lucien. It was a huge animal, a kind of dog or wolf, a monster. We wanted to make protectors who could fight it off once and for all. We had no choice."

"You didn't even ask us!" I cried.

"Aurélie said we couldn't. Your mother was dead and Aurélie…she didn't think you'd understand, that you'd say no. It was better to just make you strong and teach you how to wield that strength."

"You're right. I would have said no, but the choice should have been mine."

The metallic scent of blood stung my nose. Madame LaClaire paled slowly, incrementally, the warm hue of her cheeks fading back to gray. I didn't know how much time she had left, but it wouldn't be long now. I hoped Sebastian realized this too and steeled himself against the certainty of his mother's death. By the way he gazed at her, with a shiny, wet sheen of hope in his eyes, I guessed he didn't. It would hurt more, then.

His mother wheezed and coughed. She brought a delicate hand to her mouth and held it over her lips. Her fingers came away with red flecks covering them.

"We made you to stop the killings."

My throat tightened and a flash of heat rose through my body. This woman did not *make* me.

"I was already here; we were here and you used your own magic to wreck us."

Sebastian's mother waved her blood-spattered hand. "You're powerful and you have a chance. That's more than so many of the children here have."

She wasn't wrong—we'd buried many small coffins in this village. Perhaps more than most.

"How do I get rid of it?" I finally asked.

Sebastian's mother shook her head. "That would be harder than you think after so long."

"But if she doesn't want it, surely you can take it away?" Sebastian asked from where he knelt beside his mother. My heart beat a little faster at his words. He wanted us to be free too.

Madame LaClaire turned her head slowly toward her son. "It's not whether I want to or not, Bastian. It would be hard and dangerous to undo. I could read the spell, yes, but it would take more than that. We bound the spell with a Queen of the Night...a flower that blooms only once every two years and only at night. It used to be grown in the garden at Versailles, so I had a dried one. A gift. They aren't grown there anymore."

I gripped at the remains of her dress where they fell around her, my fingernails digging into the stained silk. My cloak gaped open, but I didn't care. I couldn't stay like this. I *would not* fade into a monster, trapped in the body of an animal until I lost all sense of my true self.

"I am not a beast," I said.

"No, ma chère. You are not."

Her voice hovered just above a whisper and it was obvious there wasn't much time left. Tears stung the corner of my eyes as I stared into one of the flickering flames making a halo of yellow light around the room. I let go of the fabric clutched in my hand and turned away from the only person who could have saved Ama...and me.

"Say goodbye, Sebastian." I forced my words to be steady and hard because we couldn't both fall apart.

He laid his head on his mother's heart. A sob broke through the quiet in the room. Madame LaClaire's breaths didn't even register anymore. They'd been rasping before, but now they didn't sound like anything at all. Soon they'd be gone, and her chest would still.

Sebastian wept into his mother's chemise and I only looked back over when he seemed to have spent himself.

"She's dead."

I nodded. "She's been dead for a year."

He wiped his eyes with the back of his hands and tried to pull the broken pieces of her beautiful blue dress back over her stained chemise.

"I thought I was keeping her somehow. Like if I didn't let death fully claim her, I could stop her from leaving."

"I don't think even magic can bring people back from death."

"Then what's the point of it at all?"

I shrugged, tired and out of answers. Magic didn't seem to bring anyone anything good. It was a weapon, and not always a very effective one.

"We don't need magic to stop all this horror from happening, Sebastian."

He slipped from his mother's side and took a few heavy steps toward me. Without hesitation I opened my arms to him, and he fell against me, leaning down to rest his head on my shoulder. I wanted to hold him, smell him, find comfort in his warmth even though I was angry at his lies, the things he hadn't told me. We stayed like that a moment, swaying lightly and breathing in the scent of each other.

"What do we do?" he said into my hair.

"Your mother said the monsters were like dogs. Emméline has a kennel full of hunting dogs."

"Yes, dogs. Not monsters."

"But a dog, one of those huge red mastiffs, could be bred with a wolf. And think what kind of monster that could create. I found a tuft of russet fur near the seamstress's body. I thought it was Ama's, but it could have been one of theirs. Those wolves that came to your windows? Perhaps they were more than just wolves. Maybe it's what you saw last night."

"You still don't believe it was Ama?"

I searched my splintered and sore heart. I just couldn't live with my sister being a killer of children. It wasn't possible.

"I don't want it to be her. Plus, Emméline knew about Ama. She figured it out somehow while spending so much time in the woods. She wanted Ama and me to turn against each other. Just more chaos, more upset."

Sebastian shook his head. "And how do you think Emméline controlled this monster of hers?"

"Dogs learn commands."

I'd thought the killer had been a person wielding a blade to make it look like a beast attack, but the killer's weapon could be an animal instead. A dog bred with a wolf wouldn't have claws as long as Ama's, so its cuts would be shallower—just as the cuts had been on Maurice and the seamstress. If Emméline had control over her creation, she might be able to call it off before it devoured its kill, which would explain how much of the bodies had been left behind. Her father might have been breeding these monsters for years before he died—that would account for the deaths Sebastian's mother had been trying to stop by transforming Ama and me. Emméline could have easily continued his work, having reason to want to drape the valley in fear.

"The beast you saw last night ... it must have been Emméline's. Not Ama."

Relief swelled in my chest at this final piece falling into place. The candlelight flickered around us and Sebastian's mother's body took up too much space in the room. I wanted out. I needed to breathe fresh air.

Heedless of whether or not Sebastian was ready to leave, I swung open the door and followed a little hall lit by a small window looking out into the garden. The outer door opened easily. Outside again, I pulled in greedy gulps of the stinging cold air, tasting the snow on it. Sebastian tumbled out behind me.

"Marie, if you're right, we must kill Emméline's creation before it attacks the town again."

I nodded, already visualizing her farm in my mind. A small barn served as a kennel for her numerous hunting dogs. They may not have been killer beasts, but they were dangerous enough.

"We can't go alone."

Sebastian raised an eyebrow. "Are you going to recruit the townspeople who wanted to kill you just last night?"

Even though it made no sense, a giggle bubbled to my lips. As soon as I'd made the sound, I clasped my hands over my mouth and shot a look at Sebastian. He smiled but without much enthusiasm.

"It's all right, Marie."

Everything felt too fresh. I was a beast too, just like Ama, but I didn't really know when I'd transform or how I'd been doing it without Ama finding out. I must have killed some-thing, when I transformed, if not humans. And Sebastian's mother had said there's no way to turn the curse back. No matter what she said about protectors and strength, I refused to think of this affliction as anything other than a curse. I hadn't chosen it—it had been chosen for me, done *to* me. If that wasn't a curse, I didn't know what was.

And of course, I couldn't forget that whatever she might have done to me, she was Sebastian's mother. Who'd died min-utes ago. I wasn't even sure how he stood there beside me in the garden instead of balling himself up into a sobbing mess.

Maybe it wasn't quite real for him yet. That happened sometimes. Shock stopped the real feelings from penetrating too deep. I'd have to watch for him—he couldn't fall to pieces while we ambushed Emméline's farm.

"This will be dangerous," I said. "But there's one person who can help us."

"Who?"

"Ama."

CHAPTER FORTY-FIVE

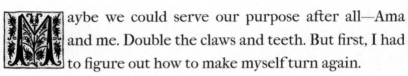aybe we could serve our purpose after all—Ama and me. Double the claws and teeth. But first, I had to figure out how to make myself turn again.

Sebastian and I sat on the great stone steps outside his house, the cold radiating from the rock through my skirt, numbing my skin. I'd rushed to my room to put on a plain dress while Sebastian reloaded his musket. I'd half expected Emméline to still be stalking the garden, but there was no sign of her. I glanced up to Lucien's glowing window and the shadow of Madame Écrue passed in front of it. Lucien was safe at least—or as safe as he could be for now.

We stared out at the peaks of the town. Smoke curled up from chimneys and birds flew from tree branches to shingled roofs. It was idyllic, like a painting. The details blurred into a soft, sweet haze.

"When does it happen for Ama?" Sebastian asked.

"She turned once a month and she could feel it coming, like a buzzing beneath her skin . . . She always turned at night, but she knows it will happen that morning. That's when I'd mark out her victim. But now I don't know. She changed again before a month was up this time, perhaps during the day, and now she doesn't seem to be able to change back."

Sebastian picked up my arm and let it drop again in my lap. "Do you feel anything?"

I curled my arms in on myself, irritated at his question. I wished it were that easy. "Of course not."

"Well, how are we going to do it then?"

I tore my gaze away from the town and shifted it to the trees. I was certain the woods were the key. Even before I found out about myself, I'd felt the forest reach out to me. I'd thought I just liked it there, but perhaps it was more than that.

"I think it needs to be in the forest."

"In the forest where the beast roams?"

I smiled without any humor in it. "Of course."

"All right."

We stood and crunched the gravel under our boots. I wore Sebastian's cloak over my dress, and he wore his jacket over leather breeches. I'd always asked Ama to go naked when she turned so as not to ruin perfectly good clothes. I shivered now at the thought of slipping this dress from my shoulders in this frigid air.

The trees swallowed us as we stepped under their canopy. That familiar pull tugged at me, and I answered it this time, recognizing it, letting my feet take me deeper into the woods. Sebastian followed behind with light, quick steps. His face was grim when I glanced back at him. Maybe he didn't relish the thought of me turning into a monster either. How could we be sure I wouldn't go after him? Ama had never attacked me when she'd first turned. I'd always thought she'd recognized me. Perhaps I'd recognize Sebastian too.

It was a hollow wish, but I clung to it anyway. I had no choice unless I was willing to send him back—and I wasn't. I needed him here with me.

Emméline lived in a large farmhouse a little outside town. We could follow the edge of the forest, skirting my own cottage, and end up on her property.

"How will you call her?" Sebastian asked as we stood in the deep green of the pines and the bare branches of the tall oaks. A biting breeze lifted my hair from where it tickled my cheeks, and the tip of my nose already tingled with cold.

"I have to be like her, I think."

He nodded and ran his hands through his curls. I'd told him to wear a hat against the cold but he hadn't listened.

I knew how and why Sebastian's mother and Aurélie had made us, but I didn't know how to trigger the transformation that happened at the bottom of the oubliette. Fear, maybe. Determination. I knew what it felt like now, though. Perhaps that would help.

Without a word, I walked away from Sebastian toward a thick, fallen log. Maybe he understood what I was doing, because he didn't follow. I sat on the rough bark and pressed my eyes closed, reaching for the wild heart of the woods. After a few moments of nothing but the low whine of the wind, the cold numbed me. Then every sound, every scent grew and heightened. I listened with a part of me that had been buried but now I set free. I wanted this to happen. I welcomed the wildness in my heart and let it take over, the buzzing of it running through my veins. It was as Ama had said, a thrumming under my skin.

Despite the cold, and Sebastian lingering a few feet away, I shrugged off my cloak and slipped from my simple dress. My feet came free from my boots with gentle tugs. The icy air hit me, and gooseflesh erupted over my skin.

Sebastian glanced over and then quickly away when he took in my nakedness, but I didn't care this time.

"Marie," he called over his shoulder. "Are you sure about this?"

I stared at him, holding the picture of him in my mind. *Don't hurt him*, I told myself. *You might love him despite everything.*

The image of Sebastian standing there in the golden winter afternoon light, shadowed by the trees around him, tugged at my heart. After all that had happened, he was still here. He hadn't run away or vowed to fix me. Sebastian had accepted everything about me from the moment we met—even if I hadn't been able to recognize it.

The strong line of his broad shoulders dipped as he shrugged, perhaps tired of waiting for my response.

"Sebastian, this is how it must be . . . how I want it to be."

His shoulders rose now, as though he took in a deep breath, and he nodded. "Just don't eat me, please."

The tremor of humor in his voice made me smile. "I'll try not to."

I closed my eyes again and reconnected to the wind, the trees, the earth beneath my feet. The forest called to me and I answered with an open heart.

A flash of pain broke through my body. It burned through my bones as they bent into the shape of a beast. My skin tingled and stung as the fur pushed through it. A rough, growling scream tore from my throat and filled the still air with its terror.

The pain drained away. I groped with my body—both familiar and strange. I knew how to stand on four legs and tilt my nose up to the sky to sniff out the wind. The fur covering my skin was as familiar to me as Ama's had been. My thoughts pulled back and surged forward with such intensity the human part of me jolted from the shock. The animal in me was strong, sucking in the scent of warm blood.

I whipped my head around to where a man stood shaded among the trees. His chest heaved with fear—I smelled it rolling off him in waves.

Sebastian.

Colors shone too bright, the scent of pine and snow, dirt and muck stung my nostrils. My ears pricked with the hum of a beating pulse. There was a warmth to it, a tantalizing *beat, beat, beat* of blood. My muscles moved without decision, springing toward the delicious smell. A shout echoed in my ears, but it wasn't louder than the rhythmic pulse.

In an instant, I had it under me. The body thrashed wildly, but my heavy paws pinned it to the ground. The throat gleamed like a target, the expanse of bared flesh an invitation for my teeth.

I luxuriated in the moment and pulled in the heady aroma wafting from the soft skin. But then a familiarity caught at me, and the blurry shape of a man filled in with features I knew.

Soft brown eyes and brown, freckled skin. Hair curling over his forehead and around his ears. He stared at me with wild fear and suddenly I became aware of my hands—paws. I jerked back from Sebastian with the fluidity of a four-legged animal. I knew this body. I knew how to move, how to be. The strong legs moved naturally under me and I drank in my heightened senses. It was as if someone had pulled a caul from the world. The woods sparkled with clarity.

"Marie?" Sebastian sat up from the ground with wet moss and twigs clinging to his back.

I nodded my head and relief relaxed his strained features.

Not being able to talk was going to be a problem. I couldn't exactly use my paws to draw words into the dirt either. I turned from his questioning gaze. I'd call Ama, and once she was here too, we could ambush Emméline's farm and kill her monster. Sebastian was armed with his musket and a hunting knife, and Ama and I would be armed with our own claws and teeth. It would be enough. It had to be.

I wasn't sure exactly how to go about calling my sister, but I, like everyone else living along the edge of the woods, had heard the strange growls in the night. It seemed like a good thing to try.

The growling call built in my belly and ripped through my throat off into the night. I pushed it out from deep within and tried to shape it into my sister's name.

Ama!

If she was out here, somewhere, I could only hope she could hear me and would come to me. I wanted to see her so badly, I ached with longing.

Minutes passed. The wind teased me by blowing the dead leaves from the ground and playing through the bare branches of the trees. It wasn't that I could see everything, but between sight and sound and smell, nothing could happen in my part of the forest without my knowing. I'd be aware as soon as Ama's padding footfall turned toward me. And there was nothing yet.

Sebastian waited too, muscles tight and stiff.

I felt her before I heard her. My heart leapt with a faint familiar scent tracing its way toward me on the swirling breeze. Then her careful, padding steps reached my ears. Joy spread through me and I circled my sister as she bounded into our clearing. She seemed to know me right away. Our eyes locked and she tipped her large head toward mine.

I dipped my head a fraction, the short fur around my nose rubbing against hers.

The sharp bark of dogs pierced the air as their warm,

musky smell filled my nostrils. Ama pulled away. Sebastian started and spun around toward the tree line. Torches bobbed in the distance, their fire flaring in the night, coming closer. A search party.

"They've discovered you're missing from the oubliette," Sebastian said.

I narrowed my keen eyes. The men at the front held crudely fashioned spears and a couple muskets someone must have squirrelled away against the law. I was strong, powerful, but not more powerful than a bullet blast.

"Look!" A woman's voice broke free from the mob. Emméline. "I see something there!'

Sebastian shouldered his own gun, but I nudged him behind the legs to tell him to run. Then I looked to my sister and leapt over a fallen log, diving into the trees.

CHAPTER FORTY-SIX

ma ran beside me. The wind slid over her fur and gave me the gift of her familiar scent. How I'd missed her, despite everything.

Sebastian wasn't nearly as fast as we were, but I kept him with us as we wound through the edge of the woods toward Emméline's farm. The sounds and smells of the mob behind us marched steadily closer. We outpaced them, but fear nipped at all four of my heels. They'd followed us right into the jaws of the beast, and I couldn't be sure they'd pick the right one to try to kill.

Emméline's house spilled over its plot with extra rooms added as the father and daughter's wealth grew. It didn't match itself—the plaster of the main section colored with age and the new additions much too white.

A wooden barn stood sentinel on the edge of the property beside an open, empty field.

A thinner building ran parallel to the barn. Its wooden slats had been spaced carefully and close together. A metal door lent the thing the look of a prison. This must be where they held the creatures.

But a guttural howl, so much rougher than mine or Ama's, told me the monster wasn't in there now.

Sebastian spun, his musket aimed at shadows. A chill breeze brought the gasps and shouts of the townspeople to my finely tuned ears. Ama must have heard them too, because she looped around and came to a rest in front of me. She angled herself between me and the sounds of a hundred furious people looking for something to soothe their desperation.

They wanted blood, but I was determined they wouldn't get any of Ama's or mine. I peered out into the trees and waited for the glow of the torches to come closer.

Every few moments, I glanced behind me, but the creature didn't spring from the shadows between the barns. I had to rely on my senses—the deep pull of a breath through my sensitive nose, the shift in the air to tell me of movement, the taste of salty sweat and fear. I'd feel the monster before I saw it. Of that I was sure.

Which was exactly why it surprised me.

Red fur flashed before my eyes at exactly the same time I smelled the putrid musk of it. The animal jumped clean over me and fell with sickening grace on Ama's back. She jolted and I shrieked—a yelp scraping free of my throat. Sebastian jumped back and aimed his gun at the wrestling figures of my sister and the beast.

Please don't shoot. The aim couldn't be trusted—not with Ama twisting herself out of the monster's mouth.

In utter silence, the townspeople reached the edge of the wood and stood between the trees. Fear replaced the fury in their eyes as their nightmare came to life before them. Emméline stared at me without any expression at all. She'd let a mob come here, to her own home, as part of her evil game. The idea turned my stomach, but I didn't have time for disgust.

The monster pinned Ama to the ground. In a blinding rage, I bared my teeth and sunk them into the animal's russet-colored back. It growled and released Ama's neck while I tore into its flesh. Blood filled my mouth with a thick, metallic taste and I had to let go before I choked on it.

I stepped back and took my first real look at the monster. It was a giant, almost bigger than me and Ama. The long legs of a wolf topped with the muscular body of a mastiff. Bred for hunting and killing. It came at my sister again. I leapt and brought my long claws down on its back. Ama's legs kicked at the dirt and pine needles until she could stand again. Then she clamped her jaws around the animal's neck, holding it there for a moment before it threw her off. Ama and I stood with our tails flicking each other, cornering the wolf-dog against a row of fir trees. Her golden eyes held mine, and it was almost as if I could hear her in my head. I just knew what she was going to do next by the stance of her legs and the set of the dark crest of fur on her neck. I imagined I looked the same.

She went for the animal's back legs and swept them out from under it with her snout. I angled my body and launched myself at its neck, sinking my teeth into its flesh for the second time. Ama rolled the beast over with her paws and opened her jaw so that her sharp teeth hovered just over the soft white fur of the beast's belly.

Sebastian kept his gun trained on the injured monster and I tried to scream at him with my eyes, *Get back behind me!*

He didn't listen and I couldn't make him.

"You see?" Emméline's strong voice split the crowd at the tree line. They parted for her and her loping hounds. "Three of them. No wonder they pick us off so quickly."

The animal caught on the ground beneath us snarled and snapped at the air. On the other side of the field, the hounds grumbled low, tentative growls.

"Kill them all!" Emméline said. "We'll send their bodies to Versailles and the king will reward us with more than we could ever dream of. We can show him what we're really worth."

Shouts of agreement rang out through the frozen air, and I wondered why they weren't more afraid. Did they think they could kill us so easily?

Sebastian dropped to his knees in the cold, snowy dirt beside Ama and me. "Marie," he whispered. "Change back, now. We can explain . . . tell them what happened."

He'd be revealing his mother as a witch, along with my aunt. It was a sacrifice from him, and I took it without question.

The townspeople seemed to move as one, bursting from the trees like bees from a hive, surging toward us with their makeshift weapons. Papa pushed his way to the front of the group and rounded on them.

"Stop!" he yelled.

They didn't listen. I concentrated on my muscles, the feel of them, the ache. I imagined slipping out of this body like a snake shedding its skin.

A warm tingling started in my hind legs and burned its way through me. I knew without knowing how that I was turning back. My body broke around me, the golden fur falling away to reveal the human skin underneath. Screams echoed in my ears, and the snarling and snapping of the monster behind me sent shiver after shiver down my naked spine.

"Behold the face of evil," said Père Danil as he pushed through the crowd with a crucifix squeezed tightly in his hand. He stretched it out toward me as if expecting me to flinch. Sebastian rushed forward and covered me with his jacket, and I was glad to have something between my skin and the searing gaze of the crowd.

They'd stopped moving and stared at me. It was as if they were all waiting to see what would happen, as if this was a play and not their real lives at all. The only indications of life were the flittering of eyelids and the wispy plumes their breath made in the icy air.

I didn't owe these people anything. They'd never accepted me—some had hated me, hunted me. I'd always been on the edge of their world, never invited in. But their behavior had nothing to do with me. Now I got to choose exactly who I was, who I wanted to be, and I was no monster.

Papa reached out and clenched his hand around my wrist to pull me back to him, but I twisted away.

"Marie," he said, his voice barely a whisper. "You too? You're one of them too? Please, come."

I wouldn't act to please him either. This was for me. I wanted to know I could do it.

"My lord," Père Danil said to Sebastian. "We must execute her to keep the village safe."

Murmurs of agreement spread through the crowd behind me.

"Kill her right away this time, so she can't escape," came a voice from the crowd.

"Shoot her!"

"Slit her belly!"

Fear gurgled up through my throat, but I refused to let it show. I stared into the faces of the townspeople who wanted me dead and silently dared them to come try to kill me themselves.

"She was meant to save you!" Sebastian cried, and the shouting died down. He still held some power as their lord, it seemed. "That's what she and her sister were supposed to be . . . protectors. And we pretended she was a witch to trick the killer so we could capture them! Everything Marie said that night was a lie, but you believed it because it was exactly what you were all afraid of. That thing, the animal that killed your children, was not Marie."

A few heads nodded, but most still stared at me with a mix of burning fear and hatred in their eyes.

"And that *thing* wasn't created by God," I said, pointing at the wolf-dog under Ama's paws. "It was Emméline."

The sudden absence of sound shocked me. Tension wound around us like a hangman's rope, tying us all together. I had to explain.

"Emméline and her father before her made the monsters," I went on. "They bred their great mastiffs with wolves and trained the pups to be killers. And when their animals wouldn't obey them, I think they killed their victims themselves. They wanted to create a panic so they could be the heroes."

Emméline gripped the hunting knife in her hand and raised it toward me. "Liar! You're only trying to save your skin."

Shock zipped through the crowd like a spark—lighting frenzy in people's eyes. They started to shift and churn together.

"Lies!"

"It can't be!"

"It's true," Papa said, and my heart warmed a little. "My daughters could never be monsters."

Daughters. He'd given Ama away, but I guessed that didn't matter anymore. All our secrets were laid bare and the villagers were still deciding what to do with them.

"Kill her before she changes into the beast again!" Emméline shouted, spittle coating her lips.

I stepped closer to her. She towered over me, but my presence seemed to make her shrink into herself.

"What have you done, Emméline?"

The monster twisted in Ama's grip and my sister squealed with pain. It was weak, but its legs were still long and powerful. The animal launched itself between me and Emméline. I ripped a pitchfork from the baker's hands and swung around. The tines sunk into the monster's belly with just a little resistance. Nausea swept through me, but I clamped my lips together and willed it away. I'd seen blood before. No need to be squeamish. This one was dead now, and that eased the knot in my belly, but it was only the latest in a long line of kills. We'd all have to live with the deaths forever.

"See how it protected Emméline?" Papa said from beside me.

"It was her creature," I said. "You see that now, don't you? She set it loose on our village, your children."

"Lies!" Emméline said, backing away from us, the lines of kennels behind her.

We moved with her, closing in. Sebastian reached for her arm, but she tore it away.

"Don't touch me! You're just like the rest of them. You can't see anything beyond this village. I could have won us glory."

"No, Emméline," he said. "You've only given us terror and grief. The magistrate can decide what to do with you."

"Père Danil!" she shouted.

The priest had retreated back into the crowd; the only thing setting him apart was his stark black robe.

He shook his head. "You let the devil in, didn't you, child? And you and your father both tricked me."

"You're all wrong! Small-minded! There are bigger things happening in Paris, you know. We could have been talked about, rewarded!" Emméline said, and pulled open the latch on the nearest kennel.

Lucien stumbled out, blinking, legs unsure.

My breath caught in my chest. I lurched forward, Sebastian matching my steps. Emméline wrapped an arm around Lucien's neck and held her hunting knife to his throat.

"When?" Sebastian asked.

"Marie led me so helpfully back to the house when she escaped the oubliette, and it gave me the idea to take him. It was the first time I realized it wasn't just her sister who turned into a beast that my babies could never quite catch. So I went upstairs to see Lucien, to get myself some insurance. Madame Écrue was so pleased to see me." Emméline smiled and I wanted to run her through with the pitchfork.

"He's so sick, isn't he?" Emméline continued. "I grew the oleander flowers in my garden in the spring and made the tincture before the cold came. All it took was a few drops while you turned your back when I visited that day and he sickened so quickly. I knew that would keep you distracted while I churned up more panic."

"*You* did this to him?" Sebastian asked.

She nodded. "And I told him he'd benefit from the fresh air on my farm and he came with me just like that, didn't you, Lucien? Probably bored of being in bed all day."

It wasn't a surprise that Emméline knew oleander was poisonous—most people did—but I couldn't believe she'd given it to a child. Foxglove didn't have as bad an effect as oleander. Oleander could easily be deadly.

A trickle of blood ran down Lucien's neck. His hair was slick with sweat and sticking to his forehead. Dark circles hung like upside-down moons under his eyes. He barely reacted to being pulled from the kennel and held with a knife to his throat, he was so ill. My chest filled with heat, rage burning through me.

I understood a bit better how Maurice's parents felt, what Vivienne's parents must have gone through. And then I realized every vagrant, every person I'd marked for Ama had a family somewhere. Once upon a time, they'd been someone's child. They'd been loved. And I'd stolen them away. Regret tightened my chest, soured my stomach. I'd also been a monster.

"What will it be, Sebastian?" Emméline said, turning to him. "Should I sink the knife into his skin or are you going to let me go?"

Sebastian glanced over at me and I recognized the determination in his eyes. He'd do anything to stop Emméline hurting Lucien. Emméline was counting on it, but I knew Sebastian better than she did now. He wasn't going to let this happen without a fight and I was right there with him.

"Yes, yes, whatever you want. Just let my brother go," Sebastian said.

"How do I know you won't come after me?"

"I don't care about you, Emméline. I only care about Lucien."

"Hurry, Sebastian!' I said, filling my voice with panic. It came easily.

"Let go of him, Emméline, and we'll give you whatever you want!" Sebastian pled.

She laughed. "This is what makes you weak, you know. Your attachment to your brother..."

She stepped backward with Lucien in her grasp and flicked the latch on another kennel. A red mastiff loped out, snarling, teeth glinting in the pale, early winter sun. The people behind us leapt back. But Sebastian and I remained.

I met Ama's eye and nodded my head. She growled and jumped for the dog. Emméline's head whipped around to see what happened and I tackled her. This body wasn't as strong as the beast's, but it was enough. I knocked into Emméline and Lucien, sending them both sprawling. Emméline flailed and a searing pain went through my shoulder where her knife split my skin. The blood trickling down my chest was warm in the cool air. I knocked the knife out of her hand, into the dead grass. Lucien crawled away. Emméline held me and I struggled in her grip, fighting off her desperate strength, until I could reach the knife. In one swift motion, I picked it up and plunged it into her chest. Her eyes opened wide and she let out a little breath. My second kill of the day. It didn't feel good or bad. Just numb.

Ama whined and I looked up. While I'd been trying to save Lucien, the mastiff had injured my sister. She rose on shaking legs and fell again. She spasmed and her body broke apart. Fur shriveled into skin.

My sister shimmered back into her human shape. Papa threw his coat over her, and she crawled through the dirty snow toward me. I ran to her and fell to my knees, pulling her close. I'd been waiting for this, to just have her here, to have her back. I let the feeling of it settle over me and bent my face to her head. Her hair smelled like the fir trees all around us. That's who she was now. A little bit of the animal and the forest always inside her. Just like me. I couldn't strip my sister of her curse because she'd never been cursed to begin with—neither of us had. Sebastian's mother might not have asked our permission to do what she did, but Ama had embraced it now, and I could too.

Lucien leaned into Sebastian and I took them both in, trying to capture the moment so I could always remember it. They were both safe. We were all safe.

"Another one?" the baker said, pointing at Ama and me.

Sebastian took a step toward us, Lucien clinging to his leg. "They saved you, all of you. They're our protectors."

I didn't know what I was now. All I knew was that the townspeople couldn't tell me, and neither could Sebastian or his mother or even Ama. I had to find out for myself.

EPILOGUE

My stitches itched. I hated looking down at myself when I slipped my chemise over my head and seeing the black thread tying my skin together. I wanted to be healed—whole—but I wasn't sure I'd ever be in one piece again. The scars would remain, a puckered red reminder.

Ama moaned and gripped the bedpost while a fresh spasm tortured her. She was human again now, the animal body fading with her strength after her injuries. But she wasn't totally right.

I'd gone back to Aurélie's cottage to demand she heal Ama, but the cottage had been empty. As full of dust as if it had been abandoned for a hundred years. I had no idea where she'd gone.

I mixed salves and potions and crushed herb after herb under my mortar that first week, but nothing worked on Ama's wounds.

"Here," I said, putting a steaming cup of ginger tea by her bedside. "It will help with the nausea."

"No, it won't. The nausea comes from the pain, and the pain doesn't stop," Ama said.

She was right. Her injuries from the mastiff were deep. Cuts along her back from its teeth. Bruised ribs, maybe broken, from the weight of the animal. I wanted to help her heal faster or at least take away her pain, but neither Sebastian nor I could make the words in the spell book work like they had for Madame LaClaire. Not for Ama and her injuries. Not for Lucien and his consumption.

Ama had stayed human ever since the day at Emméline's farm. She had to heal first before being able to turn back—I was sure of it. Her body couldn't handle the transformation into a beast right now. But when she finally healed, and when she could turn again, I wanted to teach her control, how to live with the curse and only hunt rabbits and deer. No one had to be hurt anymore.

"Stop being like that and drink it. I had to go to the market for the ginger, you know. It's expensive."

Ama's eyes darted up at me. "You went to the market?"

I almost bit my tongue. Ama wanted to leave the cottage so badly, to be out among people in town, to be among the trees in the woods, to be free to flit and fly wherever she wanted. I shouldn't have mentioned it.

"Just quickly. For the ginger, only," I said. "And a few people stared, but no one was rude."

My sister leaned back on her pillow. "I want to go next time."

I smiled at her tenacity. "As soon as you can sit up again."

"Don't tease."

"I'm not!"

Ama tossed a pillow at me but softened the blow with a smile.

"You know I'm bored here. And you go out so often, it's not fair."

I sat on the edge of her bed now, placing one hand on the blanket draped over her legs. "I've been experimenting, testing myself. I can change when I want now if I focus on the sounds of the forest and the smell of the wind. It's just a matter of practice. You'll be able to do it too."

"I wish I'd known it was happening to you too," Ama said. "I could have helped you."

I shrugged and squeezed her leg. "I don't remember much of it before the night in the oubliette anyway, so it wouldn't have mattered."

"We could have run through the forest together though, just the two of us and the trees. That would have mattered."

"We still can. We will, as soon as you're better."

"And Papa? How will he handle it?"

I pressed my lips into a frown. "He'll just have to."

For now, Papa did his best. He brought her cloths and bowls of cool water to wipe her brow. He also disappeared into the night and came back smelling sour with his eyes screwed up in his face because it wasn't that easy to let go of drink. I couldn't work out how I felt about him. He'd hurt me, drove nails into me with his absence and his drunkenness. Even if those nails were removed now, the holes still remained. And yet, perhaps I hadn't understood everything. Perhaps he'd loved us as much as he'd been able. He didn't have to stay now to take care of Ama, but he did.

Sebastian knocked lightly on our cottage door. I didn't know if the townspeople whispered about the lord coming to visit me in our humble cottage, because I didn't listen for their mutterings anymore. The only gossip I cared about were the activities of Père Danil. Sebastian had given him two books of religion from his own library, along with a heavy purse of coins, and asked him to study the vast variety of God's creations before leveling judgment on my sister or me.

The door stuck in the jamb and I had to shove it with my shoulder—which made my stitches sting with pain. Sebastian jumped back from the door and into a slick patch of mud.

"Careful, Marie."

"Like I did it on purpose."

Something hung between us now, ethereal but tangible. Any anger we'd had at each other had melted away in the face of danger. With Emméline's monster in front of us and the mob behind us, we hadn't had time to let anything get in the way.

But now his betrayal and my half-truths stretched between us like a bog. Pick our way across carefully, and we'd be fine. One wrong step and we'd sink in our own anger.

Sebastian followed on my heels into the cottage. He

shuddered at the sound of Ama's moan upstairs, and I put my fingers on his arms and squeezed.

"Bring the laudanum."

He appeared at the top of the ladder moments later with the little green bottle in his hand. I'd traded five bottles of lavender scent for it. The liquid did seem to give Ama a little peace.

"She'll heal," I said, after I'd spooned a little through Ama's cracked lips. She quieted immediately and sunk deeper into her pillow. Her features softened and some of the tightness left my muscles. She slept.

"And then?" Sebastian asked.

"Then she and I learn to control ourselves together. We live as we are, and we don't hurt anyone. Perhaps we can even protect the valley if needed, just like your mother intended."

Sebastian sighed and put a hand on Ama's blanketed leg. "Protect the people who threw you in the oubliette?"

"We'll protect the children who are too young to be bad."

A smiled ghosted Sebastian's lips. "Emméline and her monsters are dead."

"There are still wolves in the woods and evil people in this world."

Sebastian moved his hand from Ama's leg to my hand. The warm touch of his skin against mine sent a thrill through my body. Part of me wished he'd pull me into his arms and wrap me in his musky scent. Worry and guilt were lonely burdens to bear and I yearned for the comfort of him.

"Yes, there are bad people. But I won't let them come for you, Marie," he said. "You know that, right? I'll protect you from the villagers."

I smiled. "Well, I'm the one who can turn into a beast. I'm pretty sure I can protect myself."

He chuckled softly. "You know what I mean. I know you've never liked how these things work, but I *am* a lord, and Père Danil can't just do whatever he wants without my say."

"The church is out of your reach, Sebastian."

"Not our church, the one in the village. I can make it the richest church for many miles around, and that's what the priest wants."

I toyed with a string on Ama's blanket as we both watched her sleep. Sebastian moved first, motioning for me to follow him back down the ladder. We settled in two chairs pulled near the hearth.

"How is Lucien? Did you tell him I miss him?"

Sebastian's eyes darkened and I reached out to take his hand, lessen his pain in some small way. I'd promised, hoped, the spell book would have a cure for illness, but even if it did, we couldn't make it work. We had to care for Lucien as best we could for the time he had left. Make him comfortable. Help him enjoy his life.

"He's been coughing more, and there's always blood. Madame Écrue will barely let him out of her sight."

I felt bad for being suspicious of the woman before. She'd

cared for Madame LaClaire and her sons through everything. She simply loved them.

"Spring will come, and he'll be able to go outside and breathe in the fresh air. Hopefully that will help," he said, and stood, pulling me up with him.

Sebastian's curling black hair fell in front of his eyes as he spoke, and I leaned over to push it back.

His full lips cracked into another smile, but this time I cut it off with a kiss.

It started slow, our lips moving against each other with the softest of whispers. Then his fingers curled into my hair and pulled me closer to him so my body pressed into his. My mouth opened and I'd never tasted anything so right.

When we pulled apart, I ran my own fingers over my tender lips. I couldn't deny it—Sebastian felt like home. I wanted him with me in this new life, through every part of it.

"Let me show you something," I said, and went to the door. We stepped into the brisk air and I breathed it in, letting it clear my head and calm my heart. The trees called to me.

Under their canopy, I slipped a shoulder from my dress. Sebastian watched the other shoulder emerge and then dropped his eyes as a blush crept up his cheeks. I let the dress and chemise pool around my feet.

I focused on the woods around me and felt the thrumming beneath my skin. The pain still made me gasp, no matter how many times I experienced it, but I let the animal tear through me. My body broke around me and arranged itself into a beast—one I could control.